fission

Based on a true story

Also by
Tom Weston

The Alex and Jackie Adventures:

First Night: *being a ghost story*
The Elf of Luxembourg: *being a love story*
Feathered: *being a fairy tale*

Tom Weston

fission

Based on a true story

tom weston media

FISSION

Copyright © 2011 by Tom Weston.

Printed in the United States of America.

Library of Congress Control Number: 2011903961 (Hardcover)

ISBN 978-0-981-94137-0

tom weston media

To Larry

CONTENTS

Fade in . . .

 "*N*o apology! There is no reason to apologize.*"

"You have told us that you had qualms about helping to organize gas warfare, and that you spoke to Haber about your scruples."

"This again? Why must we keep going over this? What more is there left to say? It is ancient history best forgotten. I am history."

Otto Hahn, formerly aged 88, yet soon to become timeless, bristled at the questions which he had dodged so often throughout his life but was compelled to answer now. The Wars, the Nazis, the Bomb! The cheap shots at his honesty and integrity always hurt, but now the questions were not accusations, they were . . .? . . . data collection, as if asking for place of birth on a passport application or directions to the railway station. Otto had always felt the story misrepresented and inconvenient, but now the interrogator appeared aloof and matter of fact, and this made the questions all the more searing.

"Remain aloof also! This person will try to make you feel inferior. Do not give him the satisfaction."

"I knew that the Hague Convention prohibited the use of poison in war. I didn't know the details of the terms of the Convention, but I did know of that prohibition. Haber told me the French already had rifle bullets filled with gas, which indicated that we were not the only ones intending to wage war by that means. He also explained to me that using gas was the best way to bring the war to an end quickly."

Otto sipped from the brandy glass in his left hand; his right held a cigar. He sat in a comfortable, leather club chair, in an oak paneled room, library fashioned and full of tired, leather-bound books; and beyond the perfume of the cigar he could smell the age of the room. A setting so familiar and relaxed that the conversation could have been taking place in his old staff room at the Kaiser Wilhelm, for God's sake.

"And you found those arguments convincing?"

"Except for the projection screen!"

"You might say that Haber put my mind at rest. I was still against the use of poison gas, but after Haber had put his case to me and explained what was at stake, I let myself be converted. I then threw myself into the work wholeheartedly."

"You have also told us that you saw with your own eyes the effect of poison gases on enemy soldiers. And you also say that what you saw made a very deep impression upon you?"

The light from the projector cut through the cigar smoke and demanded his attention, as if the Bat Signal bled into the night sky of Gotham City. On the screen flashed remnants of Otto's past life: the decisions made, the roads not taken, the effect of his life on others. He tried to pretend that the projector and the images did not trouble him. He could not completely ignore them and he stole a glance whenever the interrogator looked away to write down an answer.

A grandfather clock to the left of the projector chimed the hour. 6:00 PM. The projector of Otto's life displayed the date - April 22nd, 1915 - World War One - The battle of Gravenstafel. After the alternating cold and mud of the winter months, the campaigners found the spring evening surprisingly warm and lazy, and the cloudless sky shone a handsome, brilliant, sapphire blue.

In the German trenches, soldiers with improvised masks around their mouths, simultaneously open 6,000 metal canisters. With an accompanying discharge of sound, as if a hundred steam trains departed from the station at the same time, the yellow-green chlorine gas rises. The gas carries on the wind, over no-man's land, southwest towards the French trenches, turning the sky the color of a fairy tale golden sunset, beautiful and beguiling to the men who had never before seen its like. This graceful, serene, man-made cloud, four miles wide, rolls gently over the allied soldiers.

Otto remembered the scene in sharp detail not dulled by the passage of time, and shook his head in a futile attempt to change the past. Thanks in part to his ingenuity and industry, six thousand men would die before the clock chimed the quarter hour.

Overpowering the retreating air, the gas flows downwards into the trenches, blocks out the daylight and embraces its victims, first in soft, blanket warmth but quickly turning to ruthless, hellish fire. In a sudden panic, men start to abandon their posts. Others stagger around, blinded and choking.

Although the German soldiers could not see the pandemonium in the French trenches, they could hear it well enough. The screams of men and horses, cows, sheep and dogs all screaming in a sick, doleful, choral requiem, to the rhythmic drum beat of rifles and large guns, fired indiscriminately and without discipline into the cloud, as if the soldiers battled an ethereal enemy. But the sounds did not escape the cloud for too long, and as it settled in the bottom of the trenches the Germans then only heard the silence.

Smoke filled the screen. Otto felt it flow down from the screen, where it danced on the floor and billowed around his feet.

He knew the interview had concluded. He had answered the questions truthfully and factually, but he felt that his answers lacked something - was it context? - No, that wasn't it. Humility, regret, shame? - Again no; the interrogator seemed as indifferent to these emotions as Otto had in life.

The smoke, instead of dissipating, rose again, gained strength and thickened. The interrogator, never much more than a silhouette at the best of times, became obscure. Otto gulped down the last of his brandy, but it tasted of vinegar. The fire in the cigar died and the ash from its tip fell into the smoke.

Otto remembered.

What he missed was the pain, locked deep within him, yet almost always present, almost always intrusive - almost, but not quite. And he longed for life again. Not that he would behave any differently, but perhaps so that he could experience the pain he had avoided the first time.

"Yes, that is true. I felt profoundly ashamed - was very much upset. First we attacked the soldiers with our gases, and then when we saw the poor fellows lying there, dying slowly, we tried to make breathing easier for them by using life-saving devices on them. It made us realize the utter senselessness of war. First you do your utmost to finish off the stranger over there in the enemy trench, and then when you're face to face with him, you can't bear the sight of what you've done and you try to help. But we couldn't save those poor fellows."

"The old lie: Dulce et decorum est pro patria mori."

"How sweet it is to die for one's country?"

"Just so."

Death

"I believe all young people think about how they would like their lives to develop. When I did so, I always arrived at the conclusion that life need not be easy, provided only that it is not empty."

Lise Meitner

... *Bramley, England, 1968*

T he funeral procession was small - just a hearse and two other cars, but then that was only to be expected: she had outlived the majority of people who had known her well enough to call her a friend. For some, advanced years and frail bodies prohibited their attendance. Still others, who should have respected the protocol, remained too proud or embarrassed to show their faces; having snubbed her in life, they seemed unable to set aside their prejudices even now.

Her burial in the sleepy village of Bramley, so far removed from her home in Cambridge and so distant from her life, helped to cull the numbers further, but she had wished to spend her after-life next to her beloved baby brother, Walter.

Trailing the hearse, the second car held her nephew, Otto Robert Frisch, Otto to his friends and other family members, but always Robert to her - even before the second Otto entered her life. With Robert sat his wife, Ulla, and their two children, Tony and Monica.

Little specks of fragile, sapphire sunlight skipped through the leafless trees, as children would, and danced and sparkled on the windows of the car. The cold, damp autumn air caused the windows to fog, and the occupants wiped away the condensation with the sleeves of their coats. The sun hinted at warmth, but the suggestion was little more than momentary optimism, for the hard breeze at ground level betrayed the presence of the faster moving air above, and grey clouds quickly closed ranks against the blue.

Robert's grip on the steering wheel tightened. "It wouldn't surprise me if it snowed," he mused, as he squinted through the car windshield at the clouds. He wrestled with his thoughts and dismissed them, judging the day as miserable enough without his gloomy predictions. "Of course it's still too early to snow. It's only just November."

No one replied, the conversation muted and redundant.

In silence, the Frisch family car pursued the hearse through the narrow country lanes which led to the Church of St James. When they arrived at the church, they ambled up the gravel path, their tread light for fear of breaking the mood; Tony and Monica assisted a walking-stick ancient from the third car to the grave-side, where the competent but unfamiliar vicar read a formulaic and impersonal eulogy.

The cold air pressed against their faces and caused their skin to tingle and contract.

Urged by intuition, Robert turned his head towards the sky. A single snowflake caught his attention. It tumbled so slowly he could make out its unique pattern. As it glided toward his nose, Robert blew gently into the air. The snowflake rose again on his breath, visible in the cold day, before it resumed its slow downward spiral and came to rest on the headstone.

Lise Meitner:
a physicist who
never lost
her humanity.

Two more snowflakes appeared and pirouetted around each other, in the manner of coy lovers. Then four more, then double again, and again in a choreographed Strauss-like waltz.

"Only just November," reflected a disappointed Robert.

Within minutes, the snow dance had turned into an all out assault. It fell hard and fast. It massed on the ground and on their clothes. The mourners pulled their coats around them, the vicar's delivery of the funeral rites quickened, but Robert smiled and his dour mood dissolved into the background of the increasing whiteness.

"Is this your doing, Lise?" he thought. "One last joke on me?"

Robert pondered his sudden change of mood. Was it disrespectful? He didn't care. She had always worn a prim and proper persona in public; she had observed propriety always. But not with him - with him she had laughed, teased and joked - she called him the exception to the rule - he didn't know why.

The funeral proceedings wound down, but the wind had picked up. Underneath the whispered moans of the trees, the conclusion of the vicar and the footsteps of the small gathering returned to the gravel path, Robert imagined that he could hear the noise of a large and boisterous crowd. It was there - he felt it - a sudden hush which greets a celebrity who walks into a packed room, then the bustle of people as they rise to their feet, and the applause and warmth of friends as they raise their glasses. Her exile was over. She was home.

"Goodbye, Aunty."

. . . Vienna, 1906

The lecture hall in the Türkenstraße building of the Institute of Physics at Imperial University of Vienna smelt of decay - a decrepit room with rotted window sills and cracked, lime plastered walls, the white wash long since tinted with a brownish hue. Hard wooden benches, seemingly stacked on top of each other, rippled out from the podium and groaned up toward the ceiling. If required, the room could hold as many as two hundred and fifty people, not necessarily in comfort, but typically at a lecture such as this, attendance peaked at only five or six of the more dedicated students.

So why did today find more than six hundred people packed into the room? Three hundred students, of whom only a handful actually understood the physics required by this lecture, rubbed elbows with members of the faculty, visiting members of other faculties, assorted nobility and government officials, the gentlemen of the press, the general public, sausage and pie vendors, and the proverbial one man and his dog, out for a walk and who only came in to find the cause of all the commotion.

Swarm-like, they crammed into this modest room or lined up in the stair-wells and corridors and asked for the proceedings to be relayed to them, or pressed from the outside against the windows and tried to catch a glimpse of the action within; so tight that they blocked the little daylight which would normally have penetrated the dirty glass.

To enable those inside the hall to see their hands before their faces, the faculty called for gas lamps, which the wardens procured and lit. If a fire had broken out, few would have escaped with their lives. On the other hand, a fire requires oxygen - something the room severely lacked.

So why had they all come? Why had bankers and bakers closed their businesses early? Why had students deserted the coffee shops to risk an encounter with their professors? Why had editors ordered their underlings to hold the presses?

The answer in a word: *'Boltzmann.'*

Ludwig Boltzmann: Director of the Physics Institute, part time lecturer, full time luminary. In Vienna, as Beethoven was to music, so Boltzmann was to physics. Larger than life in many ways, he was a giant of a man, a short-sighted colossus with a big bushy beard which gave him the appearance of a grizzly bear wearing glasses. He enjoyed enormous popularity with the public, but remained controversial within his chosen field, despised by his academic enemies and embarrassingly frustrating to his government.

People regarded his lectures, reported and embellished by the press, as better than a night at the opera house: full of passion, comedy and profound insight. They sat around the coffee houses of Vienna and debated whether to idolize him as a savior or hang him as a heretic. But love him or hate him, they could not ignore him, and his public appearances - more performances really, audacious, unscripted and bubbly - attracted adoring fans in numbers which would make today's celebrities green with envy.

Today he bubbled in particularly good form. Although the crowd, loud and boisterous, came precariously close to anarchy under the cramped conditions, Boltzmann had them eating out of the palm of his hand. In the manner of a hypnotist, he could reduce them to hysterical laughter with an aside and a roll of his eyes, and then total silence with the gentle press of his index finger against his lips. And the crowd obeyed instantly.

"Now I know that some of my colleagues doubt the existence of the atom," Boltzmann continued.

The laughter erupted again, mingled with a few jeers and feigned cries of shame. For the audience participated in the joke. Boltzmann, the leading advocate for the existence of the atom which had proved intangible to date, had proposed that a new approach to physics, based on theory instead of experiment or observation, may unlock its secrets. His chief rival, the powerful and well-connected Ernst Mach, famed discoverer of the speed of sound, argued that theory was meaningless and irrelevant - anybody and everybody could have a theory, so what?

"Why can't you experts ever agree on anything?" shouted out a voice from the back of the hall.

The laughter rose and people stamped their feet.

Boltzmann raised his hands. "Please, please a little decorum, Gentlemen."

The noise subsided as a suddenly serious and offended Boltzmann obviously wanted to address this attack on him and his colleagues.

"As a young boy I visited a farm," Boltzmann answered the heckler. "There I noticed that some of the pigs' tails curled to the right while others' curled to the left. Do pigs group together and take sides based on this, I can't say."

The laughter erupted again.

"No, no, Gentlemen please," Boltzmann pleaded in a sham condemnation of their coarse interpretation of his anecdote.

Six hundred men attempted to stifle their enthusiasm; six hundred men and . . . one woman.

"No, no, I stand corrected - Gentlemen . . . and . . . Lady," Boltzmann acknowledged the presence of Lise Meitner in the auditorium. The audience responded with more laughter and jeers.

A voice shouted out above the din.

"Like the atom, some do not recognize the existence of female students, Professor."

More laughter.

The heckler was Niels Bohr, neither a student nor a resident of Vienna, but on a prolonged visit from his native Denmark and, as with everyone else, not about to pass up the chance to see the legendary Boltzmann in action.

Boltzmann responded, "Many may share your observation, Sir, but she exists nevertheless. Some do not see her . . ."

He paused, not for dramatic effect or because an appropriate response had escaped him, but because his last statement had triggered a puzzle in his mind and he wrested to solve it before he continued. The audience waited in silence.

"Some do not see her . . . perhaps this smacks of obstinacy . . . perhaps of genuine affliction. If I take off my spectacles, quite possibly I also could not see Miss Meitner." Boltzmann removed his glasses. "So what do I do now? Is there a woman in attendance at my lecture? I cannot see her, therefore she does not exist. I cannot see her, but I have heard whispers and rumors of her presence. Do I curse my poor eyesight and say, 'Let's defer the question until my vision improves?' Or do I say, 'Perhaps I can find another way to confirm the reality of Miss Meitner?' Are we imprisoned by our senses or can we break free of them? Can we even trust our senses? Without my spectacles I cannot see, but . . ."

Boltzmann shook his head, sighed, returned his glasses to his nose and searched through the audience.

". . . No, she is still there . . ."

The audience erupted again.

". . . And most persistent," he shouted above the roar. "But perhaps my eyes deceive me? Perhaps I am the misguided and obstinate one? And so I have to ask: who else sees Miss Meitner?"

The response could be heard on the Ringstraße.

Lise Meitner, aged 27, diminutive, shy and socially awkward, squirmed at the attention and the commentary, some fairly crude for genteel Viennese society. She led a sheltered life. Over and over again, people - friends and family included - told her that she should not meddle in a man's world. Defiantly, she had come anyway, but she had wanted to keep a low profile, not to rock the boat or cause trouble.

Boltzmann waved the crowd back into silence. "Some will never see what goes against their beliefs," he sighed again. "Others - and I hope for inclusion in this category - will structure their beliefs around the empirical evidence, yes, but also the conclusions of thought and reason. If the empirical evidence eludes me, but the logic of an object's existence is irrefutable, should I amend my beliefs?"

Cries of 'yes' and 'no.'

"Do you claim to have discovered her, Professor?" shouted Niels.

"Publish! Publish your results!" went up the roar from the crowd.

Boltzmann's commanding voice rode above the clamor, "It is easy to mistake a great stupidity for a great discovery. Yesterday we did not believe that female students existed, but then where do male students come from? Something is missing from the picture, so we must theorize as to the nature of that missing piece. 'I have it,' says one, 'we need women!'"

More laughter.

"We search for the elusive women and look . . . we find them! We discard the old theories and adopt new ones. So yes, some doubt the existence of the atom. And some who ask the question, 'then where does life come from?'"

Cries of God, God!

Boltzmann waved the crowd to silence and dropped his voice to almost a whisper so that they had to strain to hear him, "Is God the answer?" he sighed. "If science is no more than a series of miracles then why are you all here? I am not God and I cannot teach you. Can we have an explanation for the workings of the universe which does not reference God? In the dark ages before Newton and Leibniz, until the so called enlightenment of our own age, humanity has avoided the answer to this question.

"I do not seek to deny God. I seek to understand why wood burns and birds fly and the planets orbit the sun. I do not seek these answers merely to satisfy my intellectual curiosity. I believe that understanding leads to practical application. That is the aim of science. If we stop at some arbitrary point and say 'no more, leave it to God' and throw away all the awareness which came before . . . I seek therefore to understand the atom. And I believe that all the energy of the universe can be harnessed to our advantage when we finally do understand the atom.

"Still, theory is just theory, they say. Forgive me if you regard conjecture as a waste of your time. Everyone is entitled to a theory or two, even me. But what purpose does it serve if I can conduct no experiments, no machines which I can build, and no patents which I can file? No profits which I can turn, eh?"

The laughter this time, muted and nervous, scarcely rose to an audible level: for society held it unseemly to talk of money or to hint that it was the grubby motivation behind much of their noble endeavor.

"I have none of that," Boltzmann whispered. "I just have this little atom. Here it is." He held out his left hand, palm up and empty. At least it held nothing tangible which the audience could discern.

"Is it really there? Can you see it? How many of you would care to hazard a guess as to its true nature? Who will devise the experiments? Who will build the machines? Some of you, perhaps only a few, will understand why, in the absence of proof, it is still important to try. So here is my atom. I give it to you. Take it."

Boltzmann raised his palm to his mouth. He looked again into his audience; his eyes scanned them, one by one, and made each feel as if Boltzmann spoke only to him - or her.

Lise leaned forward and her eyes locked onto her hero - for Boltzmann was her hero, her mentor, her inspiration - and she imagined his eyes locked on her in response. Boltzmann gently blew on the invisible atom, as if he dispatched a feather into the air.

"Catch it if you can," he said.

* * *

Lise packed up her notebooks and shuffled from the auditorium, carried along by the departing hordes. As she walked down the corridor away from the lecture hall, a voice called out to her. She turned and saw Niels approaching rapidly, weaving through the crowd and sometimes bumping into them, for which he would shake hands and apologize profusely, even as he kept moving.

"So, Lise," he puffed when he at last caught up with her. "That was quite a performance you gave in there."

"Professor Boltzmann does tend to the theatrical," Lise replied. Niels was a friend and she felt at ease with him. But Niels quickly made friends with everyone and Lise coveted his easygoing nature.

"Oh that's just a front," said Niels. "Underneath is a core of melancholic, romantic goth."

"It takes one to know one, Niels." Lise knew that Niels shared with their celebrated professor a wistful quality, hidden underneath the exterior of a joker.

"Too true, but the real person resides below the surface."

"I must remember to take note of that."

Niels laughed. "I hear that you are quite a note-taker. I must confess that my own preparation leaves much to be desired - somewhat sketchy at best; but I do have some new papers from Jacobi. Maybe we can get together for coffee and exchange notes?"

Lise hesitated. Viennese etiquette and personal ethics prohibited the acceptance of a casual date. And although he had already established a reputation for brilliance, Niels was several years her younger, not Austrian, and she felt his behavior during the lecture betrayed a certain immaturity.

She was also acutely, painfully aware of her novelty status at the university - that all eyes were on her and that many detractors would use the slightest excuse to argue for her dismissal. As much as possible, she preferred to walk in the shadows. The university, until recently the undisputed domain of men and never before breached by anyone of her sex, would severely frown on misconduct by a woman.

She carefully mulled over the consequences of his offer before she finally decided that, Niels being Niels, he probably just meant coffee after all and any reasonably independent observer would interpret her actions as innocent and appropriate.

"Yes, that might be mutually beneficial - I have not seen the Jacobi papers."

Their walk took them by the office of Professor Friedrich Hasenohrl, Lise's assigned tutor. For the second time in the space of a few minutes, Lise heard someone call her name and the professor's head appeared from behind the door of his office.

"Miss Meitner, a word if I may?" Hasenohrl called out. The professor's voice betrayed the awkwardness of his assignment as her tutor. As one of the more progressive academicals who had championed her admission, he had welcomed the assignment, but in the face of the criticism and sometime ridicule of less enlightened colleagues, his approach to the task resembled a man who walked over a mile-wide beach of eggshells.

Niels sensed that three made a crowd and did not slow his pace. "Catch you later; for coffee," he forcefully reiterated, with a wave of his hand to deflect further argument.

Lise entered the professor's office.

"Please, Miss Meitner, take a seat," said Professor Hasenohrl. He decided to overcome the awkwardness by coming straight to the point. As a consequence, he sounded harsher than he had intended. "I have your thesis here on the calculus problem. I see you claim to have detected an error in the analysis?"

"Yes, Professor, I believe so," said a defensive Lise. She sat down. Compared to her academic polish, Lise's social graces remained undeveloped and she felt as uncomfortable as her tutor and equally brusque. Even in informal settings, conviviality could not be said to be one of her redeeming qualities.

"Good work, good work indeed," complimented Hasenohrl. "When will your paper be ready?"

"Ready? . . ." What could he mean? It was already ready. She had handed it in on time and the Professor had obviously reviewed it, otherwise they wouldn't be having this conversation. "Sorry Professor? Ready? I don't . . ."

"For publication," added Hasenohrl.

"Publication? Oh no, Professor."

"No? What do you mean, no? Why ever not, woman?" The professor, while not as reserved as Lise, also felt awkward in the company of the opposite sex, especially at the university, where females roamed as rare as unicorns. But Lise was his student and he did not discriminate; her work was good enough to be published and he saw no reason for modesty, false or otherwise.

"Well, it is not my work," Lise offered, by way of an explanation.

"Are you telling me that you cheated?"

"Oh no, Professor! It's just that . . . I mean . . . it's not entirely my work . . . Your help! I couldn't have reached the conclusion without your help."

"That is what I am here for Miss Meitner . . ." the professor took the compliment warmly and basked in its glow for a second before getting back to business. ". . . But that is my job. It is your thesis! It is a good one and you should publish."

"No, Professor, it would be wrong for me to claim the discovery. I feel that it is a collective effort."

"I see only your name on the paper . . . But you would bring collective credit to your professor and your university if you published."

"Perhaps if your name was also on the paper?"

The warmth dissipated. Why the Hell had this woman fought so hard to attend the university if she did not make the most of the experience? Did she think that she could stay cocooned forever?

"Don't be so modest, woman. There is no place for it in the world of academia. If you want to make a name for yourself you must publish."

"I am not here to make a name. I am here to study."

"Miss Meitner, as you are aware, the university received much criticism for allowing your entry to this prestigious academy," the professor said angrily. "Some of us fought hard for the admission of women. You are a pioneer for your sex, Miss Meitner, and you owe it to them, and to the university, to use your time wisely."

Lise struggled for an appropriate response to placate the professor. Compliance would be easiest: 'Yes, *Professor, you are correct, Professor, thank you for your confidence in me, Professor,*' but Lise had a hard time doing the easy things. Before she could find an answer, Ludwig Boltzmann appeared at the door and entered without a knock, treating the office as if he owned it.

"Ah Fritz," boomed Boltzmann. "Devouring another victim, eh?"

Hasenohrl did not take umbrage at this sudden appearance or at the cavalier manner of his old and close friend. And he welcomed the possibility of Boltzmann's support in this battle with his pupil.

"Ludwig, perhaps you can explain to Miss Meitner here?" he asked. "While all work is built on the earlier work of others, insight is not theft. It is a point which Miss Meitner fails to grasp."

"Fritz, Fritz," said Boltzmann. "Don't be too hard on our young femme fatal. She has been helping me with my lecture today and perhaps that has left her just a little bit weary and befuddled. What's all this about?"

Professor Hasenohrl summarized the circumstances.

"You must forgive your tutor, Lise," said Boltzmann. "He is a traditionalist, but he means well. He has the interests of the university at heart; and yours also."

"Yes Professor." Lise felt shame at this admonishment cloaked as an apology. She esteemed Boltzmann - more than that, it bordered on worship. In an ideal world, she would have found Boltzmann, not Hasenohrl, assigned as her tutor. Boltzmann was the reason she had come to Vienna University to study physics and defied the social mores of the time, and endured the looks and snide comments. Criticism from Boltzmann cut to the core.

"You see, Lise, there is more to the university than study," Boltzmann continued. "For the university to attract the best teachers and students it must advertise. Placing an advert in the daily papers or putting up posters on the Ringstraße would be too crass, too commercial. And so we do it this way. A published paper brings prestige and fame to the university, as well as to the author. And let us remember the other little comforts which fame and prestige attract."

"Yes Professor . . . I must seem very rude. Professor Hasenohrl credits me with insight, but his guidance in that direction showed me what and where to seek. I only arrived at the destination which he had already mapped out for me. I don't think that I am cut out to be a mathematician."

"Not one for the heady delights of pure thought, eh?" He laughed. She was more of a kindred spirit than she realized. His reputation and accomplishments as a scientist had bought fame and glory to the whole of Austria. His rewards included the Physics Department at the university; but he was not an academic at heart, he remained an incorrigible dreamer who took an almost childlike delight in the discovery of new wonders, but quickly became bored with the familiar.

"No Professor," replied Lise. "As you said today, science must lead to discoveries of a practical nature."

"Is that what I said? . . . perhaps, but what I meant was . . . that we should pursue the truth, wherever that takes us. To Heaven or to Hell, Lise, seek the truth."

. . . One Week Later

T he living room could serve as the perfect example of late Victorian ethos: confused, cluttered and the epitome of middle class values, with flock wallpaper, frayed carpet, dusty crystal kerosene lamps and warped, creaky bookcases with well thumbed tomes. And this very ordinary room seemed much too small to hold the Family Meitner, at least all at the same time. But as with most families of the time, the Meitners had perfected the art of living in such a small space in relative harmony.

Auguste Meitner, Lise's older sister and called Gusti for short, and Fritz Meitner, Lise's older brother, played a duet on the upright piano: Brahms Hungarian Dance No. 5 for four hands. All the Meitner children, Lise included, had received musical training, but Gusti proved the more talented by far and had the calling of a concert pianist. To tease Fritz, she randomly changed the tempo; slowing down to make sure that he paid attention and then speeding up until he could not keep up with her.

Gusti's husband, Justinian Frisch talked - struggled to raise his voice above the general din - to their mother, Hedwig Meitner, who cradled the youngest member of the Meitner clan, doomed to live his entire life with the moniker, baby Walter. Justinian also held a child, his son, Otto Robert, just old enough to walk, but currently proving a bit of a handful and Justinian labored to hold on to him.

Today, rounding out the numbers in the Meitner living room, Gisela, Lola and Frida - Lise's other sisters - waltzed around each other and all chattered at once, oblivious to the others' voices, as if they had become impervious to them.

Into this mini maelstrom entered Lise. She carried a basket of groceries which she had picked up on her way back from University.

"Here is Lise with the bread," cried Lola, breaking away from the circle of sisters and taking a loaf of bread from the basket. "Dinner is saved."

"Hoorah," said Frida, who snatched the bread from Lola's hand and two potatoes from the basket, and began to juggle with them.

"But Lise, haven't you forgotten something?" Lola teased. "Where are your books? You enter a room without a book in your hand. Unthinkable!"

The standard joke in the Meitner household held that they had never seen Lise without a book - that she preferred the company of books to people; although her mother swore that once upon a time, before the birth of her younger siblings, Lise had enjoyed a more social lifestyle.

"And it gives me a free hand," cried Lise, as she took a playful swipe at Lola, who avoided the blow but instead came close to careering into the assorted parents and babies.

"Hey, watch out there," warned Hedwig sternly. "Here Lise, you hold Walter while I check on dinner."

Lise and her mother exchanged the grocery basket and baby.

"And how is Brother Walter today?" Lise smiled at the baby, who, of course, did not reply but just stared up at her blankly, with dribble on the corner of his mouth. Lise's smile turned into a wide grin. At times it seemed that Walter was the only one able to get Lise to crack a smile.

Applying additional stress to the room's sagging floorboards, Philipp Meitner, the symbolic head of the clan Meitner, and Lise's father, now entered the fray. He carried the day's mail, but appeared lost in thought, as if pondering some monumental issue. The family recognized this behavior from Philipp Meitner as normal. He preferred quiet, thoughtful conversation to party atmosphere and had successfully managed to reduce family gatherings to mere background noise.

"Ah husband, about time too," said Hedwig, jostling him out of his meditation with a small kiss on the cheek. "You come home later every day. Did you forget that Gusti and Justinian were coming for dinner?"

"No, I didn't forget!" Philipp lied.

"Well, you are only just in time," Hedwig admonished. She took the bread mid air from the juggling Frida and retired to the kitchen.

"Papa," said Lola. "Lise has lost her books."

But Philipp did not hear her; he had already retreated to his inner sanctuary. He scanned the mail in his hands and muttered incoherently to no one in particular.

"Bill . . . mmm . . . bill . . . Oh, Lise, here is one for you."

Lola and Frida took up the chant, "Lise has a letter, Lise has a letter."

Lise handed Walter off to Gisela and grabbed the letter from her father, taking note of the official stamp on the front before she tore it open. She already suspected its content and so hope and disappointment battled within her in equal measure. After a quick scan of the pertinent parts of letter, disappointment easily vanquished hope. It read in part:

Dear Miss Meitner,

Thank you for your enquiry as to the position of physics assistant at the Institute. Unfortunately we do not think that your application is suitable at this time.

"Another one for the coal scuttle," said Frida, who saw the look of frustration on Lise's face and construed the content of the letter without the need to read it. Frida had seen that look many times.

Although her parents had shown extreme patience with her, Lise knew that time had begun to run out on her quest to find a career in the field she loved. Soon she would graduate from the University with a PhD in Physics. For a man, such an achievement as good as assured a successful future. But as a woman, people expected Lise to cease playing at science, retire from the academic scene and find a good husband. And in spite of their support, her parents expected the same thing.

"Don't worry, Lise," comforted Gisela. "It's the same for me. No one wants a female doctor either. We must persist until they have no choice but to accept us." Gisela also knew the frustration of struggling to make it in a man's world, this time in the field of medicine and she had encountered equal resistance from the Austrian Establishment.

Philipp Meitner raised his hand to Lise's chin. "Keep your head up Lise. They can't all turn you down."

"And we shall never want for warmth as long as the Meitners keep getting rejection letters to burn," added Frida cheerfully.

Hedwig Meitner returned from the kitchen.

"Let's eat," she said.

. . . *Summer*

L ise had eventually accepted Niels's offer of coffee and it led to a much more amicable and social Lise, not yet the life of the party by any means, but more assured, if still not comfortable around others.

Niels made it easy. He came from a successful and celebrated family. From his father, who headed the Physiology Department at the University of Copenhagen, he had inherited an unquenchable thirst for knowledge. From his mother came the fiscal security derived from a wealthy line of Danish bankers and politicians. And as icing on the cake, Niels shared the athleticism of his brother, Harald, an Olympic medalist.

In spite of this privileged upbringing, Niels had the common touch: generous and outgoing; and he made friends readily. Partly because of the money, partly because of his reputation as a man on the fast-track of science, but mostly because of his personality, he became the natural focal point for a group of like-minded people, and Lise found herself accepted as a member of the clique.

But with Vienna now firmly in the warm grip of summer and the university life of study and examinations behind her, Lise's goal of landing an interview, let alone a job, seemed as unattainable as ever.

Coffee had become a morning ritual for the unemployed graduates. Vienna had many coffee shops where the students gathered to exchange potential leads and complain about their misfortunes.

Lise and Niels headed over to Café Central, near the University. Niels grabbed a newspaper from the rack at the café entrance and on taking a bench at an open table, opened it to the help wanted section; not that he needed a job - he planned to return to Copenhagen to continue his studies - but he knew that Lise supposedly hunted for work.

Supposed was the operative word, for Lise's father had made this assumption based on the fact that his daughter had now graduated and finally finished with this educational nonsense. Instead, Lise had the idea that she would like to stay on at University, perhaps as one of Boltzmann's assistants. To work with Boltzmann was her dream assignment. To get a job at the University would prove as difficult as her acceptance as a student, but given her connection to the Great Man, and his genuine opinion of her abilities, she considered the dream not entirely beyond the realm of possibility. It was also a dream which she had yet to share with her father.

"Horseless carriage mechanic wanted," Niels read aloud. "Must be of good character. No Protestants or Jews or Protestants who used to be Jews." He invented the last bit, in the knowledge that

Lise's family, although born Jewish had converted to the Protestant faith, to better fit in with Viennese society. Lise did not overtly practice either religion, but she had welcomed the conversion; for on top of the sexism which she encountered every day, anti-Semitism also lurked around every corner; an encounter she preferred to avoid.

"Too technical," replied Lise, sitting down beside him.

"Baker's assistant? Bring your own rolling pin," Niels continued.

"Damn, I just sold it."

"Well, how about . . . no, no, no! How can they expect a woman to do that?" Niels snapped the paper shut in mock disgust. "Well I give up then. There just isn't any work for a woman of your poor abilities. Maybe you should go back to kindergarten and start all over again."

"Maybe I should marry a prince and lead a life of ease."

"Well that would be a step down of course, but then you can't expect to start at the top. You have to work your way up."

"Speaking of not starting at the top, do you still have the run of your father's laboratory in Copenhagen?"

"Well, yes, but it's really a very small laboratory, nothing more than a broom cupboard."

"Small?"

"Yes, it's rather sad really. All the equipment has to be scaled accordingly: thimbles for test-tubes, matches instead of a Bunsen-burner. I can only conduct little experiments."

As Lise attempted to stifle a laugh, she heard the sound of a familiar voice from the café doorway. It belonged to Emma Planck, daughter of the physicist, Max. Planck It could have equally belonged to Emma's identical twin, Grete; for few people could tell them apart. Although the twins didn't attend University, they had taken up temporary residence in Vienna, and in a trait they shared with Niels, they exhibited relaxed and playful personas; and soon after meeting them, Lise counted them amongst her closest friends.

Lise peered beyond Emma for a sign of Grete, for they always appeared as a double act. Grete obliged Lise's curiosity and appeared in the doorway. The twins scanned the café, spotted Lise and Niels, and made their way to the table.

"Make room," said Grete, forcing herself between Lise and Niels onto the bench. Emma sat down at the end of the table. At the other end of the café, a heated debate of a political nature took place among three men, loud enough to turn heads.

"What has Russia got in place of such a middle class?" yelled the man at the centre of the argument. "The new middle class, the professional intelligentsia: lawyers, journalists, doctors, engineers, university professors, schoolteachers?"

"Who's that?" asked Emma, for the men did not have the usual appearance of malnourished students.

"Bolsheviks!" replied Lise. "You just missed the lecture. They've been going at it since we got here."

The three men consisted of Vladimir Ilyich Lenin, Lev Davidnovich Bronstein, who people called Leon Trotsky, and who held the floor and yelled the loudest, and Baron Rothschild, the famous banker. In addition to hosting unemployed graduates, Café Central was a popular place for the three men to meet, play chess and scoff at the state of world politics.

"Don't worry that you've missed anything important - Lise took notes," teased Niels. "Apparently, Professor Bronstein there wants to start a revolution in Russia."

"Well they won't do it sitting in Vienna, drinking coffee," scoffed Emma. She noticed that Niels had a newspaper. "What news of the world there, Niels, other than great unrest in the Balkans? Has Einstein discovered cheese on the moon?"

Although none of the Vienna Set had met Einstein, for he moved in the lower social circle of the patent office in Berne, they harbored more than a little hint of professional jealousy at the amateur Einstein's growing fame.

"Just some social gossip in the personals," replied Niels. He quoted from the paper in mock formality, "The Emperor Franz Joseph wishes to announce the engagement of his nephew, Arch Duke Ferdinand to Miss Lise Meitner, of the Vienna Meitners, and late of the University of Vienna."

"He's already married, isn't he?" objected Grete.

"But the current princess is not suitable," replied Niels. "They are looking for a replacement."

"Lise, I'm disappointed in you," chided Emma. "You never tell your best friends anything?"

"It was meant to be a state secret," pouted Lise, taking up the horseplay. "In case it upset too many people and threatened unrest."

"Actually, Ferdinand is not the first," said Niels. "Prince Rudolph committed suicide when told that Lise was unobtainable." Although he didn't know it, for the Crown Prince had indeed committed suicide many years before, Niels had gone too far with his joke.

"Oh, not a good choice of words, Niels," said Emma with a frown. Lise and Niels looked at each other in puzzlement, and Grete positively squirmed between them.

"What?" demanded Niels. "What have I said?"

"You haven't heard?" asked Emma.

"Heard what?"

"Father told us this morning. We thought that you would have heard - that Lise would have heard at least."

The quizzical expressions on the faces of Niels and Lise showed that they obviously had not heard.

"We have some news," said Grete. "It's not in the papers yet, but it will be . . . Professor Boltzmann . . . He's dead . . . Suicide they say."

. . . Another Funeral

Four black horses, with black and gold harnesses and black ostrich plumes atop their heads, pulled the hearse through the streets of Vienna. The hearse, also black of course but tailored with sides of glass and silver, and layered with gold leaf decoration, glided silently and in slow motion, as if over a carpet of fine lace. A canopy of more black ostrich feathers shielded the hearse, its driver and whip-hand from the sun. Inside the hearse, the coffin lay surrounded with flowers. And inside the coffin lay the body of Ludwig Boltzmann.

Various foot attendants, pallbearers, feather men, pages and mutes - the official mourners - walked behind the hearse in somber pomposity, while at least two dozen official coaches followed behind them, carrying family, friends and dignitaries. And behind this authorized entourage, two hundred more unauthorized coaches of various sizes and splendor formed a mile long black ribbon.

All along the Ringstraße, the procession slowly passed the university and the museums, the Opera House and Musikverein, with its magnificent Golden Hall, and the Belvedere Palaces, home to Franz Ferdinand. Tens of thousands of Viennese lined the streets to pay their respects to the Great Man or at least, to participate in a story which they would tell to their grandchildren.

Such an extraordinary sight of pomp and ceremony was typically reserved only for the funeral of a head of state, but in the eyes of the Viennese, whose numbers swelled dramatically the closer the procession got to the Central Cemetery, Ludwig Boltzmann ranked equal to any head of state: a visionary, a leader and a man of the people all rolled into one previously larger than life package.

Eventually the funeral parade arrived at the gates of the Central Cemetery on the outskirts of the city, and made its way to the church, passing along the Ehregräber (Graves of Honor), with its monuments to Vienna's greatest citizens, such as Beethoven, Mozart and Strauss.

Finally the hearse arrived at the church and stopped. The other coaches stopped behind it in a line which stretched back to the cemetery gates and beyond. The mourners climbed out of their coaches and entered the church - the tail required to run and push through the crowds to get inside before the ushers closed the doors. Inside the church, hundreds more, a group which included Lise and her friends, had arrived hours ahead of the procession and already occupied the unreserved seats.

* * *

With the last mourner, out of breath and covered in sweat, finally seated, noted dignitaries, friends and enemies alike, stepped to the front to deliver effusive praise for the fallen Boltzmann. His old friend, Professor Hasenohrl, chosen to deliver the eulogy, did so in a practiced, stilted voice, intended to cloak the emotions which churned within him.

> "The successes of the scientist require talent and intellect, but the teacher must have his heart in the right place. Characteristic of the good teacher, at the elementary as well as the university level, are ability to understand those who are learning, interest in their development, good will, and sympathy."

"What will you do now, Lise?" Grete whispered to her friend.

"Meyer will probably be the new Chair, I suppose." Lise whispered back. "I need some time to think about it."

Lise would have preferred to remain silent out of respect for her hero and mentor. Grete meant well, but the Planck twins were always impatient and inattentive. If Lise did not reply they would just become more insistent. Response was the lesser of two evils.

For Grete to talk of the future at a time such as this could be construed as insensitive, but her friends understood what Boltzmann's death meant to Lise - that Lise's job prospects had taken a severe blow, perhaps fatal - perhaps they would be buried along with Boltzmann.

"Come to Berlin," whispered Grete.

"What?"

"Come to Berlin," echoed Emma. "Without Boltzmann, Vienna will stagnate anyway. Niels there is deserting us and going back to Viking Land."

"It's pronounced, 'Denmark'!" an indignant Niels whispered out of the side of his mouth, his eyes still focused on Hasenöhrl.

"In a word, the good teacher is characterized by a kind heart."

"I can't come to Berlin," protested Lise.

"Why not?" demanded Grete. "What future is there for you here?"

"I need a job. I don't know anybody in Berlin."

"Those were the personal traits that made Boltzmann a brilliant teacher and that assure him of the everlasting gratitude of his many students. The way in which Boltzmann got on with his students has remained indelible in their memories."

"We will be in Berlin," whispered Grete. "You know us."

"Can you give me a job? I don't think so."

"Father knows lots of people," whispered Emma. "And they in turn know lots of people. Come to Berlin and carry on Boltzmann's work."

"He never played up his superiority: everyone was at liberty to ask questions and even to criticize him. One could converse with him in an uninhibited way as if between equals, and often one noticed only subsequently how much one had learned from him once again."

"Boltzmann's work? I can't even get an interview."

"If you stay here, you'll end up teaching kindergarten and marrying the grocer," pushed Grete.

"Hush, be quiet, Grete. You say too much!" admonished Niels.

> "He did not measure others with the yardstick of his own greatness."

"You must talk to father," continued Emma.

"I can't do that," protested Lise. "He doesn't know me."

> "He also judged more modest achievements with goodwill, so long as they gave evidence of serious and honest effort."

"Then you must come to dinner," insisted Emma.

"Yes, come to dinner," echoed Grete.

"No!"

Heads turned in their direction. Even without looking, Lise could feel their burning stares and disapproval. The twins remained oblivious to the displeasure their behavior caused, but Lise felt the anger and embarrassment rise in her. Why couldn't he have stayed alive just a little while longer - until she had gained that first vital position? The thought was unworthy and her anger turned to guilt. She wanted to tell Boltzmann how sorry she felt. She had failed him as much as herself. To have worked so hard, to have endured so much, to have come so close - and to lose it all now was too much to bear. She wanted to run away and hide.

"For God's sake, Lise, agree to dinner," whispered Niels. "They'll never shut up otherwise."

. . . Hotel Bristol

L iving in Vienna, Lise had obviously heard of the Hotel Bristol: the temporary home of nobility, presidents, opera singers, actresses and the other well-heeled when they had occasion to stay in the city. And Lise had walked by its front door on many an occasion, but moving in a different social circle, she had never stepped foot inside the place before this night.

The hotel stood opposite the State Opera House and it matched that place for grandeur in every respect, with crystal chandeliers and marble floors. The Plancks occupied a suite at the hotel during their visits to Vienna. The dining room, where they held court at this moment with Lise as their overwhelmed and nervous guest, rivaled any prince's ballroom for opulence.

"Yes, Boltzmann was a prodigious talent. You were lucky to study under him, Miss Meitner," spoke Max Planck, the twins' father. "And I say this as one who did not always see eye to eye with him."

Fifty years of age, small of frame, slight of build, bespectacled and bald; Max Planck struck no one as an imposing figure, especially in the dinner jacket, two or three sizes too large for him at least, which enveloped him as if a child's security blanket, and the stiff collar, reminiscent of a medieval neck stretcher.

But Lise knew of his work in the world of physics, his reputation as a scholar without parallel and the respect he commanded from his peers; and of his sometimes heated disagreements with Boltzmann. And as Lise sat opposite him, a proverbial fish out of water, she wished she had refused to heed Niels and accept the twins' invitation to dinner.

"Yes," she barely whispered in a thoughtful and measured response.

"I must confess that it took more time than it should have for him to win me over. I still wrestle with him and he still slaps me down occasionally, even now."

"Lise plans to carry on the good professor's work," interrupted Emma.

"But you are a doctor already! What more do you want?" queried Max, with a shake of his head.

The pessimistic observation met Lise's expectations. Planck's views of women reflected the standards of the day and, he would add, were reinforced by the capricious behavior of his daughters.

"I would like to gain some real understanding of physics," croaked Lise.

"We think that Lise should come to Berlin, Father. Vienna is such a backwater," said Grete, charging to Lise's aid. Naturally, the twins knew their father better than most, sans the public reputation, and as familiarity bred contempt, they relished the opportunity to stand up to him.

"Berlin is not as liberal as Vienna, Miss Meitner," Max shook his head again. "Women are not invited to study at the University, or made to feel very welcome. They have a reputation as disruptive. Professor Fischer. . ."

"Oh, Papa, don't tease," interrupted Grete. "Do not mind him, Lise, it is just his way."

Grete knew when her father played games. She had suspected he did so now; and the mention of Professor Fischer confirmed her suspicion. Emil Fischer, a Nobel Prize winner, headed the Chemistry Department at the University of Berlin. The Plancks loved him as an old, dear and generous friend, but he occupied the body of a stuffy old fashioned traditionalist.

"Professor Fischer has a constant worry that female students will distract his chemists from important work," Emma explained to Lise.

"He's such an abbot," added Grete. "We call him 'Father Fischer.'"

"Grete, do not speak ill of our good friend," chided Max.

"Oh, Papa, you are an abbot too. And you are being rude to Lise."

"I am merely pointing out the realities. For a woman to make it in a man's world takes special qualities."

"Lise has them and more," argued Emma. "You've always encouraged us. Don't pretend now to be a regressive. Lise was Boltzmann's best pupil. She will be yours."

"No, no, out of the question. You know I have never permitted women to attend my lectures."

"Then it's time to make an exception," said Grete.

"And Lise is exceptional," said Emma.

"She would have to be!" said Max.

"Come on, Papa, this is the 20th century, not the Stone Age," said Grete.

Max raised his glass of wine and sipped it, to give himself time to fashion a response. He loved his daughters more than any thing else in the world, and indulged their wishes more than an attentive parent should. But business was business, hard and brutal - and no fit place for a woman.

On the other hand . . . Max knew more of Lise Meitner than she comprehended - from Boltzmann - of her papers, her work ethic, and her promise. He put the wine glass back on the table and proceeded to speak slowly and deliberately, as if he had reviewed a theorem and found a flaw.

"If a woman has a special gift for the tasks of theoretical physics - which does not happen often but happens sometimes - and moreover she herself feels moved to develop her gift, I do not think it right, both personally and impersonally, to refuse her the chance and means of studying."

"Papa says 'yes'," interpreted Emma, with glee.

"But Berlin is not Vienna," Max shook his head. "There is nothing of the comforts or pleasures of Vienna. It is cold and austere, especially so for the gentler sex."

"Papa says 'welcome to Berlin'," interpreted Grete.

Max took a deep breath, looked reproachfully at his grinning daughters and then fixed his eye on Lise.

"Very well," said Max. "I shall consent to your admission, on a trial basis, to my lectures and practical courses."

"Thank you," Lise managed weakly.

"On the other hand," hedged Max. "I must keep to the fact that such a case should always be regarded as an exception."

"Oh, yes, always!" mocked Grete. The twins knew when their father joked, even if Lise did not.

"It cannot be emphasized enough that nature herself prescribes to a woman her function as mother and housewife," continued Max.

"Father is always lecturing us for not being married yet," said Emma.

"We are such a drain on the household budget," said Grete.

"The laws of nature cannot be ignored without grave danger," said Max.

. . . *The Next Night*

"Lise, are you playing or just observing?" asked Philipp Meitner. Lise and her father sat at the dining room table and played chess. Lise had the rudiments of a competent player, but Philipp played at the level of a Grand Master and he showed no mercy, even to his daughters.

The sun had dropped below the horizon; and in doing so had shed its warm, peaceful, orange blush on the Meitner household. Fritz worked late. Gisela and Lola enjoyed an evening of free Strauss at the Belvedere Gardens. Hedwig Meitner settled baby Walter for the night, and then settled herself in an old, soft chair in the living room and relaxed with a book.

Frida, too languid to accompany her sisters and too impatient for chess, occupied herself at the piano with a slow, quiet rendition of the Moonlight Sonata. Frida never could master the more demanding passages of Beethoven's work, so she contented herself with repeating the easier opening bars. In spite of this, the notes emanating from the piano added to the tranquil atmosphere rather than disrupted it.

Warm and peaceful; and Philipp welcomed the respite.

"What? Oh sorry Papa," replied Lise. Even when Lise concentrated, she could hope for no better than to hold her father at bay for a little while, but today her mind wandered. She looked at the chess board half-heartedly and made a move. Philipp responded instantly with a move of his own.

"And how is the job search coming?" Philipp enquired nonchalantly, without looking up from the chess board, but he sensed that his daughter had something other than chess on her mind.

"Professor Boltzmann advised me to follow the truth," she replied, accepting his soft, opening gambit.

"And what of your father's advice?" said Philipp, clearly irritated. "Boltzmann! Much good following the truth did him. The truth did not make him happy."

"No but . . ."

"The truth does not put food on the table."

"No, Papa, it does not."

As he never found any of his daughters this compliant, Philipp deduced that whatever troubled Lise called for a gentler touch.

"I'm sorry Lise . . . Professor Boltzmann was a good man. I know you thought highly of him. We are all sorry that he is gone. It is only to be expected that those who knew him feel his loss the most, but life goes on."

Philipp looked up. Lise looked down.

"What is it?" He asked.

Lise knew that it was now or never. She saw her opening and pressed.

"I think that without Boltzmann, the truth is no longer to be found in Vienna," she said.

"But where is the truth other than with your family? The truth is not a theoretical abstract."

The moment had come. Lise plucked up her courage and looked into her father's eyes.

"Papa . . . I want to go to Berlin."

"Berlin? Whatever for? What is in Berlin?"

"Max Planck is in Berlin. He is the natural successor to Boltzmann. If anyone is to further the science of physics, it is Planck."

"No, you should continue to look for a job. Trips to Berlin can come later when you can afford it."

"No, Papa, not a trip. I want to move to Berlin to study under Professor Planck."

"Berlin? But your family is here in Vienna. We know nobody in Berlin. If you can't find work in Vienna, what chance do you have in Berlin?"

"Well, I was hoping Papa that you, perhaps . . ."

"No, Lise, do not ask. Don't you think that I have given more than enough already? More than we can afford. I think you already know that. It's time to stop this nonsense."

"Yes, Papa. You have been more than patient with me, but . . ."

"But, but! - Always an argument with you. Why don't you behave like your sisters? Fall in love - get married - teach! You would make a good teacher."

"When you fell in love with Mama . . ."

"Now, don't bring your mother into this. I have a difficult enough time without the women of this family ganging up on me."

"Mama is the love of your life. If she had been in Berlin, would you not have gone there to be with her?"

"Not a good analogy at all. Your mother is not a science experiment."

"But I love physics just as you love Mama. And right now physics means Berlin."

"Who will pay for this folly?"

"Please, Papa; you and Mama have sacrificed so much for all of us."

"Yes, we have. I'm glad you admit it, young lady."

"Have we come so far just to stop now? Then it will all have been a waste. I would hate for your sacrifice to have been wasted."

"Now, Lise, don't try reverse psychology on me; I am not a science experiment either."

"Please, Papa, for a little while longer. Just one semester to find out what Max Planck can teach."

"But Lise . . . where will it all end?"

"Just one term; then I'll come back and take up the life of a kindergarten teacher."

"Your mother . . . Money is tight . . . She . . . I . . ." His anger subsided.

"Please, Papa, one more term."

"I'll have to discuss it with your mother. She's not going to be pleased."

"Thank you, Papa, just one more term, I promise."

Lise's heart pounded. She had won, but she knew that it had come at a cost. She knew that if she went to Berlin things would change forever. Whether she went for a term or a year or a decade, it would make no difference. She had now severed the ties to her past life in Vienna, her childhood, her family, the protection and warmth of home. In an instant, her parents, brothers and sisters had become distant strangers.

She suddenly felt all alone in the world, as if she had fallen; and she did not know if she could land on her feet or if anyone would catch her. Her heart filled with mixed emotions. It would take but a word from her father and she would gladly abandon her dream and stay with her family, where she belonged, secure and wanted. She could not look him in the eye, but she inwardly pleaded with him to tell her no, to take charge, to relieve her of this burden - just one word.

Philipp Meitner nodded at the chess board. "It is still your move," he said.

Pride

"I don't believe that atoms exist!"

Ernst Mach

. . . After the funeral, Cambridge, 1968

T he cottage, small but picturesque and cozy, nestled in a slightly overgrown flower garden, protected by a freestanding stone wall. Inside, along with the white-washed plaster walls which failed to hide the dry rot, and a preponderance of tarnished brass decoration, the cottage held the scattered remnants of a life: faded, yellow books on a sagging shelf, grey photographs in silver frames and brown envelopes in cardboard boxes - not nearly enough for such a long life, but the diminutive size of the cottage helped to magnify their effect.

Typically, slate coals in the fireplace heated the living room to tropical levels, even in the summer, and the heat combined with the English dampness to make for a humid sauna-like environment in which Robert always struggled to avoid sweating. But today, as with the past week, the coals in the fireplace remained dormant and waited for someone to put a match to them. So now, the atmosphere inside the cottage resembled that of the weather outside, which tended to the chilly.

Robert raised a hand, rubbed his eyes and then passed his fingers through his hair. He sat at a hinge-top cherry side table, which did double duty as the dining table when she entertained guests - when she dined alone she had preferred a tray - and he lifted a handful of papers from a stack at one end of a table and placed them at the other end.

He had started to sift through Lise's belongings a few days earlier. He understood the importance of preserving as much of the history as possible and he worked with meticulous care, but he hadn't appreciated just how much the documentation needed sequencing and categorizing - and just how much this brush with the past would drain his emotions. Now he had succumbed to a mental numbness and he found himself just going through the motions.

"If you like, I can make a fire, Professor."

The voice jarred Robert back into consciousness. It belonged to Lise's housekeeper. Well, not so much of a housekeeper than more of a minder whom Robert had hired to keep an eye on Lise in her declining years. Lise remained far too independent, even at the end, to accept any offer she perceived as charity. She and Robert had argued for months before Lise finally caved in and permitted the help of a daily. And it had taken months more before Lise had become comfortable with the housekeeper's company.

"What? Oh, no thank you. We won't be much longer," said Robert.

"No bother," said the housekeeper. "She was never much bother either; always very prim and proper."

"Yes, I suppose she was. At least that's what people said of her. But she still managed to make an impression in her day."

The housekeeper continued, "Something of a celebrity too, I hear; rubbing shoulders with Mr. Einstein and Presidents and the like."

"She probably would have preferred fewer Presidents and more Einsteins," Robert replied.

"No, no bother. Never heard her complain neither, not never." The housekeeper waddled back to the kitchen, where Robert heard her converse with his daughter, Monica. Wanting to leave him with his thoughts, they talked in hushed tones as if they stood in a cathedral.

Robert got up to stretch his legs and walked to the mantel, where he picked up a photograph and looked at it. The picture showed three women seated on a grass embankment. One woman was his aunt, Lise - then a young woman, for the photograph came from a bygone age more than sixty years previous. The other two women he recognized as the Planck twins, Emma and Grete. A photo which featured both twins was rare, for usually one posed while the other operated the camera. The twins wore, daringly for the time, bright summer clothes and straw boaters, and looked perfectly charming and radiant, in a manner designed to attract husbands. Lise, on the other hand, looked thin, fragile and uninviting; with black shadows under her eyes, for she never did get enough sleep, and her customary, unyielding, conservative black dress.

"You should have been a nun, Aunty," thought Robert. "You always dressed as one."

His mind wavered between seeking the comfort of human contact in the kitchen and drifting back into his lethargic stupor when he heard the sound of car tires on gravel and a short toot-toot of a horn, which signaled a welcome end to the day's exertions.

Monica entered the room.

"Father, the taxi is here; we have to go back now."

Robert replaced the photograph on the mantel, but as he did so, he noticed that Lise, above her frown, also wore a straw boater. He had missed it the first time, for people usually see only what they expect to see. Ah yes, the hint of playfulness was still there - always there for people to see - for the ones who really knew her. He smiled.

He would continue tomorrow, refreshed and cheerful.

... *Berlin, 1908*

The successful and brilliant Max Planck garnered much well deserved public respect, attention and many business propositions, which included an offer to replace Boltzmann in Vienna; and which he declined. In private, he earned further admiration from those who considered him a warm, loyal and generous friend.

But when it came to commanding and captivating an audience he was no Ludwig Boltzmann. During his lectures, Max stood expressionless at the podium and delivered his speech with a dry, monotonous, robotic, clanging voice which grated on the students' ears and wore them into submission.

Today, the lecture room baked under lazy, hot, humid air; and Max preferred that the windows remain closed, to cut down on the distractions. His students, not the most attentive even in the best conditions, sweated and dozed.

Unlike the other students, Lise, captivated and enchanted, gripped the edge of her seat to avoid floating away with the words which came from Planck's mouth. He may have lacked Boltzmann's delivery, but she recognized the greatness in him and she refused to waste a moment of the time given to her to absorb everything which he had to teach.

Next to Lise sat the well groomed, elegantly dressed and waxed mustached Max Theodore Felix von Laue, aged 27. As with most of those present in the room - i.e., the non-female - Laue weighed the merits of learning something useful from Planck against the temptation of taking a little nap. The nap held a commanding lead.

Max Planck continued his drone:

"The recent spectral measurements made by O. Lummer and E. Pringsheim, and even more notable those by H. Rubens and F. Kurlbaum, which together confirmed an earlier result obtained by H. Beckmann, show that the law of energy distribution in the normal spectrum, first derived by W. Wien from molecular-kinetic considerations and later by me from the theory of electromagnetic radiation, is not valid generally. In any case the theory requires a correction, and I shall attempt in the following to accomplish this on the basis of the theory of electromagnetic radiation which I developed. For this purpose, it will be necessary first to find in the set of conditions leading to Wien's energy distribution law that term which can be changed; thereafter it will be a matter of removing this term from the set and making an appropriate substitution for it . . . Blah, blah, blah."

A loud crash jolted Lise from her focus. A student had fallen to the floor: whether faint from the heat or just another nap taker who had overestimated the ability of the wooden bench to support his sagging body, we do not know.

"Oh," cried Lise, but the other students barely batted an eye lid.

"Don't worry," said Laue, without looking up or even opening his eyes. "It happens all the time; like Icarus flying too close to the sun - or is that moths to the flame? Anyway, they can't help it: they are in awe of the great man."

Two other students helped the hapless man to his feet and brushed the dust of the lecture room floor from his clothes. Then all three returned to their seats and the dust slowly swirled and settled over them. Max Planck continued his lecture as if nothing had happened.

"In my last article I showed that the physical foundations of the electromagnetic radiation theory, including the hypothesis of 'natural radiation,' withstand the most severe criticism; and since to my knowledge there are no errors in the calculations, the principle persists that the law of energy distribution in the normal spectrum is completely determined when one succeeds in calculating the entropy S of an irradiated, monochromatic, vibrating resonator as a function of its vibrational energy U . . . More blah, blah, blah."

Lise leaned forward in admiration of Planck's focus and will power. Max von Laue continued his nap.

* * *

In spite of the hardship of her life in the unforgiving city, and although she had promised her father just one term, Lise always seemed to find an excuse to extend her stay. And so the days turned to weeks and the weeks turned to months; and the time passed in equal cloudy measures of tedium and discrimination, with the occasional outbreak of the Planck twins.

In fact, the entire Planck family, which included the twins' brothers, Karl and Erwin, went out of their way to keep Lise included and entertained. Max had taken on himself the duty of Lise's surrogate father during her residence in Berlin and insisted that she dine with the family several times a week; for which she was extremely grateful, as her meager allowance scarcely extended to such luxuries as food.

And she also established a solid friendship with Max von Laue, whose affected mannerisms, fake vanity and dry wit made for one of the few sweet oases in the desert of academic Berlin.

On Wednesdays, Lise attended the Physics Colloquium of Professor Heinrich Rubens. This Wednesday, Lise noticed a new face in the crowd at Ruben's lecture, but this did not strike her as unusual - people came and went all the time - so Lise made nothing of it and soon became absorbed by the lecture, attentively taking in every word and scribbling notes furiously.

The lecture proved nothing out of the ordinary either; perhaps one or two points of interest, which she had already figured out for herself, but mostly unmemorable. So Lise anticipated its conclusion and looked forward to some coffee, to which she had become addicted.

"Okay, if there are no more questions that about wraps it up for today," said Heinrich Rubens. The assembly rose as one and began to file out of the lecture room. Lise moved towards the door, but heard the professor call her name.

"Frau Meitner," said Rubens. "Frau Meitner, Herr Hahn."

"Professor?" Lise turned and replied.

The newcomer, a man roughly the same age as Lise, also stopped and turned. He was obviously the Herr Hahn to whom the Professor had called.

Rubens spoke to Lise. "Professor Planck has approached me about the possibility of arranging a workspace for you, is that correct?"

"Yes, Professor," replied Lise. "I am hoping to continue the research I started last year."

"Well, workspace is always tight, as you know. I've considered the request most seriously, but I'm afraid I don't think I have anything suitable. Too many researchers and not enough university, you understand," said Rubens. "Although, if you are interested, I may have a requirement for a student to assist me with my work - under supervision of course."

Under the circumstances, Rubens' offer was a generous one and any student would have jumped at the chance.

"Thank you, Professor, but I was rather looking to pick up where I left off in Vienna." Lise did appreciate the offer, but had little desire to abandon her research to work on Ruben's pet projects.

"That's too bad, too bad. Oh, sorry, I don't mean to denigrate your work. It's just that I don't think that I can help you there. I don't know of anyone who could. You know that competition is tough and you have the disadvantage of being a woman. Most professors will dismiss your request out of hand."

The Professor displayed kindness and had treated Lise better than most of his colleagues, but he obviously could not, or would not, buck convention for her sake.

"Well, thank you again, Professor, for your time." Lise turned away. The professor's negative response, while disappointing, simply added to the long list of rejections. Rubens, however, had not finished.

"Frau Meitner, you have not met Herr Hahn, I believe?"

Lise turned again. "No, I'm afraid not."

"Then let me make the introductions," said Rubens. "Lise Meitner, meet Otto Hahn - Otto Hahn, Frau Meitner."

"Hello, nice to meet you," said Otto, with his hand extended. Lise hesitated briefly but then shook Otto's hand. He held her hand with a firm but warm and gentle grip, as if he cupped a baby bird; and Otto's smile extended from ear to ear in a half moon of pearl white teeth.

"Herr Hahn has just joined us after spending a year in Montreal with Earnest Rutherford," said Rubens. "Although he's a chemist by nature, he has been kind enough to attend my Physics Colloquium."

Otto's smile widened even further at the compliment. "I'm researching radioactivity. Most of my colleagues have never even heard of radioactivity," he said.

"Herr Hahn knows of your research in the same field and wondered if you would be interested in collaborating with him?"

"Collaboration?" asked Lise, cautiously.

"Yes," said Otto. "Chemistry can only take me so far. I need someone who knows their way around an electroscope. Professor Fischer seems to think that there is no instrument more sensitive than the human nose."

(The aforementioned Fischer was the Head of the Chemistry Department and, because of his antiquated views, the butt of many a joke from the younger generation.)

"I do believe there is some common ground between chemistry and physics," agreed Lise. "But as you must have just heard, I don't have a workspace, let alone an electroscope."

"I think I may be able to resolve that," said Otto. "There's a possibility of a shared workspace over at the Chemistry Department. I'm sure Professor Fischer can be persuaded."

"Then you are further ahead in the game than I," said Lise.

How Otto Hahn, a newcomer to Berlin, could be further ahead in the game was open to speculation. Because of the gender thing? Definitely! But that did not explain it all. Hahn also exuded just the right blend of charm and confidence. And a year with Rutherford attested to his ability as a chemist. His career obviously fast tracked, Otto Hahn was destined to go far.

Still, having just turned down Professor Ruben's offer, Lise had no desire to work under Hahn either, even if he dangled the temptation of a workspace before her eyes. She began to decline the invitation.

"Well, don't say yes right away," interrupted Otto. "Why don't we go and discuss the possibilities over a cup of coffee; I'm addicted to the stuff."

* * *

Over coffee, Otto made it quite clear that he did not seek an assistant: Otto would handle the chemistry, Lise would handle the physics, and he proposed an equal fifty-fifty partnership. And the brief, relaxed conversation proved that Otto certainly knew his chemistry, but more importantly, that he also felt as she did: that searching in the grayness between the black and white worlds of physics and chemistry could unlock the mystery of the elusive atom.

Charm and confidence! Lise took an instant liking to him.

Of course, Otto argued, as long as Lise remained technically just a guest at the University, it would prove easier to let him handle any negotiations. Lise agreed - the opportunity to obtain a workspace overcame her aversion to the discrimination. If Otto wanted to take up that crusade, then more power to him.

They finished their coffee and, now full of caffeine and optimism, Lise and Otto went to plead their case with Professor Emil Fischer, head of the Chemistry Department.

* * *

"No, no, no! Quite out of the question. The rules forbid it," an agitated and hurried Fischer waved them away, as he strode down the corridor which led to his office. Otto shuffled along side him. Lise brought up the rear.

"But Professor, we need access to the equipment and workspace," pleaded Otto.

"My dear Hahn." Fischer stopped and sighed. "It is a well known fact that women and chemistry don't mix."

"But Professor. . ."

"It's far too dangerous," continued Fischer. "If a woman gets too close to the Bunsen burner, her hair catches fire – Poof! - The whole place goes up in smoke."

"Professor, I . . ."

"This is nothing personal you understand," Fischer waved a dismissive hand towards Lise in a form of apology. "We simply do not have the facilities to accommodate a woman."

"You know Rutherford is going to win the Nobel this year for his work on radioactivity."

"Rutherford?"

Otto knew he had hit a nerve: the rivalry and jealously amongst the Nobel contenders equaled that of any sports contest. Otto pressed his argument.

"Professor, Frau Meitner is the only person here in Berlin with experience in radioactivity," said Otto. "It is a golden opportunity for us to establish ourselves as the leaders in this field."

"Rutherford?" Fischer repeated.

Otto nodded and added a sly smile. Professor Fischer weakened.

"Tell you what; I don't want to seem unreasonable - we have to keep the University current after all . . . I just don't have a workspace for you . . ."

Fischer held up a hand to silence the protesting Otto.

"No, I really don't . . . but . . . there is the old carpenter's workshop in the basement; we were thinking of using it as a storeroom, but . . . it has its own entrance, separate from the rest of the building. If you promise to keep out of sight, you can use that."

"Thank you, Professor," said Otto. "You won't hear a peep out of us. We'll be as quiet as mice."

"Thank you," added Lise, weakly.

"Now go away before I change my mind. You've already wasted far too much of my time."

Otto and Lise thanked Professor Fischer again and turned to go.

"And don't tell anyone of this; otherwise they'll all want workspaces."

"Quiet as mice," shouted Otto as they walked away.

"And keep out of the Chemistry Department!" Emil Fischer shouted after them.

... *The Orient Express*

The Hahn-Meitner Research Department, as it came to be called, flourished. And although Lise failed to secure any pay for her work - unlike Otto - and although she continued to live in relative poverty, still relying on her father's generosity long after her promise to him had expired, she did not complain. Their research proved fruitful and they published several important papers. The University had begun to accept her and her contributions to science, even if the world at large still showed hostility.

In her time away from the workspace, Lise joined Emma and Grete on walking tours of the Alps, where the twins would coax her to defy convention and attempt to climb mountains in dresses entirely unsuited to the purpose.

Lise was happier than she had ever been.

In addition to science, Otto and Lise shared a love of Brahms; and they had taken to singing duets as they hunched over the laboratory equipment. Otto performed the role of baritone, and a very good one. Lise just accompanied him as best she could. But to see her at these times, smiling, joking and laughing, one could easily refute the reputation she had developed as a shy, cold wallflower.

Otto stopped singing.

"No, no Frau Meitner," laughed Otto. "You keep slipping into the counterpoint. Please keep to the cantus firmus."

"You keep leading me there," giggled Lise.

They resumed the song, but Lise forgot the words and started to hum instead. The song deteriorated into laughter, which only abated when a knock at the door commanded their attention. Lise saw the sparkle of the Geiger tube on the work counter; it could only mean one thing.

"The post is here, Herr Hahn," sang Lise.

"The post is here, Frau Meitner," echoed Otto.

Lise went to the door and opened it. The postman stood there. Lise feigned the mannerisms of a mind reader and held a hand to her head, palm outward.

"No, don't tell me . . ." she said. "Wait . . . wait. . . . Ah yes, you have a package for me. It is from Rutherford."

The mailman took the package from his sack. "I don't know how you do it." he said, shaking his head. "We think you are psychic back in the office."

"She's a witch, Herr Postman," cried Otto.

"You could take that act on the stage and make a lot of money with it," said the postman.

"My work is unsullied by the taint of money," said Lise, clutching the package to her heart.

"Hers is a labor of love, Herr Postman," mourned Otto.

"Well still, it's uncanny, if you ask me," said the postman. He turned away; blissfully unaware of the radio active nature of the package he had just delivered. Lise closed the door. Simultaneously, the face of Max von Laue appeared at the window.

"Are we scaring the mailman again?" scolded Laue. "Now, I've had cause to reprimand you wicked children on prior occasions."

"Hail, Max," said Otto. "No, he doesn't know about the Geiger counter."

Max von Laue glided into the workshop through the open window.

"Hello, Max," said Lise. "What brings you to our humble abode?"

"Actually, I am also here in my official capacity of mailman," said Laue, standing to attention.

"What is it now?" asked Otto. "Has Fischer received more complaints about the singing?"

Max von Laue turned grim and serious, and silently handed a paper to Otto. As Otto read its contents, Laue's frown turned back into a smile.

"The Salzburg conference is rearing its ugly head," informed Laue. "Planck is going and Planck says he is dragging the three of us along for the ride."

"Ah, a day out at last," said Otto. "Who's in the firing line this time?" He read the paper. "Oh, we have a special guest speaker - Mr. Albert Einstein."

"Bow your head when you speak that name," said Laue. "Moses is coming down from Mount Sinai."

"Einstein? Moses? He's not even a member of the flock, is he?" asked Lise.

"No, but he is ruffling some feathers," laughed Laue. "Oh, I'm mixing metaphors. Anyway, he's bound to make some waves - oh, there I go again - shut up, Laue."

"He's not the only one who'll be getting some feathers wet, by the looks of this next speaker," said Otto.

"Who's that?" asked Lise.

"You!" replied Otto.

* * *

The journey to Salzburg entailed an excursion on the cross-country train to Stuttgart and connecting with the cross-continent train - The Orient Express. Being a strictly first-class mode of transport, the Orient Express had no sitting compartments other than the dining car; and when not dining, passengers kept to their sleeper cars.

Lise and Max Planck each had their own sleeper, while Otto and Max von Laue shared. But the shortness of this leg of the journey - a matter of a few hours - precluded them from any significant sleep, even though they travelled in the small hours of the morning.

And so the academics from the University of Berlin crowded in Max Planck's sleeper compartment, which with the bed stowed away, converted to a small office with sofa and table.

Otto, Max Planck and Max von Laue played three-handed bridge and engaged in small talk. Lise had volumes of paper spread out on the sofa beside her. She muttered under her breath as she tried to memorize her upcoming speech.

"Oh, for God's sake, Lise, take a break!" cried Otto.

"But this is important," said Lise. "I don't want to look like an idiot when I stand up there."

"You'll do fine, Lise," soothed Planck. "You'll be much better prepared if you rest."

"They won't know what hit them," said Otto. "From her publications, most assume that Dr. Meitner is a man anyway. It'll be quite a shock, I expect."

"The novelty factor of being the first woman speaker in the history of the conference will guarantee you a captive audience," added Laue.

"I am well aware of the novelty factor, thank you very much," said Lise. "This is exactly why I need to rehearse this stuff. I don't want to let the University down."

"The conference is just an excuse for a bunch of old men to get together for a free lunch," said Planck. "You'll do fine."

"I need some coffee," Lise sighed. "Which way is the buffet car?"

"It's towards the front, two cars down," answered Laue.

"Anyone want anything while I'm going?"

A series of 'No thank you' echoed around the car.

"Bring me back a breakfast menu, if they have one," amended Otto.

Lise rose from her seat, bundled her papers together, put them down in a tidy pile and exited the compartment.

A few minutes later, she found and entered the buffet car. With the lateness of the hour, no diners occupied the tables and, save for the beat of the train's wheels, a hushed and sleepy tranquility presided. At the center of the car stood the bar, tended by a steward, who straightened his jacket and stood to attention as Lise approached. One other person, a passenger aged about 30, also stood at the bar, sipping a cup of coffee. His dress betrayed a man of careless habits, for his rumpled clothes would have benefited from a steam press, and his hair from a comb.

Lise asked the steward for coffee and, feeling the passenger's gaze on her, looked steadfastly to the back of the bar while the steward fulfilled her request. The steward eventually turned back and she accepted the steaming cup of coffee from him. Unsure of the protocol, or whether first-class passengers received free coffee, she offered him a small coin in exchange, which he acknowledged with a nod of his head and pocketed.

She turned to exit the buffet car, holding on grimly to the coffee cup, the rattle of the cup in its saucer magnified by the rattle of the train.

"Be careful," warned the man in the rumpled suit. "I've already spilled my coffee twice, and it is very hot."

Lise smiled politely, but having no desire to be drawn into a conversation with this stranger, did not reply.

"I wouldn't mind but it's my best suit," continued the man.

"That is unfortunate," Lise responded, her mouth engaged before she could prevent it.

"One would think somebody would invent a train which didn't shake its passengers about so much. A little easier on the bones - and on the clothes, eh?" added the man.

"As you say," replied Lise as she tried to edge by him towards the buffet car exit.

"Would you care to join me?"

"I'm sorry, but we have not been introduced."

"Of course, please forgive my forwardness."

The man bowed and Lise hurried from the car, spilling her coffee as she went.

The Orient Express pulled into the Salzburg station just as the sun came up, and Lise, Planck, Otto and Laue departed the train. As the others identified the luggage and gave instructions to the porter, Lise scanned the station for the exit. To her dismay, she spied the rumpled-suit man standing on the platform - and he had seen her.

With a theatrical flourish, he removed his hat and bowed, elaborately and somewhat comically. Her face turning red with embarrassment, Lise returned her attention to her colleagues and they exited the station.

. . . Salzburg

The interior of the Salzburg auditorium did little to calm Lise's nerves. It loomed over her, cavernous and Cathedral-like; and its occupants engaged in broken conversation with hushed reverence. The colleagues from Berlin huddled together, as the speakers for the 81st Annual Scientists and Physicians Conference came and went, and Lise's level of distress rose exponentially as her turn at the podium crept ever closer.

"Calm down, Lise; you'll do fine," said Otto.

"Yes, I know, but . . ." A figure entered Lise's peripheral vision, causing an involuntarily pause in her train of thought. "Oh God, it's that rude man from the train," whispered Lise, as the rumpled suit came into view.

The man saw that Lise had recognized him, waved and approached; the big smile that played on his face complemented his unkempt appearance.

"Hello again," said the Rumpled Suit.

"Hello," said Lise, coldly.

"Is this seat taken?" asked the Rumpled Suit, indicating the empty seat next to Lise.

"Er . . ." replied Lise.

The Rumpled Suit sat down without waiting for a confirmation.

"I'm sorry," he said. "We still have not even been properly introduced . . . You are?"

"I am Frau Meitner - from Berlin."

The Rumpled Suit beamed in delight.

"Dr. Meitner? But this is an honor. I read your paper on the Dispersion of Alpha Rays - I think you are onto something."

"Thank you," stuttered Lise, taken aback that anyone, especially the Rumpled Suit, could have remembered - let alone, named - any work of hers. "I'm surprised that anybody read that."

"Yes, this is an honor. I don't know what to say. I must apologize again, but this is all new to me and I'm not quite sure what to expect." A gesture of his hand and a small nod of his head showed that he referred to the conference, not Lise. "In fact, to let you in on a little secret, until this conference I had never met a real physicist before - you are my first. The renowned Dr. Meitner! What a day I am having."

"And you?" responded Lise. The man's nervousness displayed a humble sincerity which reflected and slightly reduced her own inner turmoil, and she warmed to him a little.

"No, I'd like to be. One day, perhaps. But today, I am a just an amateur."

"No, I mean your name? How shall I address you?"

"Me?" He laughed at the misunderstanding. "I am . . ."

But before he could answer, the Conference President had returned to the podium to introduce the next speaker.

"Oh, I believe that we are about to begin," said the Rumpled Suit.

> "Colleagues and distinguished guests," said the President. "May I present to you, Mr. Albert Einstein."

The Rumpled Suit rose and gave Lise another little bow, his grin wide and mischievous, and he turned and shambled to the podium. With the surprise openly registered on Lisa's face, the embarrassing realization of the identity of the man behind the scruffy appearance dawned on her.

Einstein faced his audience, raised his head and spoke clearly, confidently and deliberately.

> "Today," said Einstein, addressing the assembly. "I'd like to present to you some findings on the Development of our Conception of the Essence and the Constitution of Radioactivity . . .

> . . . It is therefore my opinion that the next stage in the development of Theoretical Physics will bring us a theory of light that can be understood as a kind of fusion of the wave and emission theories of light . . .

> . . . Examples of this sort, together with the unsuccessful attempts to discover any motion of the earth relatively to the "light medium" suggest that the phenomena of

electrodynamics as well as of mechanics possess no properties corresponding to the idea of absolute rest. They suggest rather that, as has already been shown to the first order of small quantities, the same laws of electrodynamics and optics will be valid for all frames of reference for which the equations of mechanics hold good. We will raise this conjecture, the purport of which will hereafter be called the 'Principle of Relativity' . . .

. . . This equation shows that the entropy of a monochromatic radiation of sufficiently low density varies with the volume in the same manner as the entropy of an ideal gas or a dilute solution. In the following, this equation will be interpreted in accordance with the principle introduced into physics by Herr Boltzmann, namely that the entropy of a system is a function of the probability its state . . .

. . . Furthermore, the equation E is equal to m c-squared, in which energy is put equal to mass, multiplied by the square of the velocity of light, showing that very small amounts of mass may be converted into a very large amount of energy and vice versa. The mass and energy are in fact equivalent, according to the formula mentioned above . . ."

* * *

Following the Einstein speech which, as history would record, changed the world, the audience's reaction to Lise's speech betrayed indifference. Even the controversial fact of her gender made little impression on them, as the enlightened buzzed and conferred at the implications of Einstein's words, and the others scratched their heads.

And one could not describe Lise's speech as memorable. Although she aspired to emulate her hero, Boltzmann, her delivery more resembled that of Max Planck. She stuttered her way through it as best she could, but she and the audience both expressed relief when it finally came to an end. Lise's colleagues, however, effused in genuine praise for her.

Post-conference, Lise stood in the foyer with Otto. Max Planck and Max von Laue had gone in search of refreshment; but along the way, Planck and Laue worked the room, shaking hands, greeting old friends and making new ones; and their return took far too long for Lise, who desperately needed a drink to quench her parched tongue.

"I am so glad that is over," croaked Lise.

"Now you can finally relax," said Otto.

"I never want to do that again."

"Oh, the first time is always the hardest. The next one will be much easier."

"The next one? There will be no next one!"

"You say that, but once you've done one there is no turning back. You are in the public eye now and fame is addictive."

"Perhaps for you, Otto, but I'd rather be in my workshop."

The two Maxes rejoined them, carrying cocktails.

"A triumph, Lise, a triumph," said Max Planck, handing her a drink.

"Yes, congratulations," added Laue. "Well done; especially having to follow an act like Einstein."

"You knew didn't you? You all knew?" accused Lise.

"Knew what?" said Planck, grinning.

"You knew that was Einstein and you didn't bother to tell me."

"We didn't know that your strange little man on the train was that strange little man," said Laue.

"You were so worried about your own speech that we didn't want to distract you," added Planck.

"But I feel like such an idiot," objected Lise.

"No, you weren't to know," said Otto. "None of us had seen him before this conference. Albert Einstein may be a Cause Célèbre, but he is still quite new to our circle."

"He grazes with the bureaucrats of the Swiss Patent Office, not at the high-table where we wear the nosebag," said Laue.

"But he won't for much longer," said Planck, cryptically.

"What do you mean?" asked Lise.

"The Cause Célèbre is coming to join us in Berlin," said Planck. "I hear he plays the violin passably well."

. . . A Paying Job

Lise returned from her triumph at Salzburg. She expected that life would continue as it had before the trip. Yes, she still depended on the generosity of her father for continued support. But now, Albert Einstein had come to Berlin! How could she leave now, when things had just started to get interesting?

But after quickly settling back into her routine of research with Otto, dinner parties with Max Planck and excursions with Emma and Grete; Lise followed triumph with tragedy. Lise received a letter from her sister, Gusti - from Vienna: her father had died; she must come home immediately.

Lise retuned to Vienna for the funeral. This turn of events implied a double loss: not only had she lost her beloved father, she had also lost her means of support. Without the allowance which her father had continued to provide long after her promise to return to Vienna had expired, she could not hope to sustain herself in Berlin.

She felt guilty. Her opportunity to stay in Berlin and follow her dreams had come about only because of her father's generosity. She had promised him that she would return within the year - she had lied. She should have returned to Vienna long ago. She should have kept her promise and honored her father as he had honored her. But now she could not turn back the clock.

After the funeral and a period of mourning, she returned to Berlin. She planned to stay just long enough to pack her meager belongings and say goodbye to her colleagues. And she would pack her dreams; put them in the case with the other useless curios and forget them. Perhaps now that she had established a reputation as Dr. Meitner, she could at last get that job as a kindergarten teacher?

On reaching her workshop, Otto, without comment, handed her a letter; the envelope bore the official stamp of the university. Inside she found a brief, hand written note from Max Planck to come to his office the instant she returned. She wondered about the cryptic nature of the order, and why Max had not just spoken to her at any of the several meetings they had had since her return. Obviously Max had official business to discuss. Had Max postponed this matter until her return from Vienna or had an issue arisen during her absence? As Max knew of her financial straits, she suspected that he meant to forestall her resignation with a dismissal. The reasons did not overly concern her - she would leave either way.

She knocked at the door of his office.

"Come in," said Max.

Lise entered.

"Oh, come in, Lise, come in."

Lise closed the door and positioned herself on the edge of the chair in front of Max's desk.

"Thank you, Herr Planck. You asked to see me?" asked Lise, quietly and formally.

"Welcome Back, Lise. How was Vienna? I was sorry to hear about your father."

"Thank you, Herr Planck."

"Your family is, otherwise, well, I hope?"

"Yes, thank you."

"A big loss for all of you, I am sure."

"Yes, Professor."

"You are still coming to dinner tonight?"

"Er . . . yes, Professor, I am looking forward to it." Lise sensed that Max's small talk merely delayed the bad news which a reluctant Max had to deliver. Poor Max - the harsh conflict of business and friendship always made him uneasy.

"But I thought it best that I should see you in my official capacity first." Lise tensed for the blow, but Max merely said, "Oh! That sounds so serious, doesn't it?"

Lise decided to let her gentle friend of the hook and preempt his announcement.

"Professor, you know that I have only been able to stay here in Berlin due to the generosity of my family, my father. My position here is unpaid . . ."

"Yes, that is why I have asked to see you."

"Well, now I can no longer rely on them for income . . . My family is . . . Therefore, I must ask . . ."

Max raised a hand to interrupt her.

"Lise, I have some information which I'd like to share with you. Oh, but first, perhaps you have already heard? Max von Laue has accepted a position at the University of Zurich. He will be leaving us."

"That is bad news for us," replied Lise, taken aback by this further delay of the inevitable.

"Yes, I had come to rely on him rather heavily. We all wish him well of course, but it does leave me with a bit of a dilemma."

"Dilemma?"

"Yes, we will have to do some shuffling around here, some rearranging. I'm afraid that we are all affected, even you."

"Professor, I understand . . ."

"Max served as my assistant. I can't allow the post to remain vacant for too long; which is why I'd like to offer the post to you."

"If perhaps I could get a letter of reference . . . Assistant?"

"Assistant! I'm afraid the pay is not much, but at least it is a paid position - finally."

"Assistant to you? That would be such . . ."

"Of course, if your heart is set on returning to Vienna, then so be it - but in my opinion that would be another loss to the university, which coming on the heels of Laue's departure . . . Well, that would reflect badly on my leadership; I would take it personally."

"I don't know what to say. This is such an honor. Thank you Herr Professor."

Max stood and moved around to Lise's side of the desk, as the confused Lise rose to her feet.

"Until tonight then."

He escorted Lise to the door and bundled her out of his office.

* * *

And suddenly Lise had her first paying job. There arose the inevitable complaints about a woman on the staff, and the usual government bureaucratic delays in confirming her appointment, but Germany regarded Max Planck in the same way which Austria had regarded Ludwig Boltzmann, and so Max won the day.

93

Max had warned Lise that the pay would not amount to much - but it was enough. It enabled her to stay in Berlin, to continue her research. And her work at the university with Otto proceeded to become increasingly important. Lise's reputation in the scientific world also grew and she won the respect of many contemporaries, albeit grudgingly from some of the old-school academics.

The university passed through an important chapter of expansion and renovation, which culminated in the creation of a new organization, the Kaiser Wilhelm Institute, the grandest, modernist, most prestigious monument to the sciences ever built. Max had accepted the position as the institute's first Director of Physics.

The Government and university made elaborate plans for the official opening ceremonies; celebrities from the academic world and political dignitaries were lined up to attend, less well connected purchased tickets on the black market; the Kaiser would cut the ribbon.

A party entered the institute's new location of the Hahn-Meitner Research Department. The renowned Ernest Rutherford, Otto's old boss, and included on the official guest list along with his wife, Mary, came into view.

"Ah, here we are at last," said Professor Fischer. "Sorry for the detour; I'm still learning to find my way around the new grounds. Otto, someone here to see you."

"Professor Rutherford!" exclaimed Otto. "We knew you were coming, but I expected you this evening. We would have met you at the station."

"Otto, it's good to see you again," said Rutherford. "You remember Mary?"

"Mrs. Rutherford, welcome to Berlin," said Otto. "And here is my colleague, Dr. Lise Meitner."

"But Dr. Meitner - you are a woman!" said Rutherford, taken aback.

"Yes, I get that a lot," responded Lise, tired of the accusation.

"Dr. Meitner has become quite an authority in radioactivity," interrupted Fischer, before the conversation turned frosty.

"Yes, yes. I know. I know of your work with Otto, but forgive me, I should not have assumed," Rutherford apologized.

"We are making great strides in the battle of the sexes as well as in the sciences," said Otto.

"Still, this is fortuitous," said Rutherford, brightening up. "Mary is eager to take in the shops. Her German is non-existent. It would be such a help, Dr. Meitner, if you could perhaps accompany her?"

Lise looks pleadingly at Otto for an excuse, but he just eased her towards the door.

"Why not take Mrs. Rutherford to the Kaufhaus. And then we can join you at the Rutherford's hotel later for coffee. You are staying at the Kaiserhof, yes? Of course!" said Otto.

"Let me get a cab for you," added Fischer.

"Oh, no need for that," argued Rutherford. "Mary would like to see something of Berlin while she is here. It's a nice day for a walk."

Stifling a protest from Lise, Fischer bundled her and Mrs. Rutherford from the workshop. Ernest Rutherford turned to face Otto.

"Well that works out well for Mary," Rutherford beamed.

"It really is good to see you again, Professor," said Otto. "I have not yet congratulated you on your Nobel Prize."

"Yes the Prize; I great honor. It will be your turn one day, Otto. You are making some exciting discoveries here."

"I would like to dream it possible, Professor."

"Your paper on actinium, for example, most interesting!"

"Thank you," said Otto. "You are too kind."

"However, credit where credit is due, eh?"

"I'm sorry?"

"I seem to remember some work in Montreal, by my student, Harriet Brooks. Remember Harriet?"

"Professor, I must defend myself. Brooks' observation was of radium, not actinium," Otto bristled. To accuse one of taking credit for another's work was a serious matter in the scientific world.

"Well, never mind that now," said Rutherford, nonchalantly. He put a friendly arm around his former pupil and steered him towards the workshop door. "What say you show me around the Institute?"

... *Gala Day*

T he big day arrived - the grand gala opening of the Kaiser Wilhelm Institute. In the open square in front of the semigothic main building, the importance of the day called for top hats and tails. Max Planck and Fritz Haber, Planck's opposite number at the institute's Department for Physical Chemistry, shared the makeshift stage with Germany's political and scientific elite.

As these things always have a habit of taking longer than expected, Lise, Otto, Albert, Emma and Grete sat and fidgeted on the white wooden chairs, arranged with German precision, in neat, tidy rows in front of the stage, waiting for the Kaiser to arrive. Unfortunately, the weather gods had failed to receive the memo and the rain fell in a small, steady, sticky drizzle, causing more discomfort.

"It's cold!" complained Lise. "How much longer?"

"Time waits for no man," said Otto. "Except, of course, for Albert and the Kaiser."

Albert missed the remark, as he busied himself making eyes at Grete; his ability to flirt almost matched his scientific genius.

"Albert, stop that," reprimanded Lise. "She's a married woman now."

"Which one is she, Grete or Emma?" whispered Albert. "I can never tell them apart."

"It's Grete," answered Lise. She's the married one, as you well know; you attended the wedding with the rest of us. If you have to flirt, do it with Emma."

The twins giggled. They were as guilty of impropriety as Albert, and had done their fair share of teasing in their time.

As Albert ogled the giggling twins and Lise shivered, more of their small clique arrived: Eva von Bahr, only recently admitted to the circle and the ink on her PhD still wet, Clara Haber, the wife of Fritz, and Otto Sackur, Haber's assistant at the institute. Sackur held his baby daughter, Irene.

"Eva, Otto, over here," Lise cried to them and waved a hand to attract their attention. "We've saved some seats for you; Clara, over here."

"Coo, coo, hello little one," said Albert to the baby.

"Albert, please refrain from teaching my God-daughter how to coo," objected Clara.

Albert shrugged and petulantly cooed at the baby one last time before he returned his attention to the Planck twins. Clara Haber and Otto Sackur took their seats. Otto pointed out Clara's husband, Fritz, who fidgeted on the stage, decidedly uncomfortable.

"My God, Clara, how did you manage to get Fritz into his top hat?" asked Otto. "It looks as if his head is about to explode."

"It wasn't easy," replied Clara. "We had to get everything just so or apparently the world would end. Now he won't remove the hat under any circumstances, for fear that his hair is a mess. Fritz can run a department, but he can't comb his hair."

"Max looks as if he'd rather all this was over," observed Lise of Planck, equally ill at ease next to the frazzled Haber.

"Still, a great day for him," added Otto.

A string of horse-drawn coaches arrived, the central one bearing the official seal which signified that it carried the Kaiser. On stage, the Royal Master of Ceremonies, rose to his feet and nodded towards his assistant.

"Oh, here we go," warned Otto.

"At last!" exclaimed Lise.

> "Distinguished guests, ladies and gentlemen, please rise for His Imperial and Royal Majesty William the Second, by the Grace of God, German Emperor and King of Prussia, Margrave of Brandenburg, Burgrave of Nuremberg, Count of Hohenzollern, Duke of Silesia and of the County of Glatz, Grand Duke of the Lower Rhine and of Posen, Duke in Saxony, of Angria, of Westphalia, of Pomerania and of Lunenburg, Duke of Schleswig, of Holstein and of Krossen, Duke of Magdeburg, of Brene, of Guelderland and of Jülich, Cleves and Berg, Duke of the Wends and the Kassubes, . . .

Albert rolled his eyes.

> . . . of Lauenburg and of Mecklenburg, Landgrave of Hesse and in Thuringia, Margrave of Upper and Lower Lusatia, Prince of Orange, of Rugen, of East Friesland, of Paderborn and of Pyrmont, Prince of Halberstadt, of Münster, of Minden, of

Osnabrück, of Hildersheim, of Verdun, of Kammin, of Fulda, of Nassau and of Moess, Princely Count of Henneberg, Count of the Mark, of Ravensburg, of Hohenstein, of Tecklenburg and of Lingen, Count of Mansfield, of Sigmaringen and of Veringen, Lord of Frankfurt, etc."

The assembly all stood to attention. A brass band played the National Anthem and Kaiser Wilhelm II climbed out of his carriage and moved towards the stage. His entourage frantically scrambled behind him to arrange themselves in the appropriate pecking order.

After various dull speeches about the greatness of the day for Germany and the sciences, and the implications of the new Institute for the Empire and the rest of the world, the proceedings moved away from the stage and towards the Kaiser's tour of the Institute.

In a much rehearsed dash, Lise and Otto ran in the opposite direction from the main party, around the back of the building and through the rear entrance, turning left and right down corridors, to arrive breathless at Lise's new laboratory just moments before the main party arrived and Emil Fischer said:

"And if I may present, Your Majesty, Professor Hahn and Dr. Meitner. Dr. Meitner has prepared a demonstration of a few radioactive substances."

Otto bowed and Lise curtsied.

"Doctors, you do us proud. You do Germany proud," boomed the Kaiser.

Emil Fischer pointed to Lise's shiny new laboratory. "Through here, Your Majesty, if I may lead the way."

"But it's dark!" objected the Kaiser's adjutant.

"I'm sorry?" asked Fisher, unable to understand this sudden, improvised departure from his carefully prepared script.

"The room is in darkness," explained the adjutant, as if he talked to a child. "Please be so kind as to turn on the light."

"Er!" said Fischer, searching for the appropriate response permitted by protocol.

"Your Majesty," rescued Otto. "The effects of the radioactivity cannot be seen except in darkness."

"Out of the question!" insisted the adjutant. "We cannot allow His Majesty to enter a completely dark room."

"Nonsense, Theo," overruled the Kaiser. "Never let it be said that the Kaiser is afraid of the dark."

The Kaiser pushed his way through the humming and haring entourage and entered Lise's lab; the others, wanting to prove their own courage in the face of a darkened room, tumbled in after him.

* * *

Gala day and the Kaiser came and went, but life moved forward at the Institute, which quickly established its reputation as the place to be; and Germany's finest scientific minds flocked there.

For Lise, even though the modest stipend as Max's assistant remained her only source of income, this time of her life had an idyllic quality. At the institute, she officially remained a guest of Fisher's chemistry department, and therefore, not on the payroll; but while the sexism she endured continued, she now felt it contained, tamed and manageable; and the staff and students accepted her as a member of the establishment - an insider; and although some clung to the old ways, they now did so in a less overt and confrontational manner.

Outside the institute, the world still revolved too slowly and the tide of sexism ebbed and flowed, but Lise, now sheltered and protected from its worst excesses, ignored it and focused on the work which she loved, steadily advancing the understanding, and establishing a reputation as the leading authority, of radioactivity.

As the days rolled steadily on towards 1914, talk of unrest in the Balkans began to dominate the conversation, but this was nothing new - unrest in the Empire came with the territory. And on a warm summer evening, family and friends gathered at the Planck home to celebrate one of their own. Max Planck enjoyed entertaining and held parties as often as his harried wife would allow. This time the party marked a special occasion: their old friend Max von Laue had come to Berlin for a visit and they gathered to honor him for his recently awarded Nobel Prize for physics.

They raised their glasses.

"Congratulations, Max," they cheered.

"Who would have thought I knew so much about x-rays?" mused Laue.

"Certainly not those who saw you in action in the lecture rooms," teased Lise. "Congratulations, Max."

"Congratulations, Max," the others echoed.

"Lise, you said that so sweetly I almost believe you mean it," replied Laue. "Had I known that people cared so much about me, I would have won the Nobel years ago. I was only holding out to spite you all."

The wine flowed, the conversation sparkled, the air filled with song and Max Planck and Albert entertained with a duet for piano and violin.

"Now, I'm not sure, but one of you was not keeping time there?" laughed Otto, as the duet came to an end. He only joked, of course, for they both played extremely well.

"I would say that Max's playing is constant, whereas mine is relative," Albert punned.

"Or is it the other way round?" said Otto.

"The problem with you, Albert, is that you simply can't count above three," Planck defended himself.

"Only one problem?" mused Albert. "Then I must consider my life a success."

"Let's have another song," cried Emma, bored with all the science talk. "How about a song from our baritone?"

"Yes, Otto," agreed Grete. "Give us something stirring."

"Yes, come on, Otto," urged Albert. "He who can, does; He who cannot, teaches."

"You've been reading Mr. Shaw, the English revolutionary," chided Fritz Haber.

"Irish revolutionary!" corrected Albert.

"Albert is in a revolutionary mood," complained Otto. "Then I agree with Grete; we must have an appropriate response. If you could accompany me on the piano . . ." he said to Max Planck and broke into a spirited, bellicose rendition of the anthem, *Deutschland, Deutschland über alles.*

Pumping their fists and spilling their wine, several of the other guests joined Otto in an impromptu display of nationalism.

"Patriotic nonsense," shouted Albert, trying to be heard above the clamor.

"Not now, Albert," warned Lise, who sensed that Albert viewed the response as a personal challenge. "Remember that you are amongst friends."

But the cat had escaped the bag.

"Patriotic nonsense which leads to senseless violence and war," shouted Albert louder, as the song came to an end.

"What is really nonsense," defended Fritz Haber, "is to sit and do nothing while the British Empire continues to expand. What is nonsense is to let France and Russia meddle in the affairs of brother Austria. Lise, you are Austrian, you will support me on this? We do not seek war; they bring the war to us."

"There will be no war," said Planck.

"Unless the English want war," added Otto.

"They will lose," added Fritz Haber.

"Men always want war," interrupted Clara Haber. "Why is that?"

"There will not be a war!" insisted Max Planck. He paused and then looked slyly at Otto Sackur's children. "Now who wants to play tag?"

Max Planck chased the two children out into the garden. Freshly uncorked wine replaced that lost in spillage. Emma and Grete began a risqué Bavarian beer garden song. Albert generously decided against another outburst. And the party resumed.

War

"You must not blame us scientists for the use which war technicians have put our discoveries."

Lise Meitner

. . . *Breakfast, Cambridge, 1968*

U lla Frisch prepared a breakfast of scrambled eggs and buttered toast, as she tried her best to ignore the bickering Monica and Tony. Robert entered the kitchen. He carried some newly delivered mail and sifted through the letters half-heartedly until he reached a small package: brown, tattered and badly taped. He opened the package. Inside he found a small hand-written note on lilac paper.

"What have you got there?" asked Ulla.

"A letter from Aunt Frida's family," replied Robert. He looked back into the envelope and retrieved its remaining content. "With some pictures of Aunt Lise."

"For the collection?"

"Yes, for the collection."

"Can I see?" asked Monica. She got up from the breakfast table and playfully grabbed the photos from Robert's hands. Robert gave up the pictures without a fight; even though the morning had barely broken, he had not slept well of late and his tired body refused to obey his orders.

Monica scanned the pictures and stopped at one which piqued her interest. "She is with some soldiers in this one. Are they relatives too?"

"Let me see," said Robert. He took back the photo in question and inspected it. "No, I don't recognize them at all." Robert turned the picture over. "There is a date on the back - 1915. It was taken during the First World War."

"Aunt Lise wasn't in the war," objected Tony. "You told us that she was a pacifist."

"It doesn't take much to start a war, no matter how many want peace. Aunt Lise may not have agreed with it, but she was big on duty; she felt it keenly. So yes, Aunt Lise answered the call."

"Did you go to war with Aunt Lise?" asked Monica.

"Hey, I'm not that old, thank you very much. I was only ten when that war broke out," laughed Robert.

"I can just imagine Aunt Lise going over the top of the trenches with a bayonet between her teeth. That would scare the Hell out of the enemy," said Tony.

"Tony Frisch, mind your language," reprimanded Ulla.

"Sorry," said Tony.

"Well, it never came to that, thank God," said Robert. "But she did serve: they put her skills to use as an x-ray technician at an army hospital near the Russian front. She may not have carried a gun, but she did see much of the horror of war."

"The Great War," said Ulla. "That's what they called it. There was nothing great about it; it was a terrible war. All war is terrible. I just hope you never have to find out how terrible, young man."

"Sorry," repeated Tony.

"But we fared better than most, I suppose," said Robert. "We lost my Uncle Fritz. Others did much worse. Much, much worse . . ." His voice trailed off as his mind filled with images which he quickly tried to suppress. "But luck was still with the family for that one; at least, a part of the tiny amount of what passed for luck back then."

Robert went silent again as the images resurfaced and he remembered the events from an age when he should have been too young to remember.

"It's a pity the photos didn't arrive yesterday," interrupted Ulla, who sensed her husband's despondency and wanted to allay it. "We could have included them in that last box which we shipped. We are done in by our own efficiency."

"That's okay. I'll take them with me when I go into town today," Robert responded.

"Town? Can I come too?" asked Tony.

"And me?" added Monica.

"I may be some time," replied Robert. "I have to attend to some business . . . Don't you both have a school to go to?"

"Half-term," explained Monica.

"Is this about Lise?" Ulla sighed. She had hoped that with the funeral behind them and Lise's life filed away neat and tidy, Robert would give up this quest and resume his own life.

"Yes, I have a meeting with Nevill Mott."

"Robert, it won't do any good," Ulla chided gently. "You've been trying to set the record straight for years now. You couldn't do it while she was alive. It will be impossible now that she is dead. Maybe it's time to let it go."

"Perhaps you're right; who knows?" replied Robert with an air of resignation. In both his head and heart he agreed with his wife that it had become a futile quixotic quest. Perhaps it smacked of vanity or sheer obstinacy, but something prevented him from just letting go. "One last try - I owe her that much."

"Then have some breakfast first," Ulla smiled. "Sir Nevill Francis Mott is not someone you can face on an empty stomach."

"And while we eat," said Tony, "You can tell us all about Aunt Lise and the Great War."

"And don't spare us the gory details," said Monica.

... *Lemberg, 1915*

I n contrast to the period leading up to the war, displays of
patriotic bravado had subsided by the time Lise undertook the
four day train ride to Lemberg in the company of 50 other
nurses, 10 doctors and 250 soldiers. The mood of the passengers was
somber and creature comforts were in scarce supply, but a song
would occasionally break out to lift the spirits; and at least the
women had a bench on which to grab a few hours of sleep
occasionally. They passed through a landscape of incredible beauty
and devastation; and Lise spent the journey staring out of the
window at the surreal juxtaposition of rolling hills, forests and rivers
with bomb-shelled bridges, farms and villages.

The Germans exchanged blows with the Russians and Lemberg traded hands several times during the conflict known as World War One. For the Germans who occupied Lemberg, it was incomprehensible that the battle endured - that the Russians had not surrendered a long time ago; Compared to German losses, Russian bore casualties on a colossal scale. The Russians had no food, no resources and no munitions. The Germans could scarcely believe that any Russians remained alive to challenge them. Yet the Russians would not go away.

Today, the Lemberg flag poles flew the German Eagle.

Now, in the cold, miserable, damp air, under the shadow of the Carpathian Mountains, a German Military Hospital, manufactured from the remnants of an old school, tended to the needs of 7,000 wounded and dying men; and the muddy field beside it had produced a crop of tents which served to house them all. Standing so close to the Russian Front, the hospital received the most severely wounded; those too fragile to move farther behind the lines; those who were not quite dead.

After she had volunteered for the cause, Lise's expertise in radiology was put to the test and she found herself assigned to the unit as a hospital technician - not that she encountered much technology; and in addition to operating the x-ray machine, she augmented her official duties with those of the nurse: dressing wounds, emptying chamber pots and comforting dying soldiers. Occasionally, one of her x-rays would save the life of a soldier, but more often the soldiers' fates lay beyond the help of the medical profession.

It had not taken her long to overcome her revulsion at the sight of the filth and the flies, the infected wounds and mangled bodies. She had no time for the luxury of loathing; she refused to dwell on it and only grudgingly spoke of it to her friends and family back home; not out of stoicism or decorum, but because she knew that she possessed no words in her vocabulary to describe it, and no way for those who had not experienced it to comprehend it.

The morning stirred in its infancy and the sun still lurked below the eastern horizon, when Lise walked towards one of the barracks in the converted school house. As she reached the building, a priest exited and walked towards her.

"Good day, Lise," said the Priest.

"Good morning, Father. You are here early?" replied Lise.

"Yes, I was called for in the night. The boy was not even a Catholic, but still he asked for me to hear his prayer." The Priest sighed as if he suspected that his role at the Hospital was redundant.

"You are God's representative here, Father."

"Catholic, Protestant, Jew. We all must stand before our maker."

"Yes, Father."

They conversed, awkward and stilted - to talk of death was always awkward, even for the Priest. Then, with the small talk concluded, Lise and the Priest nodded towards each other and started to move on in their opposite directions.

"Oh, before you go in," the Priest turned and added. "I have administered the Rites to the Polish boy who was operated on yesterday."

"Yes, Father."

"Good day, Lise."

"Father."

The priest walked away. Lise entered the barracks.

The ward's occupants dozed in a dark and hazy gloom. Even during the height of a bright noon-time, little of the outside world penetrated here, especially not the sun shine. Cots filled with the wounded lined each wall. Between the cots, more men lay on the floor, waiting for someone to die and give up a bed. Doctors and nurses milled around and administered precious morphine to the more vocal patients. The light of the kerosene lamps cast long, surreal, dancing shadows as they moved. The smell of the kerosene did nothing to cover the more ominous smell of death and decay.

Lise walked to a cot and looked at the man who lay on it. His eyes opened.

"Good morning, soldier," whispered Lise.

"Good morning, nurse," the soldier replied. He was the Pole to whom the Priest had referred.

"How are you feeling this morning?" asked Lise.

"I'm going to die; I know I will die," said the soldier.

"Nonsense! Why do you say that?" Lise replied unconvincingly.

"No one is bothering to check my dressing. You are not even looking at them. There is no use any more. Am I correct?"

"Yes, you are correct. You are most observant."

The truth should have felt cold and harsh, but it did not appear so this time. The boy's eyes betrayed no fear and he now seemed beyond the reach of the pain, and indifferent to his fate. The boy's head dropped for a second and then he lifted it again.

"I was always observant . . . but then again, I didn't see that shell coming, ha, ha."

Lise smiled.

"May I know your name?"

"My name is Lise."

"Good to meet you, Lise. My mother will be terribly upset. I am an only child. They tried so hard to have me. Do you have family?"

"Yes, my brother, Walter, is a cadet at the Italian Front."

"What I don't understand . . . What I don't understand is . . . Why? Take for example that fellow over there." The soldier nodded weakly towards another cot opposite. "He is a Russian, a sworn enemy. A week ago we were trying to kill him. Now we are trying to save him. And over there - the orderly - he is another Russian. He was trying to kill us. Now he is tending our wounds. I don't understand."

"I don't understand either."

"Do you think anyone would mind if . . ."

"If what?"

"Do you think anyone would mind if I wrote to my mother and told her how I died?"

"No, I shouldn't think so."

"I think that I will sleep for a while first. When I wake up, I'll write to her. She will be terribly upset."

Now with the sun setting in the west and her long work shift finished for the day, Lise, tired and hungry, headed to the makeshift hospital canteen to grab some food. She walked with her tray to an empty table. On sitting, she took out a letter she had received at mail call, but not yet opened. The envelope showed that it had travelled from Vienna. She took out the paper, which still retained a hint of the familiar lilac scent, and she began to read.

Before reading any letter from home, she braced herself for the worst; for every letter in this age held the potential for bad news. This letter was no different. And she could tell from its apologetic opening lines that the news must indeed prove miserable. She took a breath and continued.

And in the midst of the carnage of the Russian Front, amongst the trenches and howling soldiers, between the indifference and pain of death, War finally found Lise Meitner.

She no longer had a best friend.

Max Planck no longer had a daughter.

Emma and Grete were both dead.

Again, the truth should have hit cold and harsh, but in a long day, week, month and year of deaths, what did one or two more matter? Lise tried to absorb the news, to provoke some outrage and feel some pain, but her duties had made her so numb to it all that morphine could have flowed through her veins. Naturally, mothers everywhere would be terribly upset . . .

The Priest, carrying a tray of his own, appeared beside her. "Lise," he said. "Do you mind if I share your table."

. . . But Lise had a job to do and she would save her tears for a more convenient time.

"Oh, hello, Father. Please, please sit, but I'm sorry, I can't stay and chat; my shift is just starting."

She left the food uneaten on the table and returned to the barracks.

. . . Otto's War

"What are you doing here, Otto?"

Otto's Infantry Regiment had swept through neutral Belgium to get at the French by the quickest possible route; but following their latest skirmish, the German Command had selected Otto and the other members of his Company to remain behind for mopping-up operations. He billeted with 25 other soldiers, one sergeant and one lieutenant, in a large manor house on the outskirts of the medieval Belgian town of Löwen, also called Louvain by the French and English.

Otto and two other soldiers now ate breakfast in the kitchen; an elderly and terrified housekeeper and her husband, having served the breakfast, sat in silence in the corner.

"I keep asking myself the same question," replied Otto with a sigh.

The Front had moved a few miles to the north and west; it would probably move back to them at some point, but for these precious moments, they had a reprieve from the battle, notwithstanding the occasional playful shell from the French heavy artillery which kept them on their toes.

Although safer here than at the Front, Otto did not welcome the separation. He had formed a bond with his fellow soldiers and a loyal attachment to his Regiment, and felt that they should all live or die together. In spite of the relative safety of his position, he missed the exhilaration of battle, but real combat had become a scarcity as the old ways of doing things gave way to prolonged trench warfare.

"You must have friends in high places," yelled their departing comrades.

Otto fondly remembered Gala Day and his meeting with the Kaiser. Before Otto's Regiment had moved out, the Kaiser had inspected the troops. Otto stood at attention. The Kaiser and Otto did not exchange words on this second occasion.

"Here, have some sausage."

"I was told there was no sausage this side of Bavaria. Where did you get it?" asked Otto.

"There was a little accident with 12th Company, when they were standing in line for mess."

"Accident?"

"Yes, a 7 kilo shrapnel shell from a French 75, I'm told. The quartermaster wanted to take back the rations from the dead men, but some of us got there first. The quartermaster threatened to report us, but Hans had a chat with him and persuaded him not to press his luck."

Hans, a big brute of a man not known for his eloquence, merely grunted.

Otto checked the sausage for remnants of blood and shrapnel, but finding none, he bit into it greedily.

"Here, have some beer."

"Beer? What are you, a magician?"

"The beer comes courtesy of that café in Léopold Street; we confiscated it from some looters . . ."

Otto grimaced: No doubt the looters would never commit such a crime in the future; not that the soldiers needed proof of a crime to mete out punishment. Tradition demanded that once a nation's army had fallen in defeat, then that nation would cease hostilities, but rumors had spread saying that civilians continued to resist; snipers had killed German soldiers. As an example to others, Löwen bore the brunt of a deliberately bloody and brutal punishment, and the town was reduced to rubble. They had rounded up a great number of civilians, beginning with the mayor, and executed them: Women and children had also perished. Of course, counter rumors said that friendly-fire had caused the soldiers' deaths, when two German platoons, foraging for illicit supplies, had clashed with each other one pitch black night.

The housekeeper and her husband would later reflect on their good fortune, that the Germans had requisitioned their home for the billeting of soldiers, and their punishment merely consisted of serving breakfast to Otto and his comrades. And in a display of military etiquette, the Germans had even insisted on paying for their breakfast.

And now Otto worked on the clean up - to secure the town and implement the ordered Schrecklichkeit (Terror Campaign). They had systematically bombed and burned the town for 5 days until they had destroyed everything of value; and the soldiers now suspected that their vacation must soon end. To Otto's deep regret, the lieutenant had ordered his platoon to burn down the University Library. Otto felt that to burn books, especially priceless Gothic manuscripts, bordered on the criminal; Otto had argued that the petrol used to fuel the blaze was too valuable to squander in such a manner, but his arguments fell on deaf ears.

". . . It's good beer, Belgian! They make good beer, but is there anyone more stupid than the Belgians?"

"Why do you say that?"

"Well, look at us. We are German, but where are we? Belgium. Where did Napoleon and the French meet their Waterloo? Belgium. Every time there is conflict in Europe, we all come marching into Belgium to sort it out: the Germans, the French, the English, the Dutch. We destroy the country, they rebuild, and we come in and destroy it again. Stupid, no? If they had any sense, they'd move Belgium out of harm's way."

"I suppose you're right," said Otto, accepting the beer. He looked at the Belgians and wondered if they spoke German and could understand the conversation. Their stares revealed nothing beyond fear. Probably not, he concluded.

"Anyway, Otto, what are you doing here? You're a bit old for this sort of thing."

"I admit I was a little surprised; I woke up one morning and found myself drafted."

"And you're an educated man as well, eh, a professor or something; real smart like."

"Yes, something like that."

"Not smart enough to avoid the draft though, eh, ha."

"Obviously not."

"See, me now, I'm not smart at all, I'm a glazier by profession, but in wartime, all I'm good for is shooting at things and getting shot back at in return. Once this war is over, I expect I'll make a fortune replacing all those windows I've shot out. But it seems to me that you smart people should be able to get your heads together and figure out how to . . . Oh, game's up - here comes the lieutenant; and he's smiling; whenever the lieutenant's smiling we're in trouble. See, he's speaking to the sergeant. Hope he's not going to take away our beer."

The lieutenant and the sergeant huddled for a few minutes and conferred before the sergeant saluted smartly and the lieutenant turned and walked away. Then the sergeant entered the kitchen and barked at the seated soldiers.

"Okay, lads, were moving out - rejoining the Regiment - jump to it, double quick - not you, Hahn, new orders for you; report to the Duty Officer for your travel papers."

"Otto must have friends in high places," they said.

* * *

At the Kaiser Wilhelm Institute for Chemistry, in Berlin, Fritz Haber and two assistants, Otto Sackur and Gerhard Just, huddled over a bench in a laboratory, deep in conference.

"Well, this is within the expected parameters, but we need less phosgene and more chlorine from Farben," Haber explained to his assistants.

Before the assistants could agree, the lab door opened and the frame of Otto Hahn appeared, larger than Faber had remembered, thanks to the bulky uniform of an infantryman. The bright shiny buttons, newly sewn onto Otto's greatcoat, confirmed his recent promotion to sergeant.

Haber stood up and moved towards the door to greet his old friend. "Otto, Otto!" he exclaimed in surprise.

"Hello, Otto," said Sackur and Just, looking up and smiling.
Fritz Haber gave Otto a bear hug and then stepped back and assessed Otto's clothes.

"But what is this? You are still in uniform?"

"I haven't had time to unpack and change yet. I came straight here," explained Otto.

"A soldier!" Haber looked Otto up and down and shook his head. "What a waste! You'll be of much more use to the war effort here, believe me," he said.

"I hope so," Otto replied. Still missing his comrades and embarrassed by his absence from them, he remained unconvinced of the necessity to drag him away from the Front. "If nothing else, the war has impressed on me the need to put my talent where it will do some good. Hopefully, to save some lives."

Haber scrambled to remove his lab coat. "Let me buy you lunch and we can talk." He motioned to Sackur and Just. "Let's see if we can get some results up to the Ministry before tomorrow."

The assistants nodded and returned to their work. Haber grabbed a coat and shunted Otto from the lab.

The two men strolled leisurely down the gravel path which led away from the Chemistry Department.

"I was at the Plancks' last night," said Haber. "They played the trios; Schubert and Beethoven. Einstein played the violin. Albert is so out of touch. He does not read the newspapers; he says that he cherishes his innocence too much."

"I heard about Max," said Otto. "Under the circumstances, I'm surprised that he still has the strength to host parties."

"We're not giving him a choice; he tries to withdraw into his shell, but we're keeping him busy and won't let his mind wander. We all have to remain busy and focused. Having you in Berlin will be good justification for a get-together."

Otto paused.

"It's good to see you, Fritz, but what am I doing here? One minute I'm cleaning a rifle, the next I'm ordered back to Berlin." Otto wanted to forgo the small talk.

"The scientific community is a small one and getting smaller every day. I need you here, Otto."

"You need me here or Germany needs me here?"

"Today our needs are the same, we are as one."

Otto looked around the campus, full of military vehicles and uniforms.

"It looks as if the Institute is already well on its way to becoming one with the military."

"Exactly! But this is still our Institute; we can't let the military take it over entirely. Otto, you really are needed here. Our resources are stretched to breaking point. Einstein refuses to help - he signed the Manifesto against us."

"Naturally Einstein does not approve of using science in this way," replied Otto. "He condemns us. We go to save lives. Einstein calls us butchers."

"No, Otto, do not think that way. We all work to end this war and stop the killing, each in our own way. This war will be won through science. And as chemists, we have a contribution to make."

"I've heard rumors about our contribution. Coupled with my recall to Berlin, I surmise that the rumors are true."

"We are locked in a deadly race. The French will have no scruples about using gas on our troops. We must get there first . . ." Haber paused. "Martin Rothenbach was killed last month."

"Oh no!" exclaimed Otto at this news of the death of his young and popular assistant.

"I didn't have the heart to write to you. But use Martin as an example: if you stay at the Front, many more of our friends will meet the same end, perhaps even you - not that I'm questioning your courage, but we can't afford to lose you, Otto. Rather than reading of our friend's deaths, you could be saving their lives."

"How many of our friends?" Otto sighed. "I'm losing count. A few days ago I was in Belgium, watching my comrades die one by one. I can remain and watch, one by one, until it is my turn, or I can do what I am trained for, but we must do all we can to . . ."

Otto's words hung in the air as the man who spoke them and his comrade both fell hard to the ground - knocked down by the sudden wave of scorching inferno and deafening roar. The heat seared the clothes from their backs. Debris rained down on them; their orderly, cloistered university transformed into a fiery, nonsensical, chaotic nightmare.

Slowly, the smoke subsided and the men, bloodied and bruised, regained their footing. The roar of the explosion had rendered them temporarily deaf and dazed, but they shook off all offers of assistance and turned to see what had caused the explosion.

The building from which they had just departed no longer existed, replaced by confusion and desolation, fire and wreckage. Injured people staggered around and made crude attempts to put out the blaze. Otto and Haber ran back towards the scene of this devastation, fearing the worst. In the wreckage, they found the worst, in the form of the mangled bodies of Otto Sackur and Gerhard Just.

. . . A Celebration

With the absorption of the Institute by the military now complete, the war effort of the Berlin scientists had reached full stride. And for his contributions to the German cause, the Kaiser had awarded Fritz Haber, too old for the Draft or enlistment, the rank of Captain. Naturally, this called for a party. When an ailing Max Planck failed to rise to the occasion, the party people relocated to Fritz's own home.

First, Fritz had to overcome the reluctance of Clara to play hostess. She argued bitterly with her husband over the propriety of celebrating his reward for what she deemed as a misuse of science. But Fritz had won the day; and Clara, gracious in defeat, entered into the spirit of the thing: assembled the guest list, sent out the invitations, organized the food and drink and greeted the guests on their arrival, as eagerly and happily as if she had won the promotion for herself. But that was Clara!

Due to the overriding demands of the war, the number of guests who accepted the invitation did not meet pre-war levels; and Einstein, once a close friend, had made his excuses and declined to participate, which Clara thought a pity, as in Albert she felt a kindred spirit; but enough attended to do the night justice, she thought.

With the guests assembled and relaxed, Otto bade them raise their glasses in a toast to their colleague.

"Lift your goblets and share a salute; first to the Kaiser, next to Germany, but above all, to Fritz, our most noble and patriotic son."

"To Fritz," they echoed.

"To my noble and patriotic husband," said Clara with apparent pride.

"Congratulations, Fritz, a great achievement," said Otto.

"Yes, Fritz, a great achievement," repeated Clara, but this time her praise came tinged with a hint of disdain which none but her husband detected.

Fritz shot her a quizzical glance. Clara smiled sweetly and stroked his hand before she turned to ask who needed more wine She picked up a bottle and moved out amongst the guests. Fritz returned his attention to his immediate circle.

"Thank you, Otto, But I consider it to be a team effort; you also made major contributions."

"Perhaps the Kaiser will make Otto a Major for his major contributions," sang Clara from across the room.

"And what is next for our good Captain?" asked Richard Willstätter, the Institute's Director of Chemistry.

"I leave for the Russian Front tomorrow," replied Fritz. "We will continue the important work we began at Gravenstafel."

"Important work," echoed Clara.

"Clara, do you not agree that your husband is a national hero?" Willstätter inquired loudly above the drone of the guests.

Clara returned and linked her arm with that of her husband before replying to Willstätter.

"Tell me, Richard," she asked flatly. "Why is it that if I kill one man, I am arrested and sentenced for my crime? But if I gas thousands to death I am promoted to Captain?"

Willstätter, unable to think of an appropriate response, hemmed and hawed and looked to his friends for clarification. Fritz looked equally confused.

"You judge us harshly," said Otto to Clara. "We are saving lives on both sides, by working to bring this war to an end. You must see the bigger picture."

"On the contrary, Otto," said Clara. "It is you who have failed to see the bigger picture." She raised her voice. "All of you!"

Silence descended on the room.

"The most important thing in this world is life - a single life, lived to the fullest, has more worth than war and empire; and to conspire to take a single life - let alone thousands - is criminal. We are all criminals!"

A shocked Fritz unlinked his wife's arm and reared back.

"Clara, you have drunk too much. Please, everyone, ignore what she said," implored Fritz.

"Actually, I haven't had time for a drink today - too much to do. But I tried drinking and it didn't work. I've tried drinking. I've tried barbital. I've tried staying awake all night so that I'm not visited by the ghosts in my dreams, but now they visit me in the day time too. I wish I could just throw myself into my work as you do, Fritz. What it must be like to be oblivious. I wish I could empty my head of the images. What's that quote from the English' Hamlet? O, that this too too solid flesh would melt. Otto, you were there at Gravenstafel - did their flesh melt?"

"I think you are not well, Clara, we should get you to your room."

"What have you done, Fritz? What horror have you unleashed? Do you not worry that the monster you have created will turn and devour you? You did such good work for the world . . . And now this?"

"During peace time a scientist belongs to the world, but during war time he belongs to his country. I don't have the luxury of choice."

"What a country we have become when a man honored as a hero of humanity then turns his invention to the destruction of humanity. Damn the country!"

"I will not have you speak treason in my house," Fritz responded angrily.

"So, let's have another toast to my husband then - to Fritz, the savior of Germany. A toast to . . . No, ten thousand toasts."

"Clara, please . . ." begged Fritz.

"The lady doth protest too much? . . . The papers say ten thousand dead, Fritz. Ten thousand lost souls!"

"One or ten thousand, our duty is to Germany. They are the enemy and our duty is to fight them. Our responsibility is to win the war for Germany," argued Fritz.

"And Otto Sackur, was he the enemy? His daughter, Irene, our Godchild; what of our duty to her? What an irony that Irene's Godfather killed her real father. Oh, I say, it sounds more and more like Hamlet by the minute, doesn't it?"

"Otto Sackur is a casualty of war!"

"Then what is another casualty, more or less?" Clara stepped back from the crowd to give herself some space. On their realization that Clara held Fritz's service revolver, the crowd reciprocated. The guests could not say where the gun came from: one minute Clara held a bottle of wine, the next she held the gun, as if the bottle had transformed in her hand. "One more casualty of war and perhaps the ghosts will find peace."

"Clara, calm down," soothed Fritz. "You are not well, you will hurt somebody." The guests backed away nervously as Fritz tried to placate his wife.

But Clara seemed calm enough and she spoke in a soft, gentle whisper, "I think there's just enough time for one more quote: This above all - to thine own self be true."

Clara Haber smiled at her husband, placed the barrel of the revolver against her chest and, holding it there with both hands, she pressed against the trigger with her thumb. The shot was not as loud as one might have expected, but for the people who heard it, it had the roar of finality. The bullet passed through Clara's heart; peace came instantly.

. . . Max

Even though the Institute remained an infant in terms of Berlin's history, the Kaiser Wilhelm staff room appeared as old and tired as its occupants: the War had drained its energy and promise, and all its bright, young things had scurried away as if deserting a sinking ship. Only the lost, the abandoned and the defeated remained.

Max Planck slumped in a club chair in the corner of the room: His cheeks shallow; the fire in his eyes no longer shone through his spectacles; the color in his smile had faded to grey. The sunshine which came though the nearby window, although speckled and subdued, provided adequate light by which to read the newspaper which lay on his lap, but he did not read. Instead he removed his spectacles and tried to rub away the weariness from his eyes. He sat alone.

"Max?"

The voice rose soft and gentle and barely audible, as if the speaker did not want to intrude. A gossamer whisper of a voice, wafted on the air by the breeze, it tumbled onto Max almost as an afterthought.

"Hello, Max." The whisper came again and caught his attention.

Drawn out of his introspection, Max massaged his face, perched his eye-glasses on his nose and with a deep breath, drew on the miniscule amount of life which remained to put on his public persona. He looked up. In the hazy light, it at first seemed that Grete or Emma stood before him, but his heart did not leap: he had no delusions and he did not believe in ghosts. He knew that his eyes played tricks on him and he waited patiently for them to focus. Then he recognized her.

"Lise, is that really you?"

"Hello, Max," Lise replied with more certainty, but with a still faltering and timid voice.

"Lise, Lise!" Max jumped to his feet. "I didn't know you had returned. When did you . . . ?"

The words trailed into the haze as Lise and Max embraced.

"I am so sorry, Max," Lise pulled back, but still held Max's hand. "First Marie, then Emma and Grete and Karl. I am so sorry and I do not know how to tell you. I could not bear it myself. I wanted to be here, but they wouldn't let me leave. I came as soon as I could. I wanted to be here." She blurted out the words in a breathless

133

staccato. She had not meant to sound so blunt; on her way to the Institute, she had rehearsed a diplomatic portrayal of sensitivity, but the words had a taken on life of their own beyond her control.

Lise remembered the last time she had seen Max: at one of his familiar parties, a last get-together before she departed Berlin for the War. She could not get the image out of her head: of Max and his family, full of laughter, light and energy. They had milled about her, shown concern for her safety, worried and fussed, as they would have with a member of the family - they had always treated her as family.

She remembered Max had repeatedly warned her to take care, more an attempt to reassure himself than her, she considered, and she had promised him that she would come home safe and sound. She had kept her promise, but now a different Max from the one she had left stood before her; and the new Max faced an unexpected future without his wife and three of his four children.

She could not get the image out of her head: of Max and Marie, Karl and Erwin, and of course, dear Emma and Grete in a family portrait. She tried to tear the imaginary photo in two - to remove those no longer present, to leave just Max and Erwin - but she possessed neither the strength nor the will and she could not do it.

The image persisted. Nothing could tear Max from his family.

"You are too kind," said Max. "Erwin has been a tower of strength. He will not let me have a moment to myself . . . You also had a loss, I hear? Your brother Fritz is still missing?"

"Yes, nothing official yet, so we remain hopeful."

"But you? How are you? How is it at Lemberg?"

"It's not so bad, apart from the food . . ." she attempted to joke. ". . . I received a marriage proposal."

"Lise?"

"But I turned it down. A professor from Greece; I think he loved Germany, not me . . . Anyway, I'm finished with Lemberg; they finally approved my transfer back to Berlin . . . And Professor Fischer informs me that I am now officially on the Kaiser's payroll."

"Yes, congratulations - and about time too, if you ask me. I'm just sorry it took so long, but you know how slowly things change - who knew that all it took was a good war?"

"But I also know that you had something to do with it, war or not. Thank you."

"And I also know of the offer you received from Prague; that worried Fischer enough to lean on the authorities. It really didn't need any contribution from me. Are we to lose the best radio-physicist in the world to Prague?"

"No, my heart is not in Prague. It is here in Berlin."

"I'm glad to hear it. We need you here. When this war is over, there will be much to do, so much to do. Max von Laue is coming back to Berlin, did you hear?"

"No, that is great news."

"The war is lost, I'm afraid, but we shall press on. First, we shall have to rebuild the Institute. We still have a great team. I'll be glad when the military departs and we can return to peaceful endeavors and get back to normality - friends and family and . . . and . . . and perhaps . . ."

Max realized the futility of his words: that there would be no return to normality, at least for him; and Lise sensed that he had reached his breaking point and that the dam must burst.

"Max, I . . ."

But the meagerness of her own words overcame her and she suppressed them and instead moved to cradle and comfort the sobbing Max, as one would a distraught child. And finally, after waging her own war of duty, determination and denial, she realized she had also lost the fight. The tears she had suppressed for so long now welled up in her eyes and she released them: for Max, for Marie, for Karl, for Emma, for Grete, for Fritz, for Clara, for Otto Sackur, for a poor Polish boy on the Russian Front, for the thousands like him and for their grieving mothers.

And Lise and Max held each other and wept. How could they not? The time for holding back had passed. No memorials of granite, no flags at half mast, no black-eyed ravens picking at bones, no poetic prose, no requiems, no religious philosophy and no science had prepared them for this.

The War was over.

"Be strong for me, Max," whispered Lise. "We all need you to be strong. I need you to be strong."

Rise

"Scientists have one thing in common with children: curiosity. To be a good scientist you must have kept this trait of childhood, and perhaps it is not easy to retain just one trait. A scientist has to be curious like a child; perhaps one can understand that there are other childish features he hasn't grown out of."

Otto Robert Frisch

... *Cambridge University, 1968*

"P" rofessor Frisch, Sir Nevill."

Mott's secretary stepped to one side to allow Robert to enter the office; a creaky, dusty office in an equally creaky and dusty part of the building which housed the Cavendish Laboratory of Physics, the meat in the sandwich between Pembroke College and Corpus Christi College, Cambridge, and seemingly stuck in an eternal Victorian gothic time-warp. The office's few redeeming features included a window which overlooked the lake of the Botanic Garden; a view for which Sir Nevill expressed gratitude.

"Ah, Robert!" Sir Nevill roused himself, walked around his desk to shake Robert's hand and then gestured for Robert to sit.

"Thank you for granting me this time, Sir Nevill. I know how busy you are," said Robert.

"Not at all, Robert, always glad to see you. What can I do for you?"

Robert knew that Mott preferred the direct approach and had no tolerance for small-talk, so he immediately came to the point of his visit.

"I have a petition signed by many prominent scientists."

"And you want me to sign? What is the petition's subject matter?"

"It is a petition to the Nobel Academy to ask them to reconsider my aunt for the Physics Prize."

"Ah yes, Lise Meitner. I was extremely sorry to hear of her passing - please accept my condolences."

"Thank you."

"But Robert, you know as well as I do that the Academy does not award prizes posthumously."

"Yes, the petition is to ask them to wave that condition in the case of my aunt; in light of events, she deserves that at least."

"No one was more deserving, with that I agree; and I'd be happy to sign your petition of course, but I don't think it will do any good - the Academy is notoriously protective of its traditions; and impervious to external pressure. In fact, the more they are pressed, the less likely they are to react favorably. Good luck in presenting your petition."

"Er . . . I was rather hoping that you would consider delivering it to the Academy?"

"Me?"

"Yes, after all the pestering I've done over the years, I'm somewhat persona-non-grata as far as the Academy is concerned. I thought a fresh voice might bring about a fresh result."

"But why me? I know that you were not alone in your attempts to light a fire under the Academy; Niels Bohr constantly pestered them . . . How many times was she nominated?"

"Fifteen."

"Fifteen? If Niels Bohr could not move the Academy, what makes you think that I could?"

"As Bohr was Danish, perhaps the Swedes were being nationalistic and spiteful; I don't know. But you - as the Chair of the Pugwash Society - I know that you have political connections and influences way beyond anything at my disposal. You championed the Russell-Einstein Manifesto; if you can bring the Americans and the Soviets to the table to sign a nuclear arms agreement, the Academy should be relatively easy."

"Robert, it is obvious that you don't know the Academy, and you are certainly overestimating any influence you seem to think I have. Compared to the Academy, the Soviets are a reasonable people, delightful and cooperative."

"Sir Nevill . . . I'm running out of options. Now that my aunt is dead, there is a great possibility that the history will die with her. This may be her - and my - last chance. You know the history . . . what they did to her. If you had known my aunt, you would give her this last chance."

"I did know your aunt; you forget that I interned under Niels Bohr in Copenhagen. Bohr hounded the Academy for years before his own death. I maintain that if Bohr couldn't influence them, then my overtures will be in vain."

"The Academy has shut its ears to me . . . You know what the Nazis did to her; if you can't help, then I'm afraid that the Nazis have won."

"Yes, Robert, I know what they did. But aren't you being a little melodramatic? It was not only the Meitners who suffered at the hands of the Nazis. We took in many German scientists during that period, Jews and refugees. If you ask me, Hitler's loathing of science and scientists cost them the war. Germany's loss was the world's gain, but it doesn't do to dwell on the past."

"Don't dwell? How can I not? - I was there; I lived through it," said Robert. "I witnessed the history books being rewritten. The truth still needs to come out. Are you sure you cannot help me?"

"The truth is the truth, Robert; the presence or absence of a Nobel Prize will not change that - nor will it change your aunt's contributions to science . . . She was a great woman, why not let her rest in peace?"

Robert's sighed and, as his chin dropped to his chest, he brushed back his hair in frustration; He felt as if a long epic story was coming to a close, but without the happy ending.

"Face it, Robert, it's hopeless. The Academy will not listen to me any more than they did to Bohr or Einstein . . ."

Mott's criticism was not meant in malice, but he felt Robert's frustration and hated to disappoint a friend.

". . . Tell you what! I'm going down to London next week. There is a good chance I'll be dining with Sir Paul Gall-Booth of the Foreign Office; Of course, it's all topsy-turvy at the FO just now, what with that blasted merger with the Commonwealth Office, but perhaps he can oblige us and arrange a meeting for you with the Swedes; maybe we can persuade King Gustav to lean on them . . ."

Sir Nevill pushed back on his chair, stood up, walked to the window and looked out over the Garden.

". . . Did you know the King is a Fellow of the British Academy? For botany of all things - that must count for something. But I warn you, I still don't think it will do any good. Why don't you leave it with me and check back in a few days?"

"Thank you, Sir Nevill. In the meantime, could I at least ask you to sign my petition?"

"It's the least I can do."

. . . Berlin, 1927

I n the cool, bright sunshine of a late October morning, a young
man of 23 years of age, exited the train at the Berlin Lehrter
Stadtbahnhof. He carried a large suitcase; and although he
wore an overcoat, it had grown thin and threadbare and would offer
little protection against the imminent damp chill of winter. He left
the station and took a meandering path which led south over the
Moltke Bridge and under the Brandenburg Gate. He deemed a stroll
through the Tiergarten as good a way as any to begin his stay. He
looked at his watch - 9:15 AM; he had the whole day to kill.

From the station, his final destination remained a good solid walk of twelve kilometers or so. He could have taken the Berlin subway, the U-Bahn, but, as he intended to conserve every penny in his pocket and as he felt no particular hurry - he knew she would be gone for hours yet - he dawdled. He found the suitcase inconvenient: without it in tow, he may have spent the day enjoying the culture of Museum Island, but with no money for trivial recreation, the museums would have to forgo the pleasure of his company for a few days longer.

Still, the walk had its merits. Although hamstrung by the post-war conditions, prosperity had returned to Berlin. Upbeat and lively, its citizens felt a renewed optimism. The old, stuffy, austere atmosphere was swept away with the rubble and replaced by a new generation and vision. The militaristic, authoritarian band music of the Kaiser's era gave way to the carefree, syncopated rhythms of the jazz age - the Roaring Twenties. Cafes, nightclubs and decadence ushered in a new world order.

Berlin bustled with vibrant life, new and exciting. He was happy to be there.

* * *

Lise wrote an equation on the blackboard: now that she had finally attained the title of professor, the first female professor of physics in Germany, her duties included delivering lectures to bored undergraduates. Max von Laue and Heinrich Rubens, as members of the review committee, supervised her examination for the position.

"Lise, this is all a complete waste of time, if you ask me," joked Laue. "Everyone knows that you're already the foremost authority in the world on radioactivity. The only reason we've called you here for this formal examination of your expertise is because we know how much you like to show off."

Despite Otto's assurances that it would get easier with time, she had never really overcome her fear of public speaking, even here, even now in the familiar and comfortable settings of the University. Her delivery remained dry and calculated, but she amused herself in the knowledge that she was the first female lecturer she had ever met.

"Now, if only I could get the same pay as my male colleagues," she reflected.

* * *

On the Kurfürstendamm, the pulse of the city, and now alive with the sound of recently fallen leaves crunched underfoot, the sun glowed in the sky and generated an unseasonable, cruel warmth. The young man felt his suitcase gain weight with each step and the sweat started to collect in his undershirt. He paused for breath in front of a book store window; perhaps now he had graduated, he would have time to catch up on his reading - once he had his first pay packet, of course, and could afford it; and once he had a place of his own in which to house them.

The selection of books in the window disappointed him; apart from the usual fodder designed to pass away a mindless hour or two, most of the display consisted of stacked copies of a book called Mein Kampf, by a man named Adolf Hitler. As he had heard of neither, he merely shrugged his shoulders; a reflex action designed more to check the flow of the sweat beads.

"Perhaps the budget may stretch to a cup of coffee?" he mused. "If I can find a newspaper, maybe I catch up on the times?"

* * *

In the Staff Room, the lecture done and dusted, Lise grabbed a cup of coffee and sank into a chair next to Max Planck, to enjoy a brief interlude before she would return to her laboratory and her precious experiments, always at a delicate stage and demanding her personal attention.

Otto and Albert played chess and argued. Max and Albert had just returned from a conference in Brussels and the argument stemmed from the reason for that tip: Werner Heisenberg - Niels Bohr's star pupil and protégé. Although still only in his 20's, Heisenberg had developed a reputation for disarming charm and charisma. Lise could understand why the equally charismatic Bohr had taken Heisenberg under his wing and treated him as a son, much as Max Planck had treated her. Albert had taken an instant dislike to him.

Specifically, they argued about Heisenberg's paper and speech with regards to the impossibility of measuring both the position and speed of a particle at the same time, The Uncertainty Principle, as he called it.

"I think the argument has some merit," said Otto.

"Just because something is unknown does not mean that it is unknowable," countered Albert.

"That sounds like some thing Ludwig Boltzmann used to say," said Lise.

Max turned to Lise. "Albert rejects the idea of a random universe. In Brussels, Albert opined that God does not play dice."

"Absolutely; it makes a mockery of reality. And nature is very, very real," said Albert.

"Now that sounds like some thing Ernst Mach used to say," said Lise.

"Niels Bohr said, 'Einstein, stop telling God what to do,'" laughed Max.

* * *

The hotels and restaurants on the Kurfürstendamm usually catered to the tourist trade and, even though tourism remained at a low, he found them too expensive for his meager budget; so he wandered away from the main avenues and on to the side streets, where he found a small café. As he ordered his drink, confusion added to his discomfort: the waiter's dialect differed so much from his own brand of German he could have spoken a foreign language.

But eventually they understood one another; and he settled back to rest his muscles, drink coffee and read the latest news: Hindenburg's denial of German responsibility for World War One, Trotsky's expulsion from the Communist Party - and there was that Hitler chap again, addressing a crowd at some place called Nuremberg.

* * *

"Okay, Fritz, a little more carefully this time," said Lise. "Patience is a virtue."

Fritz Strassmann, almost with ink stains on his fingers from his freshly printed PhD, eagerly wanted to demonstrate both his worth and his gratitude on attaining an assistant position in the famous Hahn-Meitner Research Department. His enthusiasm had invalidated several tests, causing repetition and delay, but Lise remained a paragon of the virtues which she preached.

"Sorry," said Strassmann. "I get carried away sometimes."

"What's this?" cried Otto, who had just entered the laboratory. "Fritz, are you upsetting your boss? You should try singing Brahms to her; always does the trick."

"No," said Fritz. "It's this new equipment - we didn't have anything so sophisticated in Hanover. I haven't mastered it yet."

"You should count yourself lucky, young Fritz," said Otto. "In our day, the equipment consisted of . . . it consisted mostly of thin air, that's what it consisted of? See how lucky you are. Equipment indeed! A good scientist doesn't need equipment. Don't you agree, Lise?"

"I remember that before the war, when we conducted an experiment, we prepared the solution in the Chemistry Institute and then had to run all the way to the Physics Institute to measure the results on Baeyer's Spectrometer before the decay rendered the equipment ineffective. It was a good kilometer; how my legs would ache," said Lise.

"Ah yes, and when the half-life of the isotope was very short, we would have Max von Laue wait outside in his Audi, with the engine running, to drive us," said Otto.

"Max drove like a mad man," added Lise. She shook her head and remembered the erratic driving of Mad-Max, and the times when centrifugal forces had almost ejected her and her tray of solutions from his car. "Faculty and students would have to leap out of the way to avoid being run over, as Max cursed them for obstructing the progress of science."

"New students, who hadn't been warned, were particularly vulnerable - that's how we culled the herd back then; we didn't need an examination board. If you weren't smart enough to get out of the way of traffic, you had no future as a physicist."

* * *

He strolled through the Botanical Garden, in the South West suburb of Dahlem, and emerged on the other side at his goal, 16 Ihnestraße, where he almost met his demise as he crossed the street but forgot that traffic in Germany came from the right and not the left as it did in Austria. His confusion returned: for she had written that she lived in an apartment, but arrayed in front of him, the large stately buildings did not resemble the tenements he had expected. He re-checked the address; number 16 pointed to the biggest mansion of all, nestled in an expansive manicured landscape that rivaled the Botanical Garden he had just exited. Then he saw the plaque at the gates of the graveled driveway which led to the entrance: the Kaiser

Wilhelm Harnack House; and he knew that he had the correct place and smiled.

"Well, Aunty, I knew that you loved your work, but I didn't think that you loved it so much that you slept in your laboratory."

He stepped onto the graveled path.

* * *

The sun had long since set as Lise finally called it a day and exchanged her lab coat for her overcoat and hat. At least she had a relatively short walk to Harnack House, across the Institute's lawns and pathways; and in a bracing evening air which felt refreshing after the stuffiness of the laboratory.

Lise entered the house and turned to the stairs which led to her apartment, but as she did so, an oddity caught her eye: through the entrance to the communal lounge she saw a figure - a man - slumped in a club chair, apparently asleep, with a battered suitcase on the floor beside him. And although she instantly recognized the man, she registered a look of surprise, for she had not expected him. She walked into the lounge and gently nudged the sleeping young man.

"Robert?" she asked.

* * *

In what served as Lise's small kitchen, separated from the living area by a curtain and littered with boxes, because she had only moved into the apartment 5 months prior and unpacking remained a low priority, Lise made some coffee for Robert.

"Here, this will warm you up."

"Thanks."

"Have you eaten?"

"I had lunch near the Kurfürstendamm," he lied.

"What are you doing here?"

"I got my grant to work at the P.T.R."

"Why didn't you tell me you were coming?"

"It was all a bit of a hurry. I only got it because their first choice suddenly had a rich relative die on him. I did write to you about it, asking if you would provide a reference for me. You declined, remember?"

"Yes, I remember. I said I couldn't give an opinion because as you are my nephew I am naturally biased."

"Naturally, oh yes."

"But I did not speak ill of you either."

"Professor Przibram told me that your words were, quote, 'He is not an entirely disagreeable person.'"

"Well, it's true; you're not - most of the time."

"Thank you Aunty; coming from you that means such a great deal."

"Don't let it go to your head. But where are you staying?"

"That's the problem. It was all so fast that I have no where yet. I was hoping . . ."

"You can't stay here. There's barely enough room for me, as you can see."

"Oh, no, I was hoping that you could recommend a place for a starving young physicist, having been one yourself for so long. Perhaps you know someone?"

"We'll ask around in the morning. Tonight you are welcome to the floor."

"Thank you; the floor will be perfect. But this is quite a nice place you have here, the house and the gardens."

"I wish it were mine, but I have to share it with everyone and their dog. It's more a country club than a home. We call it the colony. Einstein is staying here right now; and Max von Laue until he can find something more suitable. Hungry? I'm not really prepared for entertaining, but I think there is some cheese in the mousetrap."

"I wouldn't want to put you to any trouble, Aunty."

"I just received a food package from Vienna; from your Aunt Frida; there's some salami left. If I'd known you were coming, you could have brought it with you - Or did you bring a package that I don't know about and eat it on the way?"

"You've found me out, Aunty - the foie gras and caviar were particularly good."

"And I have some soup."

"Soup would be great; you make the best soup."

"And drink your coffee before it gets cold. Welcome to Berlin!"

. . . February

Although nightlife in Berlin already had a reputation for boisterous exuberance, the night of January 30th, 1933, witnessed the dancing in the streets taken to new, hysterical levels. Not from the music lovers and other entertainment seekers who regularly flocked along the Kurfürstendamm, but from the hordes of NSDAP supporters who came out of hiding to celebrate their leader's appointment as Chancellor. The orders of the day called for swastika flags, arm-bands and torchlight parades. Drums and military music had returned, accompanied by the driving beat of jackboots.

As they marched through the Brandenburg Gate and along the Wilhelmstraße to the Presidential Palace, the SA and SS sang the *Hörst Wessel* song, cheered on by thousands of 'Sieg Heils'. At the Palace, Joseph Goebbels played Buckingham to Hitler's Richard and worked the crowd into frenzied anticipation. On cue, a spotlight illuminated the stage and Hitler stepped onto it.

"Sieg Heil! Sieg Heil!" the crowd roared.

It was a long night.

* * *

Two days later, a more subdued party took place in the Harnack House common lounge; not to celebrate the change in Government, but to celebrate Otto's promotion to Director of the Institute of Chemistry.

The final guests arrived: Max Planck and Max von Laue, with a visitor from Denmark, Niels Bohr. The two Maxes had greeted Niels at the station and driven from there in Laue's car. Following the angry exchanges with two Brown Shirts who made the mistake of trying to cross the street, they had to agree that Laue's driving skills had not diminished with the years.

"I thought the SA had been banned?" asked Niels. "I was surprised to see them out on the streets like that."

"That was last month," said Max von Laue. "A month is a long time in politics. Even my milkman was in fancy dress this morning. Brown is the new fashion. Didn't you see the fall collection on display from Paris? Alas, my own wardrobe is incredibly dated."

"It is the Machtergreifung," said Otto.

"Machtergreifung?" questioned Niels.

"Seizure of power," explained Lise. "The ban has been lifted."

"More like Machterschleichung, if you ask me," said Laue.

"Sneaking into power," explained Lise to Niels. "Here, let me get you a drink."

"Hang on," said Laue. "One, two, three, four . . ."

"Max, what are you doing?" asked Lise.

"Don't interrupt, I'll lose count . . . five, six . . . Six? Only six Nobel's in the room! What kind of party is this? Oh well, if six is all we can muster, it will just have to do. I hate these austere times."

"Anyway, to drink?" repeated Lise.

"Have they put you on drink duty, Lise? Is that because you're a woman or because you don't have your Nobel yet?"

"It's because I live here and you are my guest. But if I have to ask one more time, you can get your own drink."

"In that case, I'll have some of the red which Albert is guzzling."

"And for you, Niels?"

"The same please, Lise," replied Niels.

"Red it is," said Lise and turned away.

"In my day . . ." said Laue, with voice raised. "Tradition was that the rookie prize winner got the drinks - that means you, Heisenberg - I see you skulking behind Otto."

"Hello, Max," smiled Heisenberg, who had joined the Nobel club a few weeks earlier.

"Hello Werner, I'm surprised to see you here," said Niels. "I received your letter just last week; it did not mention a trip to Berlin. How is Leipzig treating you?"

"Just fine, thank you," said Heisenberg. "Like you, I'm visiting for a few days - last minute plans. I do miss Copenhagen, however, and our chats."

"Oh, Albert, I have something for you," remembered Laue. From his pocket he produced an American comic book. He tossed it to Albert.

"Amazing Stories?" said Albert, reading the title of the pulp science fiction publication, the lurid cover showing flying man.

Lise returned with a tray of drinks.

"Yes," said Laue. "The problems of atomic energy have been solved – thank you, Lise - on page one, no less. And produced such practical inventions: the atomic flying belt - as demonstrated on the cover - and ships which travel through space. All these years of research, experimentation, sacrifice and hard work - for naught! We've wasted our time and missed our opportunity. Gentlemen - and lady - we have been made redundant. We can all retire to our cottages by the sea."

Albert flipped through the pages of the comic book. "I see," he said. "That at the end, the heroic scientist saves the world and wins the girl."

"Fiction, dear boy, pure fiction," said Laue.

"If only it were that easy," said Planck.

"Who dreams up this stuff?" asked Fritz Haber. "Limitless energy from the atom!"

"Einstein, for one," laughed Heisenberg.

"In theory, I agree," said Albert. "In practice, it is far too impractical. There is not the slightest indication that nuclear energy will ever be obtainable. It would mean that the atom would have to be shattered at will. How big would the machine have to be to provide enough energy for a single purpose?"

"The size of a belt buckle, according to Amazing Stories," said Laue.

"The size of the planet, more like," said Otto.

"Lise, in that laboratory of yours, are you hiding a particle accelerator the size of the planet?" asked Laue.

"What's a particle accelerator?" asked Lise, with sly innocence.

"Albert and I agree on this. It would require more energy than it released," said Otto. "Even if we could release that energy, we could only harness it at an astronomical cost, far outweighing the benefits. The best we've been able to do is chip off a few protons; we cannot split the nucleus."

"And that is the best we'll ever do," said Haber. "The forces which hold the nucleus are so powerful, we don't possess the strength, the aim, the speed, or the sharp axe required to cleave the nucleus."

"You don't think Chadwick's neutron may make for a capable axe?" asked Robert. "Cockcroft and Walton smashed the atom . . ."

"Cockcroft and Walton disintegrated the atom in a controlled experiment that we cannot emulate on an industrial scale," said Otto. "We throw mud. Sometimes it sticks and makes the element heavier. Sometimes it knocks off a proton or two and makes the element lighter. Cockcroft and Walton threw mud until they reduced the atom to rubble. It's wishful thinking to believe that we could get energy out of this procedure in a significant way."

"You think of the nucleus as solid," said Niels. "Perhaps it is more like a drop of water than a rock. If it is pliant and elastic and its surface tension keeps it together, it cannot be cleaved, but perhaps it can be squeezed apart."

"That doesn't alter the problem. To harvest the atom's energy using the techniques at our disposal is just not possible."

"Turn on the radio," interrupted Max Planck, who wanted to break up the argument before it became tedious and threatened the party atmosphere. "It's the inaugural address."

"And I was having such a pleasant time," sighed Albert.

"Must we?" asked Lise. "Some music would make for a much more agreeable evening."

"Don't you want to hear what he has to say?" asked Otto. "It could be important."

"I will cheerfully listen to the man's resignation speech," said Albert.

"Now, now, Albert, open mind please," said Planck.

"Okay, let's hear what the new Chancellor has to say for himself," said Laue.

"Robert, you are closest; switch on the radio," said Haber.

Robert manned the controls of the radio and tuned it in as Hitler's speech began.

"More than fourteen years have passed since the unhappy day when the German people, blinded by promises from foes at home and abroad, lost touch with honor and freedom, thereby losing all. Since that day of treachery, the Almighty has withheld his blessing from our people. Dissension and hatred descended upon us . . ."

"I think Abraham Lincoln phrased it better," said Laue.

". . . The misery of our people is horrible to behold! . . ."

"He's got that right," said Albert.

". . . Millions of the industrial proletariat are unemployed and starving; the whole of the middle class and the small artisans have been impoverished. When this collapse finally reaches the German peasants, we will be faced with an immeasurable disaster. . ."

"Immeasurable disaster," said Albert. "Heisenberg, I believe that measuring the immeasurable is your department."

". . . All about us the warning signs of this collapse are apparent. Communism with its method of madness is making a powerful and insidious attack upon our dismayed and shattered nation. It seeks to poison and disrupt in order to hurl us into an epoch of chaos . . ."

"Can I assume that Mr. Hitler doesn't care for communists?" asked Niels.

"Amongst others," said Albert.

"Mr. Hitler is Austrian," said Lise. "Niels, remember those communists in Café Central?"

"Oh, yes, Bronstein and his revolution. I take it Lenin must have taken the last newspaper one day and upset him."

> ". . . This negative, destroying spirit spared nothing of all that is highest and most valuable. Beginning with the family, it has undermined the very foundations of morality and faith and scoffs at culture and business, nation and Fatherland, justice and honor. Fourteen years of Marxism have ruined Germany; one year of bolshevism would destroy her. The richest and fairest territories of the world would be turned into a smoking heap of ruins . . ."

"Unlike the smoking heap of ruins we have today," said Laue.

> ". . . But we are all filled with unbounded confidence for we believe in our people and their imperishable virtues. Every class and every individual must help us to found the new Reich . . ."

"Every individual," said Otto. "We all must do our bit."

"Now where have I heard that before?" asked Albert.

". . . The National Government will regard it as its first and foremost duty to revive in the nation the spirit of unity and co-operation. It will preserve and defend those basic principles on which our nation has been built. It regards Christianity as the foundation of our national morality, and the family as the basis of national life . . ."

"Why does everyone have to bring religion into it," asked Lise.

". . . All those institutions which are the strongholds of the energy and vitality of our nation will be taken under the special care of the Government . . ."

"I don't like the sound of that," said everyone in unison.

". . . The Marxist parties and their lackeys have had fourteen years to show what they can do. The result is a heap of ruins . . ."

"Albert, I think Hitler just called you a lackey," said Laue.

"I consider that a compliment," said Albert.

"'Heap of ruins' twice in one speech," said Laue. "Not only is that showing a lack of originality, I think he's tempting fate."

"Don't worry, Hitler is a stooge. They're setting him up as the fall guy," said Otto. "Franz von Papen is the real power who will succeed Hindenburg."

"Papen is an idiot who thinks that the Kaiser will return to rescue the Fatherland," said Albert. "Have you read Mein Kampf?

Anyone who thinks Hitler will give up power as easily as he won it is also an idiot."

"No, Hitler is a figurehead; Papen controls the cabinet."

"Hush, we're trying to listen," chided Lise.

> ". . . In accordance with Field Marshal von Hindenburg's command we shall begin now. May God Almighty give our work His blessing, strengthen our purpose, and endow us with wisdom and the trust of our people, for we are fighting not for ourselves but for Germany."

The speech concluded, Robert tuned the radio to a light classical program.

"We'll be fighting soon enough," predicted Albert.

"After listening to that, I need a drink," said Laue. "Max, come and give me a hand with some refills."

Planck and Laue headed towards the kitchen.

"Here, let me help," said Niels, who followed them out.

In the kitchen, Max von Laue turned and spoke in a forceful whisper to Planck. "Things will move fast now," predicted Laue. "It's not just the communists whom Hitler hates. I don't think Albert and Lise are safe any more."

"This pessimism is not like you," said Planck. "Perhaps things will settle down with this new Government."

"Perhaps things will get worse . . ." said Laue.

"Anything I can do to help," interrupted Niels.

The two men broke their huddle.

"Oh, thanks, Niels," said Laue. "I think the white wine is on the table behind you . . ."

"No," said Niels, as he forced his way into their private conversation. "I'm not talking about the drinks - I'm talking about events in Germany which seem to be getting out of hand."

"Another pessimist," said Planck.

"Heisenberg told me that he was warned to stay away from Einstein," said Niels.

"What? By who?" demanded Planck.

"By people who do not have Einstein's interests at heart."

"You see!" hissed Laue. "Albert is already having his lectures disrupted by these people. It's only a matter of time before it turns ugly."

"But what can we do?" asked Planck. "Not that I admit we have to do anything."

Niels leaned in to whisper. "I am not without some resources and influence in Copenhagen; and many in our community are of the same mind and determination. Should the worse . . ."

Planck started to argue, but Niels raised a hand to silence him.

"Should the worse come - and we all pray, of course, that it doesn't, but should it come, we can help. I am here to tell you of our invitation to those who may be particularly vulnerable, Albert, Lise, Fritz Haber . . ."

"They wouldn't hurt Fritz; he is a national hero, an institution!" objected Planck.

". . . A research grant to work in Copenhagen for a year; the invitation is open-ended."

"Albert is a Nobel Lauriat; they wouldn't dare harm him," objected Planck.

"Lise isn't," said Laue.

"Not for the want of trying," said Planck. "We've nominated her and Otto every year since '23. Lise should have won for protactinium alone. But Lise would never leave Berlin . . ."

"How extensive is the invitation?" asked Laue.

"If the candidate is worthy, then I'm sure we'll oblige; if not in Copenhagen, then in England or America. As I said, many of our colleagues in the international community are of the same mind."

"I cannot believe we are having this conversation," said Planck.

"Better to have it now than when it's too late," said Niels.

Max Planck shrugged his shoulders. "You are correct, Niels; better late than never does not apply in this case. I would blame myself if anything terrible happened. I hope we don't need to take you up on your generous offer, but thank you."

The three conspirators shook hands.

. . . *Goodbye, Albert*

"I have been invited to Niels Bohr's summer conference in Copenhagen," said Robert.

"Congratulations, when do you leave?" replied Lise.

"Not so fast, Aunty, I haven't accepted the invitation."

"Of course you've accepted. What else could you do but accept?"

"But my work here . . ."

"Has ended - I heard they sacked you."

"Well, sacked is such a harsh word."

"Fired, dismissed, let go, made redundant, surplus to requirements - there is no gentle way to say it. Either way, the connection to the pay check is severed."

"Which is precisely why I haven't accepted the invitation to Copenhagen - I need to nail down another job before I fritter away my money on travel."

"Robert, are you that naïve or do you think that I am that naïve?"

"Aunty, what do you mean?"

"There is no work for you anywhere in Germany, at least not as a Physicist; you know that, I know that and Niels knows that. The summer conference is merely the excuse you need to obtain a travel permit. What's more, it is an invitation from Niels; he must think very highly of you."

"Perhaps it is you of whom he thinks highly?"

"You don't think I had anything to do with this?"

"The thought had crossed my mind."

"Well uncross it. Obviously Niels has taken leave of his senses by extending an invitation to you, but don't take leave of yours by refusing it. Good God! A chance to work in Copenhagen under one of the greatest scientists the world has ever seen - or ever likely to see. If I was your age, I wouldn't have wasted time to come and say farewell to my aged aunt."

"So you think I should go?"

"I think if you don't go, I'll never speak to you again."

"If I go, you won't see me as often. If I stay, you won't speak to me."

"Yes, it's a win-win for me, either way."

". . . Aunty . . ."

"Yes?"

"The Berufsbeamtengesetz is going to make it tough for all of us to find work in Germany . . . Perhaps, you should also . . ."

"Accept an invitation from Niels?"

"Well, I don't believe that the situation in Germany will improve any time soon."

"For you perhaps, but the Berufsbeamtengesetz does not apply to me. I am exempt because of my service during the war. Besides, the KWI isn't subject to the civil service laws; it's funded by private industry."

"That may be, but even so, things are becoming rather uncomfortable for us. The anti-Semitism is growing more violent every day."

That Lise and Robert now held this conversation proved Max von Laue and Niels correct in their pessimism. But even the pessimists may have expressed surprise at the speed with which events unfolded.

A mere four weeks after Chancellor Hitler swore the oath to *'protect the Constitution and laws of the German people, conscientiously discharge the duties imposed on me, and conduct my affairs of office impartially and with justice to everyone,'* Berlin's fire department had engaged to tackle a blaze which had engulfed the parliament building, the Reichstag. Hitler accused the communists of setting the fire and bullied Hindenburg to assign emergency powers to him, which he used to arrest and expel the communists from parliament and which, therefore, gave the Nazi party a majority for the first time. Franz von Papen's stooge wasted no time in passing laws to reorganize the civil service, laws which included the expulsion of low-level Jews from the Government and universities.

"Robert," said Lise. "You've known me long enough to know that I don't give up that easily. A few thugs playing soldiers in the streets do not scare me. Besides, I'm not a Jew, I'm a Christian."

"Not according to the Berufsbeamtengesetz."

"That doesn't apply to me!"

* * *

"My mind is made up!"

In his office at the KWI, Max Planck tried to talk his old friend, Fritz Haber, out of taking a bold but futile step. Haber proved resolute.

"Fritz," said Max. "It is a noble gesture, but it serves no purpose other than to satisfy your ego. You cannot help those you wish to protect by deserting them."

"In all consciousness, I cannot obey the directive. If I cannot obey then resignation is the only course," argued Haber.

"There must be another way; the directive must be open to interpretation."

"All racially undesirable staff, all non-Aryan - the directive is most clear. I won't do it. I won't fire anyone for racist reasons . . ."

Planck sighed and sank back into his chair.

". . . Max, Max, I am tired. My health is not what it once was, you know that. This stress isn't good for my angina. Perhaps I have stayed too long. I should have retired long ago."

"No, not at all."

"This directive forces my hand, but I have mulled this decision for a while - it is time to go."

"I shall miss you; it won't be the same around here. Who else knows?"

"No one yet, just you. I have drafted my letter of resignation to the Minister, but I wanted to formulate a transition plan with you before I submit it."

"Do you have any one in mind as your successor?"

"Otto Hahn or James Franck, both are deserving."

"Franck, as a Jew, is unlikely to be acceptable to the Ministry, in spite of his Iron Cross. Would they accept Otto? He's not exactly known for his love of the current policy. He may be too ambivalent for them. In fact, he's talking about organizing a protest."

"With your recommendation they'd have to accept him. As the President of the KWI, the appointment falls under your mandate and the decision rests with you. It would be strange for the Ministry to override it."

"We live in strange times," said Max.

* * *

Lise's lack of concern for her own safety, as expressed to Robert, also lacked conviction. Although she seldom spoke her mind, and only then in private to trusted friends and family, the harassment which Albert now faced daily, slowly crept towards her. She could not help but look over her shoulder occasionally.

Albert had no such qualms about speaking his mind in public, but it wouldn't have made any difference - because his fame made him the ideal target. In the eyes of the Nazis, he embodied the worst aspects of science - Jewish Physics. The harassment would not stop. It would only get worse until it reached an inevitable climax.

Albert delighted in keeping one step ahead of his enemies and as with Haber, he had also reached a decision.

"So it's goodbye then?" said Lise. Her voice cloaked her disappointment at the news. She knew better than to pretend that she could change Albert's mind.

They sat in the Harnack House common room, just the two of them, in opposing club chairs with a table between them. The house dozed in a rare and curious, quiet stillness; as if afraid to bring attention to itself. Not even the usual hum of the radio disturbed the loneliness of their conversation.

On the table a wooden board, etched with a grid, held small black and white round stones. They played Go.

"Au revoir only," replied Albert. He looked at the board and puffed on his pipe in frustration. ". . . I was never very good at this game. I blame my teacher."

"I only taught you the rules," laughed Lise. "It is up to you to apply them."

"Ha, there is always a catch. But if I cannot beat you at Go, there is no point in my remaining."

"Don't like losing to a woman?"

"Don't like losing."

"What shall we do without you?"

"You shall adjust. The Institute will not collapse . . . Planck must find a new second fiddle, of course."

"And to sneak away as if you were ashamed? That is not right. We should be throwing you a big farewell party."

"No, the fewer people who know I am leaving the better. As a thief in the night."

"Pardon?"

"To sneak away as a thief in the night. I think that is most appropriate."

"What do you mean?"

"Because I am a thief; in leaving this way - in a manner and time of my choosing, I have stolen their thunder. They won't be able to kick me out. I'd love to see the look on Hitler's face when they tell him I've pre-empted their strike against me."

"Are you sure that you're doing the right thing? We've had bad governments before this one. This country gets worked up at the drop of a hat, but these things blow over."

"Is the state made to serve man or vice versa? Now that Hitler is chancellor I wonder. Blow over? Not this time, Lise. Not before much worse has happened. I need permission to teach. Then I can no longer teach without censure. My work is ridiculed and defamed by so-called experts. I would also advise you to leave."

"Sexism has not driven me away; anti-Semitism will not."

"This is not your run-of-the-mill bigotry, Lise. It will not blow over until everything in its path is blown over. While you remain, I will worry for you."

"If you were a religious man, I would advise you to pray."

"The most beautiful and deepest experience a man can have is the sense of the mysterious. It is the underlying principle of science and art as well as religion. To sense that behind anything that can be experienced there is something that our mind cannot grasp and whose beauty and sublimity reaches us only indirectly and as a feeble reflection. In this sense I am religious."

"Why Albert, in all the time I have known you, I have never heard you say anything so poetic. You are wasted in the sciences."

"Well, you know, every now and again, even I am capable of deep thought."

"Especially you . . ."

Albert smiled at the compliment; a small, modest smile, void of all pretense and pride. And Lise realized she gazed on the real Einstein. She had known since the first day they met that the various facets of Albert's character - the womanizer, the socialist, the joker - did not add up to the whole. Albert only ever presented a façade to the outside world and no one really understood what lay beneath. She had once guessed that, as with her, a love of science precluded any other commitment. Now she realized that answer did not satisfy at all. Albert merely dabbled in science as he dabbled in everything. Albert loved Humanity; and Humanity unremittingly broke his heart.

". . . We will be a lesser institute without you," said Lise.

"Lise, it has come to my attention that out of the greatness of your soul you are quietly accomplishing a splendid work. Small is the number that see with their own eyes and feel with their own hearts. Promise me that you will not become a lesser person."

* * *

Early next morning, Albert exited the Harnack House with a suitcase in hand and tickets for travel to the USA in his pocket. Before he could climb into the taxi which awaited him, a voice called out a warning.

"Be careful, Professor. I wouldn't want you to meet with injury between here and the station."

The voice belonged to a so-called colleague, Professor Kurt Hess; an adolescent aged about 40, and wearing a swastika arm band over his tweed jacket. Hess, a fully paid up member of the Party, had aligned with the most vocal and virulent of Albert's enemies on campus, and the warning, dipped in sarcasm, was not proffered out of friendly concern.

"Oh I think I can manage to avoid the rabble with which you associate," Albert replied cheerfully.

"That rabble, as you call them, is the future," sneered Hess. "That rabble is Germany."

"As long as I have any choice in the matter, I shall live only in a country where civil liberty, tolerance, and equality of all citizens before the law prevail. These conditions do not exist in Germany at the present time."

"Then do not bother to come back, Herr Professor. You are not welcome here any more."

Albert stopped, turned, walked to Hess, and in a low, conspiratorial voice said, "You know, I have never liked Germans." Albert suddenly raised his hand and, watching Hess flinch, lifted his Homburg hat and added a jovial, "Good day."

Before the speechless Hess could react, Albert climbed into the taxi and ordered the driver to take him to the Lehrter Stadtbahnhof.

. . . Chancellor

O f all the things which Max Planck may have received for his 75th birthday, a card from Adolf Hitler probably held a position amongst the least expected. But Max had the proof in his hands, and Hitler had personally added some warm and garrulous sentiments. Max's position as director of the KWI did require some official correspondence, of course, but the departures of Haber and Einstein had strained the relationship between the KWI and the Government; and that Hitler should make this gesture surprised Max.

Nevertheless, as badly as the recent events had shaken Max, he saw this olive branch as an opportunity. Max would draw on the last reserve of strength which remained in his frail body. He requested an audience with the Chancellor.

And subsequently a few days later, audience granted, Max found himself seated in an outer reception room at the Radziwill Palace on Wilhelmstraße, office of the Reich Chancellery. As he waited, he drummed his fingers on the top of his walking-stick, not a nervous affectation - he had lived too long and grown too old to feel intimidated by any thing, anymore - instead, as an improvised metronome to a tune which he hummed in his head, a mental exercise to keep his mind sharp. Occasionally, a note or two would escape from his lips and the receptionist would raise her head in anticipation of a question or comment from Max which never came.

The room had three doors: the one through which Max had entered from the street - inspected, escorted up the circular staircase, down the corridor, guarded all the way and deposited - and two other doors, both closed, which stood to the left and right of the receptionist. Max looked at the doors and pondered on the probability that one was fake, designed to accent the symmetry of the room.

Max waited and hummed; and as he began to tap out another drum beat, the fifth since the receptionist had invited him to take a seat before she picked up the phone and talked to whoever answered at the other end in hushed tones, the non-fake door opened and a young woman, smart and crisp, walked though it and introduced herself.

"Professor Planck, good morning, so sorry to keep you waiting," said the young woman. "I am Christa Schroeder, private secretary to the Chancellor." She held out her hand.

"Pleased to meet you," said Max, as he rose up out of his chair. They exchanged a formal hand shake, so brief that Max almost missed it.

"The Chancellor is looking forward to your meeting. If you would be so good as to follow me."

"Yes, thank you," replied Max.

Max followed Christa Schroeder through the door and down another corridor, lined with tables, chairs and guards, towards Hitler's office.

In the Chancellor's office, Adolph Hitler stood at a dining room sized table. To his side stood Albert Speer, Hitler's chief architect. On the table stood a white, wooden model of the new Chancellery which Speer planned to build.

"Excellent, excellent!" Hitler congratulated Speer. "This will prove once and for all that Germany is back on the World Stage. Build it Albert, whatever it takes, build it. The resources of Germany are at your disposal."

"Thank you, my Führer," replied Speer, "But first we need the location. I cannot build in the sky."

"Already found," smiled Hitler. "Next door, the department store, Warehaus Wertheim, and the land on which it sits."

"And you will persuade the current owners to sell?"

"Already persuaded!"

From the office door came the solid, rehearsed knock of someone expected.

"Come!" ordered Hitler.

Christa Schroeder and Max entered.

"Chancellor, Professor Planck," introduced Schroeder.

"Professor, come in, come in. Welcome," grinned Hitler. "Thank you, Christa."

The secretary nodded and, escorted by Speer, walked out of the office and closed the door behind her.

"Come, look, Professor," beamed Hitler. "Give me your opinion." He ushered Max to the table and proudly indicated the model.

Max looked at the model, unsure of how to respond. He did not know the purpose of the proposed building: government, academic, or the arts? But the square, austere and authoritarian features of the model reminded him of a factory.

"Most interesting," Max said diplomatically.

"The new Reich Chancellery," explained Hitler.

"Ah," said Max, filling in the blank which Hitler left to him for more commentary.

"Of course, from the model it is hard to judge, but when it is built it will impress every visitor with its grandeur; it will be monumental." Hitler gushed and pointed. "We'll make them enter here and walk down this long corridor - 300 meters - to the reception hall. The reception hall will be another 150 meters, twice as long as the hall of mirrors at Versailles."

"Most impressive," said Max, on cue.

"This will teach them something about the splendor of the German Reich, don't you think?" asked the Führer.

"Most . . . er . . . splendid?" offered Max.

"Exactly! I'm glad that you see it too, Professor. And a showcase for the best German craftsmanship; we will use only the finest German wood and marble," continued Hitler. "In the meantime, alas, we must make do with this . . . failure." Hitler frowned and dismissively waved an arm to denote the room in which they stood and, by extension, the palace itself. "How Bismarck could have thought it good enough to represent the Reichskanzlei, I don't know. Fit for a soap company, perhaps, but not suitable as the headquarters of the Chancellor . . ."

Hitler paused for Max to comment further, but Max did not oblige.

". . . Anyway, I'm sure that you are a busy man. Please come and sit," said Hitler, indicating a visitor's chair in front of his desk. Hitler took his place on the other side of the desk.

"Thank you, Herr Chancellor," said Max.

Max sat down and placed his walking-stick to the side of the chair.

"I am honored to have you visit me. Herr Professor. You have done great work for Germany."

"Thank you, Herr Chancellor."

"And more to come, I hope. I am proud of the discoveries coming out of your institutes, Professor."

"Thank you."

"And so, what can I do for you in return?"

"I am here to advocate on behalf of the society."

"Naturally, you are its champion; there has been none finer."

"You are too kind . . . but you are also a busy man, Herr Chancellor, with many duties. I cannot presume that the problems of the KWI are known to you in detail, so you may not know that Professor Haber has resigned his position as director of the Chemistry Institute."

"Yes, I had heard. Professor Haber is somewhat rash and foolish, wouldn't you say?"

"His resignation is in protest of the Ministry's order that we dismiss several of our most prominent and promising scientists."

"Jews," corrected Hitler.

"Yes, as you say, Jews."

"But what can I do? The law is the law."

"Herr Chancellor . . . without the work of such as Herr Haber, I feel that German science will be at a disadvantage. Is it a good law which is harmful to the Nation's well being?"

"I agree that no law should harm the Nation, but some would argue that this new law is necessary to heal the Nation from the harm

177

which the prior, soft, decadent laws have caused. Sometimes we must take drastic action to cure the patient."

"I understand, but the treatment cannot be so traumatic as to kill the patient. Can you not use your influence to make an exception?"

"For Haber? He resigned; we did not force him out."

"For the others at the KWI."

"For your Jewish scientists?"

"I repeat, Herr Chancellor, to remove them all at once, in this manner, would leave us at a disadvantage."

"Are you telling me that the Jews have such a strangle-hold on the KWI that they can hold us to ransom? This is exactly what I am talking about. It must be stopped."

"Herr Chancellor . . ."

"Don't you see the malaise which has descended on our country? I need to put idle Germans back to work; to restore their spirit and pride. We cannot sit by while Jews do the work denied to Germans. And German science is best served by German scientists! You would have our finest minds stagnate while work is done by others? Jews such as Haber are all communists, our enemies. My life is against them."

"Chancellor, Professor Haber is a good Christian and a staunch advocate of German Nationalism. And many old Jewish families represent the best of German culture."

"That is not true! A Jew is a Jew! All Jews hang together. Where one Jew is, there are others of their species. Some of the more cowardly ones may pretend to be Christian to hide their guilt, but we will root them out of all of our cherished institutions, including the Church . . ."

Hitler pushed back on his chair and lurched to his feet.

" . . . Our national policies will not be revoked or modified even for scientists. If the dismissal of Jews means the annihilation of contemporary German science, then we shall do without science for a few years."

Hitler paused for breath and turned his back. Max retrieved his walking-stick and climbed to his feet.

"I see I cannot persuade you, Herr Chancellor," said Max softly. "There is no more to be said. Of course, I shall resign as President of the Kaiser Wilhelm Society."

Without a knock this time, the office door opened and Christa Shroeder returned to escort Max from the room.

"Good day, sir," said Max and turned away, his head bowed.

As Max and Christa Shroeder reached the door, Hitler, his back still towards Max, yelled after him, so loud and angry that the guards in the corridor beyond became uneasy and wondered if they should intervene somehow.

"You know what people say about me? They say I suffer from weak nerves. Slander! Slander!"

... *Books are Burning*

Max Planck, a man of his word, resigned from his position as president of the Kaiser Wilhelm Society. Max had burned his bridges to Adolf Hitler and the Ministry; and this had other unintended consequences; including the rejection of his recommendation of Otto to replace Fritz Haber as head of KWI for Chemistry. Hitler said he had no quarrel with science, he just hated scientists; and with Planck out of the way, the Ministry could, and would, ride rough-shod over the Institute.

Max insisted that he would give a farewell speech to his friends and loyal employees at the KWI. The Ministry forbade it. Nevertheless, Max gave it. The Ministry forbade the staff of the KWI to attend the farewell speech. They attended anyway. And as the men assigned by the Ministry to take names looked on, more intimidated than intimidating, Lise and the others gathered to hear the great Max Planck one last time. The hall filled to the rafters with spectators who still couldn't quite believe it had come to this.

Max climbed to his feet, the walking-stick more a prop for effect than necessary for his infirmity. He walked to the podium. Lise had heard Max speak on many occasions; she knew with intimacy that dry, rambling, monotone style which had caused many a student, in ages past, to fall into slumber and then onto the floor.

But for once in his life, Max spoke from the heart and the speech resonated with seldom seen emotion. The quiet man of compromise spoke his mind. At the conclusion, his passion spent, he dropped his voice to almost a whisper, but the audience had so focused on his words that they did not have to strain to hear him.

> "The scientific incontrovertibility of physics leads directly to the ethical demand for veracity and honesty. And justice is inseparable from truth. Just as the laws of nature work consistently and without exception, in great things as in small, so too people cannot live together without equal justice for all."

Max finished his speech. No one spoke, no one moved, no one turned away their gaze from this little old man who had lived for so long in the shadow of tragedy, but who now stood before them noble and redeemed.

Now, as required by the protocol of the time, Max attempted to raised his hand in salute. He could not do it and his hand sank down again to his side. He tried again. Slowly his arm rose, as if gravity made the act almost impossible. But with superhuman strength, he finally overcame his reluctance to perform this vile act and he lifted his hand, palm outwards towards the audience.

"Heil Hitler," he said weakly, with contempt at the words.

* * *

The car, with swastikas adorning its wings, pulled into the driveway of the Kaiser Wilhelm Institute for Physics. The car contained three occupants: two Gestapo officers and Werner Heisenberg. The three said nothing; the atmosphere in the car as cold and tense as a funeral. Heisenberg stepped out of the car; the Gestapo remained inside, the car engine still churning.

"Thanks for the ride, guys," shouted Heisenberg. He fashioned a mock salute and grinned. The Gestapo men suppressed the urge to reply, grunted and drove away. They would have happily strangled him there and then, but their orders forbade it. The command came from the top, from Himmler himself. 'We'll get you, one day,' they thought.

Heisenberg looked at the Institute in front of him. Above the entrance, the words, 'The Max Planck Institute,' newly carved into the stone, looked back at him. As Max was now persona non grata, the Government had banned the word, Planck, and they had made a crude attempt to cover it with a wooden plank nailed into place.

Heisenberg smiled at the joke.

He had visited the KWI many times, but this visit had a different feel to it; and not just because of the swastikas flying from the flag poles. This time he did not come merely as any other visitor; the Ministry had selected him as the new Director for Physics - if they didn't shoot him first; it was a close run thing and the outcome remained undecided.

Heisenberg stood up to address the Max von Laue Wednesday Colloquium. None doubted that Heisenberg knew his physics, but he seemed to treat it as a business rather than a science and his lecture glossed over the details, leaving the impression that he believed the laws of physics must answer to the supply and demand of the marketplace, proposed by the board of directors and put to a vote by the shareholders.

> ". . . But however the development proceeds in detail, the path so far traced by the quantum theory indicates that an understanding of those still unclarified features of atomic physics can only be acquired by foregoing visualization and objectification to an extent greater than that customary hitherto. We have probably no reason to regret this, because the thought of the great epistemological difficulties with which the visual atom concept of earlier physics had to contend gives us the hope that the abstracter atomic physics developing at present will one day fit more harmoniously into the great edifice of Science. Thank you."

As the lecture ended, Lise moved forward to greet him.

"Ah, Lise, good to see you," said Heisenberg. "Thank you for coming."

"My pleasure, Werner," replied Lise. "Your lectures are always a breath of fresh air, most enjoyable. I remember when I first saw you lecture in Copenhagen."

"Thank you. Working with Niels Bohr was such an experience. Truly stimulating! As, indeed, will be working here, I'm sure. I hope my visit is not cut short."

"So do we all," said Lise. "Time will tell."

"I am looking forward to a prolonged stay. Perhaps you'll tip me off as to the best restaurants."

"Oh, I don't get out much; Berlin's night life is still a mystery to me - your man for all things chic is Max von Laue; he's the expert."

"I'll remember that. I'm on my way to lunch with him. Care to join us?"

"Sorry, I have to get back to the lab - a pot boiling on the stove, so to speak."

"Perhaps later then?"

"Perhaps, but don't wait for me, I'm not sure when I can get away. If I get the chance, I'll drop by Max's office."

"Hopefully, we shall see you tonight then."

* * *

"The whole thing is intolerable!" said Max von Laue.

He spoke to Werner Heisenberg. They had conversed over lunch and then returned to the KWI. They discussed the staff situation. Laue had openly railed against the unfairness of it all. Heisenberg appeared sympathetic, but Laue got the impression that Heisenberg had mastered the art of hiding his real opinions and at tailoring his remarks to fit his audience. Consequently, Laue did not know if he could trust Heisenberg, but Laue had reached the point where he did not care.

"Max, you must take care what you say; you know that," said Heisenberg. "If we are to survive we must compromise. I, too, have been attacked for advocating theoretical physics; Einstein's puppy they call me - a white Jew. There are those demanding my removal. I have been threatened with internment. And my love-hate relationship with the Gestapo is far too cozy for comfort. But see what happens when we make waves. Max Planck is a prime example of that."

"You don't believe in standing up for your principals?"

"I believe in looking after number one. In a hurricane, the trees which survive are the ones which can bend in the wind."

"I am not a tree!"

"Duly noted for future reference, but the point remains."

"The point remains lost on me. If we don't stop this nonsense, there will be nothing left to save. We have lost so many. Too many! German science is now the laughing stock of the world."

"That's not true. Max Born, James Franck, Lise Meitner; they are all exempt. We are only replacing some low level assistants. The talented ones we would lose to other opportunities in any case."

"Haber? Einstein? Are these low level assistants?"

"We do what is expedient."

"And what does our conscience dictate? I fear for their safety."

"But what can we do? I have written to Himmler personally, asking him to speak out against behavior of this kind."

"You see; you've just contradicted yourself. Isn't writing to Himmler making waves? Isn't that why you're constantly invited to chat with the Gestapo?"

"My grandfather and Himmler's father are old drinking buddies. I'd promised my mother that I'd keep in touch."

"It's called playing both sides and it's a dangerous game."

"Well, I play for keeps, Max, and it's important that we understand each other on this."

"Thanks for the warning. I suppose it pays to have friends in high places, but you bargain with the devil. And you are still wrong - no one is safe. What of Lise? The Ministry is questioning her status, you know."

"We won't lose Lise, I'm sure of it," predicted Heisenberg. "Her reputation is second to none. She has the support of many. You have nominated her for the Nobel Prize. I have supported you in that. The nomination alone makes her untouchable, even if she doesn't get the prize . . ."

Lise headed towards Max von Laue's office. As usual, her work had continued far into the evening and she did not really expect to find Laue or Heisenberg still inside, but she saw the door to Laue's office slightly ajar and the office light streamed out around it. As she approached, the sound of Max's voice confirmed his presence. She raised a hand to knock and enter, but paused at the mention of her name.

"She is not safe here. No one is safe," repeated Max von Laue.

"I don't believe that," replied Heisenberg. "Besides, she is Austrian, not German. She is not subject to the law."

"Not yet, but for how long?"

"Even if she were subject to the law, she is also exempt under it for her service before and during the war."

"How can something so lawless be the law?" asked Laue. "Laws can change - and for the worse, as we have seen. No, Werner, it is different for you and I, we have the Aryan blood flowing through our veins; Lise is not so lucky. Letters to Himmler will not save her. It's up to us."

Lise wanted no part of this conversation. She turned away and walked back down the corridor.

As Lise approached her office, a figure stepped out of the shadows and into her path, causing her to pull up abruptly.

"Irene? Irene Sackur? Is that you? You startled me."

Irene, the baby daughter of Otto Sackur had now matured into a grown up woman of 26.

"Professor Meitner," said Irene, between gasps for air. "Professor, may I speak with you?"

"Why do you cry? What is the matter?"

"I . . . Er . . ." Irene could not stop the sobs long enough to speak coherently.

"Come with me," ordered Lise. She bundled Irene into her office, placed her firmly in the chair in front of the desk, offered her a handkerchief, took up her own position on the other side of the desk and waited patiently for the sobs to subside before she spoke again. "Now then, Irene, what is this all about?"

A noise from outside the office window caused Irene to flinch - the sound of an angry mob, drunken and unruly. Lise stood and walked to the window. In the forecourt, she recognized some of the mob as students and lecturers, some dressed in the brown shirt uniforms of the SA. A fire burned in the center of the square. With exaggerated movements, and to cheers, they tossed things on the fire and caused sparks to fly. Lise closed the window and turned back to Irene.

"A little quieter I think?" said Lise as she returned to her seat. "Okay, we can talk now. Did they hurt you?" She indicated the crowd outside with a nod of her head.

"They frightened me, but they did not harm me; just a little shoving . . ."

Lise sensed that the behavior of the mob had added to Irene's distress but not entirely caused it. She waited for Irene to continue.

". . . Professor, I don't know where to turn. You know that I have been dismissed from my post."

"Yes, I am sorry. These are hard times. Many have been caught up in the new regulations."

"I can no longer work. I cannot get work anywhere. I must vacate my apartment."

"Is it really that bad?"

"Jews are leaving. Professor Einstein has left. Professor Haber has left."

"Is that what you want to do, leave?"

"But where will I go? What will I do?"

"There is very little in Germany, it is true, but if you wanted to consider Holland or Belgium. I am not yet without friends. I will make some enquiries for you."

"Thank you, Professor."

"Do you still have somewhere to stay?"

"I have a good friend in Mariondorf; I can stay with her for a few days."

"This will all blow over one day, I'm sure . . ."

A loud cheer and a surge of fire from outside the window caught their attention. Irene flinched again and clenched the side of her chair until her knuckles turned white.

". . . But I think it unwise to be out on the streets this evening; you will stay with me tonight. How about some dinner? It is a little hectic out there, but let's walk over to my apartment."

"Out there?"

"Yes, we are quite safe. I am still a Director. They will not harm us . . ."

Irene looked doubtful.

". . . We can go out the back way," assured Lise.

Lise and Irene exited the building and walked in the shadows, skirting the main perimeter, in an indirect route which would eventually take the pair to the Harnack House. They avoided contact with the mob, but Lise recognized some of the faces, which included that Kurt Hess, dressed in Nazi regalia, the angriest of the mob and its ring leader.

Hess shouted out; and at the end of each shout he would throw something on the fire to incite the frenzied passion of the mob. Lise strained to see what exactly could cause these normally rational teachers and students to act this way. Then she realized that the fuel for the fire was books, and Hess shouted out the name of each book before he tossed it into the flames. Each addition to the flames extracted another cheer from the mob.

"Into the flames, Sigmund Freud!" screamed Hess. "All Quiet on the Western Front! You coward! You traitor! . . . Kafka, what shall we do with you? . . . Another one translated from the Hebrew . . . Einstein! Ha, Einstein. The General Theory of Relativity! More like the Theory of Jews! On the fire you go . . ."

Lise bundled Irene away into the cover of the dark night. So they had now come here, she shuddered - to the KWI. And Lise feared that Max von Laue had spoken the truth: She was no longer safe, not even in the shadows. The sanctuary of the KWI had been breached.

. . . *Escape*

L ise sat in Max Planck's office, in the chair opposite Max's
chair; Max's desk stood between them. Of course, Max did
not occupy Max's chair; Max was gone. Lise had to force
herself to remember that. Max's replacement as President of the
Kaiser Wilhelm Society, Carl Bosch sat in Max's chair. Lise had no
quarrel with Bosch, but neither did she feel comfortable with the
man; imposed on her, as it were, by the Ministry.

Bosch had asked to see her in his office; Lise had already guessed the reason. He had received a letter from the Ministry regarding her status.

"To make sure there is no misunderstanding," said Bosch stiffly. "I shall read the pertinent passages from the Minister's letter."

> ". . . With regard to exemption under the act for military service at the front, Frau Meitner's service as x-ray technician is not considered as at the front and is therefore not exempt. With regard to exemption under the act for habilitation prior to 1918, Frau Meitner did not receive such a position officially until 1922 and is therefore not exempt . . .

> . . . Immediately therefore, for the reason set forth in paragraph 3 of the statute concerning the reinstatement of the professional civil service, I hereby revoke your authorization of professorship at the University of Berlin.

> Signed,
> The Prussian Minister of Education,
> Siegel."

The news did not surprise Lise; rumors had circulated for weeks that Bosch had been brought in to do the job which Max had refused; and that the Ministry had begun to crack down even harder, to find the flimsiest of excuses to apply the Berufsbeamtengesetz with full force. Lise had already surmised that her days as a professor in Germany had ended.

"Well, if that is all, Herr Bosch," she said coldly. She rose and with a perfunctory nod, left the office which she now understood in her heart no longer belonged to Max Planck.

She returned to her laboratory, where in keeping with the season, Fritz Strassmann had erected a small Christmas tree in the workshop. He had found some tinsel and added some candles, and merrily whistled a carol as he tried to perch a tiny angel on the top. Lise entered the workshop and exchanged her top coat for her laboratory coat.

"Morning, Boss," sang Fritz between notes.

"Good Morning," replied Lise. "And how is Fritz today?"

"Fine, just fine - la, la, la, la, pa rum pa tum tum."

Lise wondered just how Fritz remained so cheerful with everything in chaotic misery all around them, but Fritz never seemed to be fazed by anything and never less than completely joyful.

On her desk, Lise saw a square envelope, addressed to her in a hand-written almost illegible scrawl. She opened the envelope and pulled out a card, a Nazi Christmas card. In a scrawl which matched that on the envelope, the card had the salutation, 'to the Jewess Meitner from her Aryan friends'. Lise sighed, tore up the card and deposited it in the waste basket; her mood tumbled with the pieces.

As if he sensed that Strassmann's cheerful disposition needed some augmentation, if Lise's mood were to recover, Otto strolled into the workshop, also whistling a carol.

"Ah, Lise, good morning," said Otto.

"Oh, hello, Otto," replied Lise.

"What's on the agenda for today?" asked Otto.

"According to the results," said Lise. "We have a new transuranic element. Fritz needs to confirm that and then we can get the confirmation to Fermi in Italy."

"The Paris group also confirmed the findings, but they have a puzzle," added Strassmann. "Some lighter elements are showing up in the trace, lanthanum, they say. I haven't checked that out yet."

"I'm not sure Curie has her priorities straight," said Lise. "Don't go off on a tangent; let's just work with what we know, for now."

"Right, Boss."

"Our first priority, however, is coffee," said Lise. "It's going to be a long time until lunch."

"Okay, I'll be right back. The usual for you, Otto?" asked Fritz, instantly volunteering to play the role of waiter by removing his lab coat.

"No thanks, Fritz. No time this morning. I have a meeting with Max von Laue in a few minutes; but then I'll be back."

"Okay."

Strassmann exited, reviving his caroling as he went.

"I don't know what we would do without Fritz," said Lise. "He's a godsend in this day and age. Can we afford to hang on to him? Can he afford to stay?"

"Fritz will stay. He's like you; the work is more important than the money. I told him that if he joined the Nazi party then money would be made available, but he refuses to compromise his principals; says he'd rather starve."

"While Fritz is gone . . . thank you, Otto."

"For what?"

"You know of my meeting with Carl Bosch this morning?"

"How could I know? It just happened," said Otto defensively.

"You know everything which happens around here, Otto."

"Okay, I admit it, Carl told me last night; he thought I should be forewarned."

"Forewarned? Have I become an untouchable like Max and Albert? Why come here today? It is dangerous to associate with me."

"Lise, we are old friends," protested Otto.

"Yes, I know," Lise smiled. "I also know that Max von Laue was present when Bosch told you - told both of you."

"Ah," said Otto, guiltily.

"I ran into Max this morning. In fact, he ambushed me as I left Bosch's office. Max could never keep a secret."

"Ah," repeated Otto.

"Max told me that you resigned your professorship in protest of my treatment. You didn't have to do that."

"An empty gesture, given the situation; I haven't taught any real classes for years."

"Still, it is a gesture which will be noticed. I wouldn't want you to get into trouble on my behalf."

"The least I can do for a friend." ·

"I also heard that you turned down invitations to speak because they did not want my name mentioned."

"And you say that I know everything which happens around here?" laughed Otto. "Are we not partners? It's not fair that I get the credit for intellectual property which is not mine."

"Still, Otto, thank you."

"All for one and one for all!" said Otto. "At least, the loss of teaching privileges does not affect your salary at the KWI. The whole thing is ridiculous! The only reason your position was not recognized in 1912 was that no woman's position was recognized before the war; but we all know better."

"I suppose it could be worse," sighed Lise. "At least I am Austrian and not German, I still have some protection."

* * *

On the main street of the sleepy Bavarian village of Kiefersfelden, Corporal Krueger sat on the hood of the staff car, puffed idly on a cigarette, stared blankly ahead and tried not to shiver. The bright blue of the sky did nothing to allay the cold. More soldiers milled about and danced from foot to foot in the snow, in a futile effort to prevent the cold from the reaching their feet. Officers' motorcades and dispatch riders came and went on the road from Munich, as if the villagers had disturbed a hornet's nest. A group of cavalry officers arrived on horseback and dismounted.

Silhouetted on the hillside to the south, the medieval Castle Kufstein watched them warily. Kiefersfelden and Kufstein were essentially two halves of the same village; it just so happened that one half of the village stood in Germany and the other, the half with the castle, in Austria. A wooden customs gate, usually ignored by the locals, but today guarded by armed German infantrymen, marked the border between the two.

The soldiers had started to arrive at the village the day prior, mostly on freight trains which almost overwhelmed the tiny Kiefersfelden station. The armored cars and heavy artillery had arrived early that morning, woke the villagers and clogged the roads. The villagers on both sides of the barrier had come out in force to witness the spectacle. Now the army outnumbered the villagers by twenty to one.

"What's going on?" a local asked Corporal Krueger.

He shrugged his shoulders in reply. He answered honestly; and in all honesty, the villager already knew the answer to the question.

A General and a Colonel walked from the church which stood by the border gate. Corporal Krueger quickly disposed of his cigarette and snapped to attention. The General surveyed the scene in front of him, before he quietly gave an order to the Colonel.

"Okay, let's go," yelled the Colonel.

Corporal Krueger ran around the staff car and opened the door for the General and Colonel. The two officers climbed into the car and Corporal Krueger took his position at the steering wheel and started the motor. The air filled with shouts, exhaust smoke and the chorus of revved engines. The cavalry mounted their horses. The infantrymen fell in line behind them.

At the front of the procession, a cavalry officer raised his sword and urged his steed forward at a slow walk. The border guards raised the gate. On both sides of the border, Nazi flags magically appeared, large ones unfurled from buildings and small ones in the hands of the adoring, cheering, saluting crowd.

Under the sad gaze of the impotent Castle Kufstein, the Wehrmacht trampled the flowers which the villagers threw before them and marched over the border into Austria. The Anschluss, the annexation of Austria, had begun.

* * *

Inside a tiny office at SD Headquarters in Berlin, too small for the desk, filing cabinets and boxes of paper which jostled for space within its four walls, a junior SD Officer, Wolfgang Meyer, sat and lazily read the report which he had just retrieved from his in-tray. As with bureaucracy everywhere, the in-tray threatened to overwhelm him. Another SD Officer, his superior, entered and waved a manila folder.

"Orders from the Ministry of Justice," said the Boss. "The Kaiser Wilhelm Jewess, she has been seeking a passport. Send someone over there to pick her up."

"We have a man there, I'll let him know," replied Meyer. He reached for the telephone hidden under the paperwork.

"Good. I'll leave this with you then." The Boss tossed the folder to his junior and departed. Meyer picked up the phone and dialed.

"Ah, hello, hello, yes, it's Wolfgang. How are you? Good, good. Listen, that Meitner business. Well, we have to proceed. No, I've got the orders right here in front of me. I'll have to send someone with a car. No, no hurry; tomorrow will do. You know how long paperwork takes. Okay, take care."

Meyer put down the phone, lifted a stack of folders and dumped the Meitner file at the bottom of his in-tray.

* * *

Lise knocked on the door to Carl Bosch's office. Bosch had summoned her again and, because of the Anschluss, she once again had a good idea what Bosch had to tell her.

"Come!" commanded Bosch.

Lise entered. To her surprise, Otto and Max von Laue already sat in the office, in chairs in front of Bosch's desk. A third chair stood vacant and Bosch, who talked on the phone, waved at her to occupy it.

"Is it official? . . . Today?" said Bosch into the mouthpiece of the phone. "Then tomorrow . . . yes . . . and you, goodbye." Bosch returned the receiver to its cradle. "Sorry about that Lise. Now to business."

Lise looked at Otto and Laue for some indication of what Bosch meant by business, but neither man returned her gaze.

"Lise, I have received another letter from the Ministry," said Bosch. "Please, let me read it to you."

> "By order of the Reich Minister, Dr. Frick, may I most respectfully inform you in answer to your letter of the 20th of last month that there are political objections to the issuing of a passport to Professor Meitner. It is considered undesirable that renowned Jews should leave Germany for abroad to act against the interests of Germany according to their inner persuasion as representatives of the German sciences or even with their reputation and experience. The Kaiser Wilhelm Society will find a way for Prof. M. to stay in Germany after her retirement."

"Then the game is up," said Max von Laue. "Lise is not safe in Germany any more."

"No doubt we can get our colleagues abroad to offer her a position," said Otto.

"They would jump at the chance," said Laue.

"Wait a minute! Wait a minute!" cried Lise. "Would someone tell me what is going on?"

"Lise?" said Otto.

"This is me, Lise Meitner, whom you are all so freely discussing. I'm not sure that I'm ready to move out of my apartment, let alone out of the country."

"But Lise, you are not safe here," repeated Laue.

"I am Austrian, not German. I am protected."

"Not any more," said Otto.

"Your nephew has already fled to Copenhagen," reminded Laue.

"I am not Robert; my roots are here. What is this about my retirement from the KWI? I have no plans to retire."

"The choice is not yours to make, Lise," said Bosch.

"Are you asking for my resignation?" demanded Lise.

"We have no choice, Lise," said Bosch.

"You have no choice! Well, perhaps you can fire me, but I will not leave Berlin unless it is kicking and screaming."

"Lise," said Bosch. "There is more."

The statement stopped Lise in her tracks. She again looked at Otto and Laue for clarification.

Otto held her hand. "Listen to Carl, Lise," he said. "Listen carefully, it is very important."

Lise looked again at Bosch.

"Lise, the phone call I was taking when you came in . . . I have a contact at the SD. That call was from him. They are coming to arrest you."

"Arrest me? Whatever for? I have done nothing wrong."

"You are an embarrassment to them, Lise," said Otto. "They are afraid that you will cause trouble, as Einstein did."

"But . . ."

"They cannot allow you to leave Germany, and they will not allow you to remain here."

"We have to move now! Today!" said Bosch.

"Such haste?" asked Lise.

"The SD will be here tomorrow to arrest you, we must act today," said Bosch.

"I'll call Dirk Coster and get the ball rolling," said Laue.

"Wait, wait a minute," Lise held up a hand. "Dirk Coster? The last I heard, Dirk was Dutch and living in Holland. What does he have to do with this?"

"Dirk is in Berlin," said Otto. "He has come to help you escape over the border."

"Escape? How long have you been planning this? And shouldn't you have told me?"

"We had hoped it would not come to this," said Laue. "But the Anschluss removed your last safety net. The Nazis are serious about eliminating all opposition. Lise, you are no ordinary person; you are a candidate for the Nobel Prize. But your position in the community and the respect of your peers will not protect you. You are a big prize. They will have to make an example of you as a warning to others. If you don't go, you will spend your retirement in the Dachau internment camp."

"And you didn't think you could trust me with your plans?"

"Lise, we are dealing with ruthless people," said Bosch. "We could not be sure that you would not be arrested. I could not be sure that my contact at the SD would come through for us. If you knew nothing of these plans, you could not jeopardize others."

"But so sudden? I am not ready. I must go home and pack."

"No, you must not," said Laue. "Any unusual behavior may show our hand. We cannot risk someone seeing you hauling a suitcase."

"Lise, you must stay with Edith and me tonight," said Otto.

"Meanwhile, let's act normally," said Bosch. "It's business as usual. I'm not the only spy at the institute."

"No!" said Lise firmly.

"No? What do you mean, no?" asked Laue.

"You have no choice," said Otto. "If we have to drug you and smuggle you out of Germany in a sack, we will do it."

"If I have to leave Berlin, there is something I must do first," said Lise. "It won't take long; and then you can do what you want."

* * *

"Oh, would you look at this!" said Planck. "I had forgotten just how young we once were . . ."

Max sat in an old, comfortable couch in his living room; a fire crackled and bathed the room in a warm glow; a scrapbook lay in his lap, opened to a photograph of Max and his family, and Lise.

". . . But you are dressed in black, you always dressed in black."

"I still do," said Lise, on the couch beside him. "Black never goes out of style."

"Just the same, you always hid your true colors - don't you agree, Gentlemen?"

Otto and Max von Laue, opposite Planck and Lise, in equally comfortable arm chairs, concurred and sipped red wine from glasses which their host had forced into their hands the instance they had entered.

A bundle of loose papers fell from the scrapbook.

"Oh, what do we have here?" asked Planck. "Oh, my word!"

"What is it?" asked Lise.

"It is an old school report, from 1872. The things to which we cling."

"Read it to us, Max," said Otto. "Did your teachers predict a great future for you?"

"Well, let's see, shall we . . . 'Justifiably favored by teachers and classmates alike . . . and despite his childish ways, a very clear, logical mind . . . Shows great promise' . . . You know, when I decided on my vocation, I was told not to waste my time - that there was nothing new to be discovered in physics."

"You should have listened to them, Max," said Laue.

"Friends, I have made an important discovery. It is that scientific innovation rarely makes its way by gradually winning over and converting its opponents: it rarely happens that Saul becomes Paul. What does happen is that its opponents gradually die out, and that the growing generation is familiarized with the ideas from the beginning. And so, as last man standing, I win by default . . . Shows great promise? Whether I lived up to my promise or not I shall leave for others to decide. But in the meantime, there may yet be a song to two left in me; I wonder if the piano is still in tune?"

"Ah, we'd like nothing better, Max," said Otto, "But unfortunately, we cannot stay this evening."

"Oh, too bad, too bad," sighed Planck.

"In fact, we have overstayed our welcome," said Laue. He placed his wine glass on the side table and rose from his chair. "I shall go start the car and warm the engine."

"Let me get our coats," said Otto, copying Laue's actions. They both exited the living room, leaving Planck and Lise alone.

"Let me see you to the door," said Max.

"No, you stay here, next to the fire, Max," said Lise. "The cold air is not good for you."

"Nonsense, I've never felt better. I'm planning another hike in the Alps this summer."

"Yes, I do believe that you will outlive us all."

"In fact, I'm going to London, next month. If you have any letters for Lotte or Gisela, I'd be happy to pass them on for you."

"Thank you. I do have some correspondence to catch up on . . . But . . . We miss you at the Institute."

"No you don't. You need a fighter. I cannot stand up to them."

"But you did stand, Max. I know that you stood your ground in Herr Hitler's office. I know the price you paid for your defiance."

"Pah! An old man with nothing left to lose; Don Quixote tilting at windmills."

"Which is it? Max the conqueror or Max the conquered. You can't be both, you know."

They looked into each other's eyes, and Max knew instantly the reason for Lise's visit that evening.

"You're leaving, aren't you?" said Max.

"Yes."

"Of course you are; now that Austria is annexed you have no choice. But where will you go?"

"I don't know yet; Holland, Switzerland; Niels Bohr and Robert are in Copenhagen. It would be good to see Robert again. I have family in England and America, as you know."

"And as you know, Lise, you have family here, you always will." Max took Lise's hand.

"Max, I wanted to thank you . . . for taking a chance on me, for taking in the orphan on your doorstep . . . ."

"No, I took in a third daughter on that night," Max interrupted. "Do you remember our first meeting in Vienna?"

"How could I forget; the Hotel Bristol; I was so nervous; it was like meeting royalty."

"I said I would consent to your admission on a trial basis."

"Is the trial concluded, Max?"

"No, quite the opposite - that is the great joy of life; we are all on trial. And the greater the trial, the more we discover about ourselves. No, it is I who should thank you, Lise."

"Whatever for?"

"For being Lise Meitner. You have taught us all so much about courage and determination. You started teaching me that evening in Vienna. I forgot the lesson for a while, during the dark days, but you never wavered . . ."

Max gently squeezed Lise's hand. The time had come - time to say goodbye. But she could not do it. She understood that if she left she would never see him again. She tried to choose words with meaning, the last words she would ever say to him. She felt inadequate to the task. Every atom in her body screamed 'No'; every organ rebelled to prevent her from uttering the words. One more time, Max came to her rescue. He looked into her eyes.

". . . Do not waver now," he commanded.

"I do not know how long I shall be gone, or even if I shall ever be allowed to return."

"Then we are fortunate to have this chance to say our goodbyes."

"Goodbye, Max."

"Goodbye, Lise."

* * *

Whilst Lise handed Otto the key to her apartment, with a list of the things he should collect and forward to her when appropriate, the men from the SD arrived at Harnack House with the arrest warrant. They needed no key to enter her apartment, but finding it sans Lise, they quickly moved on to her workshop, where the innocent Fritz Strassmann could not help with their enquiries, and then onto the other locations around the KWI which she was known to frequent.

Lise barked instructions to Otto for the running of her department during her absence. Otto nodded and tried to reassure her.

"Lise, you are still in charge," assured Otto. "Wherever you land, I'm sure that they will have a telephone or at least a mail box. The work will continue with you at the helm."

They sat in the back of Max von Laue's car. He had insisted on driving Lise to the train station. Lise and Otto agreed that this short ride must therefore prove the most dangerous part of her journey.

At the station, Otto stayed with Lise while Laue went to the ticket office. The station buzzed with SD, SS and Nazi uniforms, as well as the general chaos of rush hour passengers. Max von Laue returned.

"Here is your ticket for the train to Munich," he said, too loudly. "Platform 11."

The trio walked to Platform 11, but their true destination was Platform 10, where the train to the Dutch city of Groningen stood ready to depart, and they walked along the platform and peered into the train's windows, searching for their Dutch ally.

"Dirk Coster is already on board," said Laue. "He has all the necessary papers for the border crossing."

"No, I can't do it," said Lise. "Is this really necessary? It's not going to work."

"Courage, Lise," said Otto. "There is nothing here for you any more. You must go. Here, take this."

Otto pressed a diamond ring into Lise's hand.

"What's this? No, Otto, I can't take it. It belonged to your mother."

"Just in case; for emergencies. You can probably still get a good price for it in Holland."

Otto and Lise embraced, and then Lise reeled off another batch of last minute orders for Strassmann. She talked for the sake of talking; as long as she talked, she could not leave.

"There is Dirk. Quickly now, onto the train," ordered Laue. Lise and Laue embraced. "Don't forget to send a post card from Munich," he added, playing the deception for all it was worth.

Lise embraced Otto again.

"You'll be back before you know it," said Otto.

And with that the two men each took one of Lise's arms and lifted her onto the train. Lise located Dirk Coster and he offered her the seat next to him, the one by the window.

As Lise looked out at Otto and Laue, who waved to her from the platform, the conductor blew his whistle, the train blew steam and Otto blew her a kiss.

Fortunately for Lise, as she could not disguise her concern, she and Dirk Coster comprised the only occupants of the compartment. She had met Dirk on several occasions, knew him well and considered him a friend. That helped, but not enough to calm her nerves. Dirk carefully explained the story they had concocted for the border crossing: for the time it took to make the crossing, she must act as his wife, Miep. Dirk assured Lise that the real Mrs. Coster approved of this arrangement.

As the train approached the border, Dirk spoke calmly. "Let me do as much of the talking as possible," he said. "The one thing we have not rehearsed is your Dutch accent."

The trained slowed to a halt and the conductor called out. "Nieuweschans, Nieuweschans! Have your papers ready for inspection, please."

The conductor moved on down the train, repeating his call, creeping ever closer to their compartment. Coster pulled some documents from his pocket. Lise saw a Dutch passport in the name of Miep Coster, but with Lise's photograph. She wondered just how long they had planned for her escape.

"Now don't worry. The Dutch know that you are coming," said Dirk. He saw that Lise absentmindedly and nervously played with the ring which Otto had given her. "Put the ring on," he said. "It will add authenticity."

Lise obeyed and slipped the ring onto her right index finger. Dirk laughed and took her hand. "Here, let me help," he said and moved the ring to its more traditional place on her left hand.

The conductor entered the compartment, accompanied by 4 men in uniform: 2 German and 2 Dutch.

"Passports please," demanded a Dutch uniform, above the sound of Lise's thumping heart.

Dirk handed him the papers. He looked them over, glanced at Lisa and then showed the papers to his Dutch companion. The second Dutch uniform nodded in agreement. The first Dutch uniform then handed the passports to the Germans, who scrutinized them further and glared at Lise with that 'don't I know you?' look, before returning them to Dirk.

"Thank you," said a German uniform.

The Border control exited the compartment, but as they did, the first Dutch uniform hesitated and remained. He waited until his companions had walked out of earshot and then turned to Lise.

"Welcome to the Netherlands, Frau Coster!" he smiled, nodded in salute and exited.

Dirk let out a sigh of relief and took the ring from Lise's finger. Lise, still frozen in fright and disbelief, did not notice.

"I'm sorry, Lise," said Dirk. "I just don't think it will work between us; I must divorce you." Lise looked up in confusion. Dirk handed Otto's ring back to her.

As the train continued on to Groningen, with the German border receding into the distance, Lise's fear subsided, but not her disbelief. In fewer than 24 hours, every facet of her life had changed. She was now a refugee, alone and unprepared in a big, cold, unfamiliar world.

But as the train pulled into Groningen station, there on the platform, she saw something familiar and her heart warmed instantly.

Robert smiled. "You are late, Aunty," he chided. "We're almost frozen to death waiting for you. Another 10 minutes and we would have left without you."

"Had I known you would be waiting for me in Groningen, I would have gone to Munich," she responded before she threw her arms around him.

Behind Robert, Lise saw the equally warm and welcome figure of Niels Bohr, who shook Costner's hand and congratulated him on a successful mission before he turned his attention to Lise.

"I am so glad to see you safe," said Niels and gave Lise a bear hug.

"Can I take it that Hitler and I were the only two people in the world who did not know of my escape plans?" asked Lise.

Exile

"We walked up and down in the snow, I on skis
and she on foot (she said and proved that she
could get along just as fast that way), and
gradually the idea took shape that this was no
chipping or cracking of the nucleus . . ."

Otto Robert Frisch

... *London King's Cross, 1969*

V iewed through the filter of a train window, every city in the world looks the same: derelict and decayed, with evidence of lost and broken lives scattered about, as if in these corners of the city they had decided not to clean up until the war had ended; and the war continued unabated.

At least today, it appeared that way for Robert, as his train pulled in to King's Cross Station. Perhaps, he considered, the window just reflected his own mood? That would explain today, as the gloomy, breaking landscape contended with an equally overcast and hesitant mind, but what of all the other times? Perhaps train journeys always made him sad.

In spite of his pessimism, Sir Nevill Mott had pulled some strings and subsequently Robert received an invitation to lunch with Sir Paul Gall-Booth of the Foreign Office. He had taken an early train from Cambridge and planned to spend a couple of hours at the British Museum before lunch. He looked forward to that part, at least.

King's Cross bustled with rush hour commuters, the general background noise punctuated with whistles and track announcements. After the tranquility of Cambridge, Robert had underestimated the jarring shock of loud and brash London. He walked from the platform to the central concourse, bumped and bustled all the way, and occasionally cursed for his unwitting infraction of the unspoken conventions of the commuters. In the concourse, he paused to get his bearings and determine the best route out of the station, when above the noise, so loud that it drown out the announcements, he heard a yell: as raucous and confident as London itself, but with an unmistakable American twang.

"Robert? Robert Frisch, is that you? Why you old son of a Colt 45!"

Robert located the mystery town crier in an instant; for the voice belonged to a man who stood a foot taller than anyone else in the concourse; and broad with it, as if King's Cross had erected a statue of Paul Bunyan.

"Shull!" Robert recognized the American instantly; how could he not? Henry Shull Arms stood at the center of the concourse, arms open in welcome and on his face a grin to rival his physique; a sight made all the more impressive because of the wide, cautious berth which the suddenly startled Londoners gave to the American.

Henry Shull Arms always introduced himself using all three words and emphasized each syllable, as if to declare that one could expect nothing small from Henry Shull Arms, not even his name. But his character contained no conceit or evil; it merely showed a man infused with supreme self-confidence; always good humored, generous and polite to the ladies; and always just plain Shull to his friends. They shook hands. It would have taken little effort on Shull's part to crush Robert's fingers, but the man with huge hands also possessed the gentle, deft touch of a neurosurgeon.

"My God, Shull," said Robert. "You were the last man I expected to see in London. I thought you'd retired to your potato farm in Idaho?"

"No, I never did go back. Found myself in Rugby after I left Harwell. Now I have a little place in Harpenden. I've never managed to escape this little island. Well, don't they say that if you stand in King's Cross long enough, you'll eventually meet someone you know? What a coincidence."

"I think that's Piccadilly Circus, but anyway, what are you doing here?"

"I'm on my way home. My baby brother, Bill, came over for a vacation. I was down here making sure he didn't miss his plane back across the pond. And how about you?"

"I'm meeting somebody from the Foreign Office."

"Are they finally going to kick your derrière out of the country?"

"Oh, no, I'm a Brit now, they can't do that."

"Say, how about we go get some of that liquid you Brits call coffee?"

"But Harpenden? I wouldn't want you to miss your train."

"Hell, there's always another train. Come on; let's go catch up on old times."

Robert admired the American's ability to make everyone feel both relaxed and important at the same time - at least, after the initial shock of the first glimpse of the man had subsided - and in no time at all, as they sat at a small café table and drank coffee, as they exchanged histories, reminisced and laughed, Robert sailed away from his earlier doldrums. They swapped pictures of family. They talked of the characters they had known and the experiences they had shared.

"Remember when we roomed in Liverpool, during the war?" laughed Shull.

"I remember that I wasn't allowed my own transport, because of my status as an alien. I couldn't work late because of the curfew. I remember you turned up one day with a bicycle and a permission slip signed by the Chief Constable for me to ride it."

"The landlady suspected that you were a Nazi spy."

"Understandable really; I couldn't talk about my work, obviously. All she knew was that I spoke very little, and when I did it was with a German accent. I wonder what happened to her?"

"She began to ask too many questions and you murdered her and disposed of the body in the River Mersey," speculated Shull.

"Not so loud, Shull," squirmed Robert, worried that strangers around them may take this theory seriously. "You sometimes forget just how your voice carries. No, you remember, it was the bombing; that night the windows blew out, she couldn't take any more of it; she just packed her suitcase and left. She didn't even stay long enough to collect the rent."

"I do remember the air raids. It was brilliant strategy by the British Civil Service to house us in the heart of one of the Luftwaffe's favorite cities."

"They knew that the Luftwaffe could never hit their targets. Liverpool was one of the safest places to be."

"I think the boarding house where we stayed was in danger of falling down without any help from the Germans. And you played the piano - during the bombing, you played the piano and the other lodgers complained that they would rather listen to the anti-aircraft guns than your playing."

"I'm not the greatest pianist in the world, that is true, but no one had tuned that piano since it left the workshop in the Stone Age. Dropping a bomb on it could only have improved its tone."

And so they drank coffee, and reminisced and laughed, and Robert completely forgot his plan to visit the British Museum, but time pressed on them and Robert's appointment with Sir Paul Gall-Booth loomed.

"Shull," Robert frowned. "It's really great to see you again, but I have to go."

"The Foreign Office?"

"Yes." A hint of his earlier depression returned.

"It's not that bad, is it?" asked Shull. "It cannot be any worse than your piano playing."

"Oh, no, it's just . . . I feel as if I'm beating my head against the wall . . ."

Shull waited for additional input. Robert explained his quest to win belated recognition for his aunt. Shull, of course, as with everybody in the scientific community, knew of Lise Meitner and the injustice done to her.

". . . But the world does not know. That is the galling thing; they don't know and they don't care. And I cannot find a way to let them know. It's more than she was my aunt - than the blood is thicker than water nonsense. The world needs to know. I just feel we'll lose something really big and important if we simply choose to forget. Someone needs to tell this story. I don't know if I am capable of it. If I am her best last hope then we are in trouble. I'm floundering badly.

"How do you do it, Shull? First you were a banker; then when you got bored with that you became a physicist, then an engineer. Everything comes easy to you. I'm just trying to accomplish this one thing and I'm inadequate to the task. What is the point of it all?"

"I'll let you in on a little secret, Robert," Shull leaned forward. "I left the farm in Idaho because I couldn't cut it as a potato farmer. It takes a special talent to be a farmer. Science is easier by far. But it's more than just that. It also takes a special talent to stick at a thing; particularly when everyone is telling you to give up. I never could stick at one thing; I don't have that talent. I envy you your dedication. It don't matter whether you succeed or not. Your aunt never gave up, now did she? It didn't matter to her. It shouldn't matter to you. Seems to me that not giving up is the point of it all."

They exited the café and walked back to King's Cross station, where they exchanged addresses, shook hands and said their goodbyes.

"Keep in touch, Robert; let me know how your meeting goes; don't forget me now."

"Shull, that svelte figure of yours tends to stamp an indelible impression on the memory; you're not an easy man to forget."

"I remember Oppenheimer looked me up and down and asked, 'Who the devil are you?'"

"Don't take it personally; he asked that of everyone - even Niels Bohr," laughed Robert.

. . . Copenhagen, 1938

C lassic Greek statues, fountains, manicured, exotic trees and shrubs, and footpaths which wove geometric patterns in and out - and that was just in the conservatory, built on such a grand scale that it could have carried the designation of Winter Garden. The house had two of them. They served as indoor promenades when the Danish weather proved too inclement to venture out.

Niels, Robert and Lise entered the courtyard of the palace which Niels called home, where Niels's wife, Margrethe, stood to greet them. They climbed out of the car and, as Niels instructed the staff in the management of the baggage, Margrethe and Lise embraced. Lise then stared at the building which stood before her.

"How do you do it, Niels, on a physicist's pay?" asked Lise. The question was merely a friendly jibe, for she knew that Niels had never lacked for money. The family house of his mother, where he entered into the world, and all his residences since, had possessed more than their fair share of the grandiose.

"Nice, isn't it," replied Niels, admiring the view with Lise, as if he had just seen it for the first time. "But it's not mine. It's a gift to the nation from Jacob Jacobsen, the Carlsberg founder. He stipulated that it should house *'a man or a woman deserving of esteem from the community by reason of services to science, literature, or art, or for other reasons.'* The residents are chosen by the Royal Danish Academy. They saw fit to bestow the honor on me. Although of course, I do have to put up with the smell from the Carlsberg Brewery next door. In the summer time it can be quite pungent, I can tell you."

"Such hardships you have always endured, Niels . . ." smiled Lise.

"Always without complaint," injected Niels.

" . . . And now forced to accept this charity from the State," continued Lise. "How it must vex you."

"Please don't pity me, Lise," said Niels.

"Do you get free beer?" asked Robert.

"The house does come with an operating budget, but alas, no beer," answered Niels. "These are hard times for us all. Nevertheless, you have not done so badly yourself, Lise. Harnack House was no hovel."

"But at Harnack House I had to share," said Lise.

"If it makes you feel better, we can move out and let you have the place to yourself; at least until we have finished the arrangements for your move to Sweden."

"No, I don't mind sharing. It is so beautiful, it will make Sweden harder to take, by comparison," Lise sighed. She had hoped that a place could be found for her in Copenhagen, near to Robert and Niels. To work alongside Niels would have turned her nightmare to a dream. But they could secure no appointment for her in Denmark and her hope turned to yet more disappointment. "When must I leave for Sweden?"

"Sweden is not so bad, although if anyone asks, you didn't hear that from me; the Swedes and the Danes do have a centuries old tradition of mutual disrespect to uphold. And your old friends, the Bahr-Bergius's are looking forward to seeing you again. Still, there are a few weeks before the Swedish Institute reopens. In the meantime you are our guest in Copenhagen; and I shall make it my personal quest to see that when you do finally move to Sweden, you will not be able to report anything negative about your stay here. If nothing else, Margrethe has declared that you cannot leave until we have replaced your wardrobe. That will be her department, of course. Physics I can handle; fashion, not so much."

"No, please don't trouble . . ."

"Now, Lise," interrupted Margrethe. "You must not protest. I have to show you Strøget."

Niels and Robert rolled their eyes and laughed; Strøget referred to the shopping district which dominated the center of Copenhagen.

"Yes, we must not forget the important things in life," scoffed Niels.

"The poor woman needs clothes," scolded Margrethe. "If you men had put any thought into her escape from Berlin, Lise would at least have arrived with a change of clothes . . ."

Niels, thus rebuked, shrugged in apology for the escape committee's failure to consult Lise with a regard to her wardrobe.

". . . I'm looking forward so much to having a companion shop with me," continued Margrethe. "My husband pretends to not even know where to find Strøget."

"Be careful of this one, though, Margrethe," warned Niels.

"When I first met Lise, in Vienna, she had - still has - an addiction to coffee and cigarettes. You need to factor that into you shopping time: one store, coffee break, next store, coffee break."

"I shall try not to keep Margrethe out all night," said Lise. "I really don't need much - Otto will send my belongings on to me when I am settled - but it is true that in the meantime I am at your mercy and I do need one or two things . . ."

Lise found it an embarrassment to depend on her friends this way, but she had abandoned all her possessions, including her savings, which languished far out of reach in a Berlin bank. She felt a failure and a coward. Part of her wished she had stood her ground in Berlin. She had never needed someone else to fight her battles. Berlin lingered only a few hundred kilometers away, but it lay beyond her reach, forbidden and hostile, and in reality, she now needed her friends; only they could help her; she could no longer help herself. Still, the independent spirit lingered . . .

". . . But please, let's not overdo it; after all, whatever I purchase I shall have to transport to Sweden. I would prefer to travel light."

"Don't worry, Aunty, when it's time I can arrange to take a few days from work. I'll come to Sweden with you and help get you settled," said Robert.

"Thank you, Nephew; after all that has happened, your help may be the most terrifying prospect of all," replied Lise.

"Come on, I'll show you around," said Niels. He hooked his arm around Lise's arm. "Care to see the elephants?"

. . . *Mystery*

"I tell you, Otto, it tracks like Barium," said Fritz Strassmann. "I can't explain it. I have never seen anything like it."

Otto's head and bones ached. His mood bordered on petulant. He pined for the long overdue break which he knew he would not get. Strassmann troubled him with a technical problem and he did not consider himself a technician, but a chemist - no, not even much of that in these later years; he considered himself an intellectual and spiritual leader. To publish papers, make speeches, inspire the students, and wrench extra funds from the tight hands of patrons of the KWI - these were his responsibilities; and in all these areas he excelled. But the mundane minutiae of the day to day? He thought he had vanquished those ogres a long time ago.

He had not fully realized just how much of the actual work Lise had born: the experiments, the ordering of equipment and materials, the operation of the laboratory and the supervision of the staff. Now, he grasped that she had shielded him from all that drudgery from the very beginning.

But Lise no longer stood between him and the details, and so it fell to him to push on, crack the whip and keep things moving. At least, that's what the people who lined up outside his office door and jostled for his attention told him.

To avoid them, he had sought out the refuge of the workshop, leaving a trail of students, staff and salesmen in his wake. Nevertheless, as soon as Otto stepped through the door to the laboratory, Strassmann had troubled him with yet another problem.

For appearance sake, Lise's lab coat still hung on the hook by the door and papers covered her desk, as if she had just popped out for coffee and would return at any moment. Had an enslaved genie granted Otto a wish, Lise would have returned in a snap of the fingers. Strassmann waved a hand at the Wilson Cloud Chamber, where the results of their latest experiment had revealed an ambiguity.

"Impossible! Let me see," said Otto. He looked in the Cloud Chamber and saw the tell-tale trail left by the ionized particles. The characteristics of the trail identified the particle, as an animal's footprint in the mud identified the beast to the hunter. Otto frowned.

"Well, where did it come from? There must be impurities from the solution."

"I've no idea."

"Let's double-check both the solution mix and the results. Run the experiment again. We must have made a mistake somewhere. Radium isotopes don't just decide to behave like Barium isotopes."

"Everything else is as predicted. It's just this single isotope which is messed up."

Otto felt that they were getting careless; perhaps due to the increased pressure of work, perhaps to the deteriorating political situation, perhaps the scarcity of qualified people made such a situation inevitable. Whatever the reason, he held himself responsible, for he knew that Lise would never have permitted such carelessness in her workshop.

And then another thought crossed his mind; the implications of which made him pray that indeed nothing more ominous than simple carelessness had spoiled their experiment.

"If we can't explain these results, it means all our work for the last four years is suspect," Otto sighed. "Re-run everything; I don't want to publish our findings until we clear up this mystery."

Strassmann nodded. Otto exited the workshop. In his heart, he suspected that the irregularity of this result required further study. If the results of a new test matched this one, then he did indeed have a mystery on his hands. But if the results did not match - if they instead ran as expected - then what? Could he just dismiss this test as a glitch and ignore it? If he did that, would he risk missing something new? Pressed as he was, where would he even find the time to research this problem? He would feel much better if Strassmann did find a contamination. He needed to take that break more than ever. He needed to talk to Lise.

As Otto walked down the corridor by the office of Carl Bosch, still followed by the buzzing crowd and still thinking about the ruined experiment, Werner Heisenberg stepped out of Bosch's office and called to him.

"Professor Hahn! Please, Otto, if you have a moment."

Otto followed Heisenberg to the office. He did not hesitate at Heisenberg's call, for he had expected the summons. And a quick glance around the office confirmed his suspicions. Besides Heisenberg, Bosch and Max von Laue sat in front of Bosch's desk. And behind Bosch's desk sat the uniformed and stern Inspector from the SD. At the Inspector's shoulder stood his SD junior, Wolfgang Meyer. Otto and the others had rehearsed for this moment. Trying to look nonchalant, Otto took a deep breath.

"Sorry to trouble you, Otto," said Bosch, "But this gentleman has a few questions to put to you."

"Professor Hahn, you were the supervisor of Dr. L. Meitner?" asked the Inspector.

"Dr. Meitner? Yes, er, no - her colleague, not her supervisor."

"Professor Hahn, are you aware of Dr. Meitner's present whereabouts?"

"No, not precisely. I understand that she is vacationing in Austria; she loves to hike in the mountains. She has family in Vienna," Otto replied, laying out their agreed on fiction.

"Vacation? Then you may be surprised to hear that the Jewess is not in Austria but in Sweden?"

"Sweden?" Otto tried to fake surprise. He looked to his colleagues for confirmation that they found his act convincing, but they offered no encouragement.

"Herr Bosch has informed the Ministry that a letter has been received from Dr. Meitner; she has requested that her pension be forwarded to that country, following her resignation from this Institute. I do not think that she intends to return from her . . . vacation."

"Really, I know nothing of this matter," protested Otto.

"She never mentioned her plans to retire to you?"

"No."

"No dropped hints or unusual behavior? You had no suspicions that her alleged trip to Vienna was just a ruse?"

"No, why should I?"

"You seem remarkably ignorant of the character of the women who worked by your side for thirty years."

"Women, eh! They never tell us men anything. We are always kept in the dark; always the last to know."

"Professor Hahn, the Ministry had expressly forbidden that Dr. Meitner leave the country. We are concerned that someone with such knowledge lends weight to the propaganda against us should they be allowed to spread lies. Do you have any idea how such a woman - your colleague - may have been able to leave Germany without the proper papers?"

"Really, this is all news to me."

"Would any other of your colleagues know how she accomplished this feat?"

"You would have to ask them."

"Yes, I will have to ask them . . . Moving on, Herr Bosch tells me that you are working on . . ." The Inspector looked at his notes. ". . . Transuranic Elements, is that correct?"

"Yes," replied Otto.

"How much of this work would Dr. Meitner understand?"

"Oh, not much, at least not in great detail," Otto lied. "She really wasn't much more than a lab technician."

"But you just referred to her as your colleague? You have published papers together, have you not?"

"Professional courtesy."

"We do not extend professional courtesy to Jews, Professor Hahn. Are you telling me that you included Dr. Meitner's name on your papers as a kindness to the woman?"

"Er . . ."

"Your generosity is misguided, Professor Hahn, it may get you into trouble one day. Perhaps it would be well to set the record straight and correct the authorship of those papers. We cannot allow Jews to take credit for the work of honest, hard working Germans, can we now?"

The Inspector paused for emphasis. Otto remained silent.

"Perhaps the Inspector would care to provide us with a list of those papers," Max von Laue pressed. "There may be some that were published without Professor Hahn's knowledge."

The Inspector glared at him.

"These are dangerous times, Gentlemen," warned the Inspector. "Our enemies use any and all methods to turn public opinion against us. It is the duty of our institutions to protect the honor of Germany." The Inspector rose from Bosch's chair. "I think that will do for now. Please, Professor Hahn, Gentlemen, if you would be so kind as to provide official statements to my assistant here . . ."

He moved towards the office door, but turned back.

" . . . Then there is the matter of Frau Meitner's apartment."

"Her apartment?" asked Carl Bosch.

"Yes; she was residing in official KWI quarters, I understand. Obviously as she is no longer an employee of the Institute, I am sure the apartment cannot stay empty for too long."

"Of course, we are already considering new candidates," agreed Bosch.

"Presently, the Ministry is examining the apartment; we are taking an inventory. Do you not find it odd that a woman should resign her position and move to a different country, but see no reason to pack for the journey?"

"Odd, yes, very odd, most unusual," they readily agreed.

"I must say that the little she possessed does not seem to warrant such large accommodations," said the Inspector. "I am surprised that you did not put the apartment to better use. Regardless, you shall be informed when it becomes available again. Good day, Gentlemen."

The Inspector departed and those that remained in the office let out a collective sigh of relief.

"Thank God the Inspector didn't ask about the missing paper clips," joked Max von Laue.

Day turned to night, but Otto still had work to do. Back in the workshop, alone for the first time in that long day, he urged his neck muscles to hold his head up from his chest and rubbed at his eyes to try to get them to focus for just a little while longer. He clearly couldn't keep up this frantic pace for much longer, not at his age. And as reluctant as he felt to admit it, he knew that he needed someone to take Lise's place in the workshop, to relieve the burden.

He convinced himself that the urgency of the situation required such an appointment; but only as a temporary measure until Lise returned. Surely, Lise would understand? No, he argued with himself - the distance between them remained unimportant. She was still his partner! It was still her workshop. Lise should decide who ran it in her absence. He would write to her and get her opinion. He sat at Lise's desk, placed a blank sheet of paper in front of him and picked up a pen to write . . .

. . . But before he could put pen to paper, the memory of the image in the Cloud Chamber popped back into his head. It had bothered him all day long, so much so that attentiveness had eluded him. Why so persistent? Why this test? Simply one of thousands they had conducted. Tests went wrong all the time. Yet he could not shake the feeling that it signified something important. He returned his focus to the sheet of paper and wrote . . .

> *19.12.38 Monday eve. In the lab. Dear Lise! It is now just 11:00 P.M. At 11:45 Strassmann is coming back so that I can eventually go home. There is something about the radium isotopes which for now we are telling only you. Perhaps you can come up with some sort of fantastic explanation?*

. . . Discovery

" . . . The body of Ernst vom Rath, whose death
at the hands of a young Polish Jew in Paris last
week loosed Nazi Germany's latest wave of anti-
Jewish violence, was brought today to Düsseldorf
for burial . . .

. . . Vienna dispatches reported the destruction of
all 21 synagogues in the city. Vienna Jews said 22
of their number had committed suicide in despair.
One synagogue in the Austrian capital was blown
up while storm troopers compelled Jews to begin
tearing down another . . .

. . . New emergency decrees to regulate Jewish life were being drafted by the German ministry. Jewish students have been expelled from all universities and other institutions of higher learning . . .

. . . As a result of the violence, fifty thousand Jews have been arrested throughout the Reich in the last few days. Of that number, seven to eight thousand were estimated to have been seized in Berlin . . ."

Eva von Bahr-Bergius turned off the radio. "In my 60 years on this planet, I have never understood this kind of hatred," she said to Lise. "I will not understand it if I live for another 60. You got out just in time."

In the scenic backwater of Kungälv, Sweden; nestled in a cozy cottage, a universe away from the troubles of the world, they sipped hot tea and warmed themselves by the fire. In such a setting, they could easily imagine that they heard only fiction on the radio, a deep and gloomy play from a classicist, perhaps - Turn off the radio and life returned to normal.

"But my life is still there," complained Lise. "And much of my family is still there. Walter and Gisella escaped to England, but Gusti is still in Vienna; her husband, Jutz, has been sent to Dachau. I pray they will be all right. I feel so helpless. I still don't comprehend why this is happening. It's all so surreal."

"I'm sure they will be alright," assured Eva. "Do not dwell on it. Concentrate on your work; that will be real enough, once you settle in at the Institute."

"I hope so. Everyone is friendly enough, but I'm left to my own devices. I've not seen Director Siegbahn since the first day."

"Not able to speak our language is tough, but that will come in time. It will get better once you are settled."

"I've written to Otto to send some of my things to me, but they have other worries on their hands. You wouldn't believe how much custom duty they want. It would be cheaper to buy new."

"I don't understand it. This cannot go on indefinitely. If this latest outrage does not spur the world to act, I don't know what will. We are headed towards another war. Well, let the politicians deal with it. My advice is to throw yourself into your work."

"Yesterday I read an article about my deuteron accelerator, but it did not mention me, not once. It listed Reddmann as the head of the project - Reddmann of all people . . . Oh, I'm sorry, Eva, you must think that I am bitter all the time. I'm not really, It's just I find no substance to my work here when everything I ever did is elsewhere, and for the first time in my life I feel useless."

"Not this week, we cannot permit it: Christmas is coming and I need your help to prepare for it. Until now, you've only visited us in the summer time, but Christmas shows Kungälv at its best. My daughter and her husband arrive tomorrow, and my granddaughter; she is a handful. Yes, I will definitely need your help."

* * *

In the Bahr-Bergius kitchen, Christmas Eve had arrived. And in the morning, Eva taught her granddaughter, Julia, how to bake gingerbread cookies. Lise drank coffee and studied a Swedish-German dictionary. Julia sang a carol.

"Concentrate on the gingerbread, Julia. We shall have plenty of time for song later," said Eva.

A knock at the front door interrupted their activities.

"Now who can that be I wonder?" said Eva. "Lise, my hands are messy, would you mind getting it?"

"Not at all," said Lise. She put down the dictionary and went to the door.

"The *Jultomten*, the tomtem," cried Julia and she ran out of the kitchen to the front door, spreading flour as she glided.

As Lise approached the door, she found Eva's husband, Niklas, who had already opened it from the outside and entered.

"Not the Jultomten," sighed a disappointed Julia, unless her grandfather had forgotten the white beard and pointy, red cap. She slunk back to the kitchen.

"Don't worry, it's only me," cried Niklas. "Ah Lise, just the person - I have a couple of things for you; first, the post." He handed Lise two letters. "From Berlin; it looks like Otto Hahn's hand writing on one of them. And second - voilà!"

Niklas stepped to one side to show that Robert stood behind him.

"Robert!" cried Lise.

"Hello, Aunty," said Robert. He then shouted through to the kitchen, "Hello, Eva, I made it."

Eva came to the entrance hall, wiping her hands on a towel.

"Robert, come in," said Eva. "Welcome to Sweden."

"He was already at the train station when I arrived, half frozen to death," explained Niklas. "We stopped by the hotel and dropped off his suitcase."

"I'll make some hot glogg to warm you up after your trip," said Eva.

"You knew he was coming?" asked Lise. "Still everyone keeps secrets from me."

"An early Christmas present for you," said Robert.

"Have you kept the receipt so that I can return you?" said Lise. She put the mail from Berlin in her pocket and she and Robert hugged. "Oh my, you're as cold as an icicle."

"Put a good measure of brandy in that glogg," said Niklas. "We need to get some warmth back in our toes."

In spite of the difficult state of affairs in which Lise found herself, she spent a warm and enjoyable Christmas Eve in the company of Robert and the Bahr-Bergius family. The conversation and glogg flowed freely, the gingerbread proved edible and the holiday smorgasbord overflowed with too much food.

In the afternoon, the real Jultomten visited and following his traditional question, 'Are there any good children here?' he produced a gift from his sack for Julia.

As the evening fell, along with a soft, gentle snow, they lit the candles on the Christmas tree and relaxed around the log fire which burned brightly in the hearth. Over the fire, a copper pot hung and Robert and Julia sat by it and dipped brown bread into its steamy content of broth, made from the remnants of dinner; and Julia explained the tradition to Robert.

"*Dipping the kettle* commemorates the great famine of . . . Oh, I forget," said Julia.

"1649," prompted Niklas.

"The great famine of 1649," Julia repeated. "When we had nothing to eat. Now we give thanks that we have bread to eat."

"Is that so?" said Robert, playing along.

"Of course, I prefer gingerbread," said Julia.

"Well, naturally," said Robert. "Me too."

Lise remembered the letters which she had in her pocket, took them out, opened the first and read. "Max von Laue sends his regards," she said to the others. Then she laughed.

"What is it?" asked Robert.

"Oh, nothing - it's just Max being Max. He say's that it's not fair that I get an extended skiing vacation in Sweden while he has to remain in Berlin and work; and could I arrange for his escape also."

Julia's mother stood and motioned to her daughter. "Okay, Julia, to bed with you; we have to be up early tomorrow for church."

"Ah, that is also my cue to leave," said Robert. "It has been a long day for me and my hotel bed is waiting."

"And you, Robert, will you join us for service in the morning?" asked Eva. "Your aunt has become a thoroughly unabashed Protestant, but I hope a good, old fashioned Catholic Mass will tug her a little further towards the true faith."

"Thank you, Eva, but I think I shall sleep the sleep of the dead tonight. Don't wait on me before you start your Mass. Goodnight anyway."

"Goodnight!" they all respond.

"Goodnight, Robert," said Lise. "Merry Christmas, Nephew."

Niklas retrieved Robert's coat and helped him into it. "Some glogg for the journey?" he asked.

"Thank you, no, I am all glogged out," sighed Robert. "It's just a short walk to the hotel; I expect I can make it without freezing."

After Robert had departed, Lise opened her second letter, the one from Otto, and read.

* * *

The sunless morning rose on Christmas Day, and Lise and the Bahr-Bergius family went to church for Mass. As a non-Catholic, Lise had not expected to participate in the Mass in any material way, other than to imitate the actions of those around her. The congregation sang a hymn and then the priest spoke.

"In nòmine Patris, et Fìlii,
et Spìritus Sancti."

Because the priest conducted the Mass in Latin, Lise could not follow it and her mind began to wander. Niklas had explained the reason for the Latin: as a device which, when coupled with the majesty of the church and ceremony, would inspire awe and mystery, and induce a hypnotic-like state, which in turn, allowed the congregation to shake-off their everyday lives and experience the Mystery of God. As a scientist, Lise didn't care much for mysteries, except to solve them.

Instead, Lise's thoughts turned to Berlin and the KWI, and specifically to Otto and his letter. As with Otto, the results of the errant test troubled her; the integrity of her work also stood in jeopardy, but that did not worry her. For unlike Otto, she did not pray for some trivial happenstance to explain it all away. She sensed that something important had happened.

The priest intoned in Latin. The congregation chanted back in unison. But the sound fell away, first to a hum, then to silence. The rich colors of the church and the priest's garments, and of the congregation in their Christmas Day best all blurred into a soft focus, dark blue.

Lise entered her own hypnotic state. Her head danced with the past; with books and lectures, with test-tubes and equations, with Max and Albert playing a duet. Her ears filled with the clicks of the Geiger-counter. She heard the words of her old teacher, Boltzmann, *'We should pursue the truth, wherever that takes us. To Heaven or to Hell, Lise, seek the truth.'* But what truth? What had Otto seen in the Cloud Chamber to alarm him? What, what, what?

The priest spoke. The congregation sank to their knees. The priest spoke. The congregation stood. And so went the Mass. But Lise sat frozen on the edge of her pew, no longer part of the ritual.

"What, what, what?"

She thought she detected something, as if she looked in a well and saw a sparkle of light at the bottom. But she could not reach it. She felt it fly around her brain, but she could not react quickly enough to grasp it.

"What, what, what?"

And then she had it!

The priest said, "Ite missa est."

"Deo gratias," responded the congregation.

* * *

At the sink in the small, cramped hotel room which he occupied, Robert attempted to shave; a task made more difficult by the sloped ceiling which forced him to crouch. The loud rap at his door caught him by surprise and he banged his head and nicked his cheek with the razor. He grimaced at the pain and at the interruption, which came too early in the day to denote the maid. The raps grew faster, louder and insistent.

"All right, I'm coming!" shouted Robert.

Without bothering to remove the soap or blood from his face, or to put on a shirt, Robert walked to the door and opened it. The diminutive figure of his aunt stood in the hall. She looked at his disheveled appearance and shook her head.

"Get dressed and take a walk with me," said Lise. "I'll wait for you in the reception." She turned and walked away.

"And a Merry Christmas to you too, Aunty," Robert called after her.

Robert found Lise intensely serious about the walk and she would not even allow him time for a cup of coffee. The weather and terrain threatened to turn any walk into a hazard. Robert borrowed a pair of skis from the hotel. Lise preferred to walk.

Two small black specks in a sea of white, they followed the trail through the woods to the towering ruins of the Bohus Fortress which overlooked the town and the grey water of the frigid North Sea. In spite of the advantage of his skis, Lise, propelled by her internal turmoil, moved the swifter of the two and Robert struggled to keep up. Eventually, he called her to a halt.

"Okay, Aunty, we can stop now; there's no one around to hear us. What has upset you?"

Lise produced Otto's letter and handed it to Robert. "Read it," she ordered. "I think it is important."

Robert read the letter and shrugged, "A failed experiment? I missed my breakfast for this?"

"No, not a failed experiment; I believe that a larger theme intrudes here."

"Something is wrong in the Lab and Otto is stuck for an explanation. He wants you to do his dirty work for him."

"Maybe he is doing my dirty work for me?"

"But Otto must have made a mistake? He used barium as a carrier and he simply failed to separate it, as he suspects."

"No, Otto is too good a scientist for that."

"But Hahn is a chemist, not an alchemist. He could not have formed barium. You know that? It would be like turning lead into gold."

"Yes, I know that."

"Then what? What has got you so riled up that you drag me out to the middle of nowhere on Christmas Day?"

"There is more; something which Otto has overlooked." Lise brushed the snow from a fallen tree trunk and sat. "I think that Otto's results are correct. I think they are correct because the uranium nucleus has split in two; barium is a fragment. It all adds up."

Robert sat beside Lise.

"The nucleus is not something to which you can just take a cleaver. You cannot split it. Otto says so himself in his letter that this could not possibly be the case. The nucleus cannot burst apart. The forces which hold it together are too strong."

Lise picked up some snow and fashioned a snow ball.

"Remember Niels' description of the atom? The nucleus is more like a drop of water than a rock. It is pliant and elastic and its surface tension keeps it together. We cannot cleave it, but perhaps it can be squeezed."

Lise demonstrated on the snow ball and Robert watched it crumble.

"Still, it does not add up," he argued. "Okay, suppose we did somehow split the uranium in two and got barium as a fragment. Where's the rest of the nucleus, the other fragments? We should have other elements which, when all put together, equate back to the original uranium? The sum of the parts does not equal the whole."

"Robert, I think I have the answer. The sum of the parts is equal . . ."

Lise picked up a twig and wrote in the snow.

$$E=MC^2$$

". . . The missing element is energy."

* * *

Also in his undershirt, and unshaven, because he had no reason that day to leave the comfort of his home in Princeton, New Jersey, Albert Einstein read a letter from Niels Bohr. Niels wrote to Albert with news which Niels had, in turn, received from Robert Frisch. Niels felt the news carried such great importance that they should act on it immediately. Albert agreed, and so in turn, he sat down and wrote a letter of his own.

> F.D. Roosevelt
> President of the United States
> White House
> Washington, D.C.
>
> Dear Sir:
>
> Some recent work, which has been communicated to me, leads me to expect that the element uranium may be turned into a new and important source of energy. Certain aspects of the situation which has arisen seem to call for watchfulness and, if necessary, quick action on the part of the Administration. I believe therefore that it is my duty to bring to your attention the following facts and recommendations . . .

. . . *Tivoli Gardens, 1941*

Many people besides Eva von Bahr-Bergius had declared the inevitability of World War II and so war came down on them. It reached the comfortable world of Niels Bohr when the Germans unleashed Operation Weserübung in 1940 and kindly offered to protect the freedom and neutrality of the Danes. In spite of the occupation, however, most Danish institutions remained autonomous and Niels still resided at his state-gifted mansion in Copenhagen.

And on a mild September evening, a relaxed Niels sat at home and read a newspaper, while Margrethe played Mozart's Sonata in A Major on the piano. The distant tinkle of a bell and the mumbled voices of his butler and some other in the hall informed Niels that he had a visitor. He put down his paper, rose from his chair and went to the hall to investigate. Under a long, black coat, the visitor wore the uniform of a German officer. Niels did not recognize the uniform, nor which branch of military service it represented, but the grinning face of the uniform's occupant was unmistakable.

"Hello, Niels," said Werner Heisenberg.

Niels took his coat and he and Heisenberg left the house and strolled east, passed the Elephant Gate and towards Tivoli Gardens. Heisenberg chatted casually and pleasantly about Copenhagen, the weather and friends, but said nothing of importance. A wary Niels kept his remarks short and guarded.

Two men followed them: Plainclothes Gestapo who kept to the shadows and well out of sight, and unaware of a third man who also trailed them.

They arrived at Tivoli, the playground of the Danes. In submission to the precautions of war time, the Danes replaced the Gardens illuminations with PH lamps, which shone their light only down, but they refused further alterations to their iconic park; it would take more than war to shutter Tivoli; and on this warm night, many others strolled through the Gardens, amused themselves on the rides, sat in the restaurants and at beer tables, and watched the entertainment in the Glass Hall and Pantomime Theater.

"I've always loved Tivoli," said Heisenberg, as they strolled. "Ever since I was a small boy and could only dream about it."

"Why have you come to Copenhagen?" asked Niels, tired of the small talk.

"P.R. for the Fatherland; it's required that we all do our bit. I am to speak at the German Culture Institute, tomorrow. You'll attend, I hope?"

"No Dane will attend. Why have you really come?"

"To see you."

"Officially or unofficially?"

"Does it matter? I'm in Copenhagen and I want to visit with my old friend."

"Officially or unofficially?"

"Okay then, unofficially. I do not serve the cause twenty-four hours a day."

"But they know you are here and have given their blessing. They are probably watching us now."

"We live in guarded times, Niels."

"Then I will be on my guard."

"Just as well; I am concerned for your security; you are an important man. We Germans are not all bad. Some of us can be trusted, should you need a friend."

"Friends are good to have at any time."

"Speaking of friends, how is Lise Meitner? Have you heard from her at all?"

"Nothing that you probably don't know already."

"And her nephew, Frisch, didn't he work for you here in Copenhagen? What happened to him?"

"He found the climate suited him better in England, as you well know."

"Still, quite remarkable to have two such geniuses in one family, wouldn't you say?"

"Quite."

"That breakthrough in fission, for example; some believe that it will pave the way for a nuclear bomb. Would you agree? I wonder about the morality of it. Is it right for physicists to devote themselves in wartime to the uranium problem? It could lead to grave consequences."

"And what about you, Werner, do you think that uranium fission could be utilized for the construction of weapons? Are you working on such a bomb for the Germans?"

"Heaven forbid! In principle it may be achievable, but a project of such magnitude would be impossible in Germany, the lack of will and resources preclude it."

"Impossible or merely difficult?"

"The Führer has other priorities."

"Just as well for civilization. But I hear that you have worked on the uranium problem to the exclusion of all else for these past two years."

"True, we have not stood idle in Germany in the long months since Hahn's discovery, but there are still many obstacles to overcome . . ."

Heisenberg paused, but Niels did not respond, preferring to avoid a technical discussion. Heisenberg remained a friend, but Germany had become the enemy and he would not say anything to help Heisenberg draw conclusions, one way or the other. Heisenberg did not wait for a response.

" . . . America, on the other hand, they have unlimited quantities of everything. And perhaps the brain power to overcome the obstacles. I still think it impossible, but if anyone could do it, they could."

"You are prudent to consider it impossible," said Niels. "I wouldn't know."

"Of course not, although there are those in Germany who think that you would. That perhaps your knowledge should be put to the test - or at least . . ."

"Eliminated?"

"Requisitioned."

"You were my best student, Werner; you know all that I know. My knowledge is irrelevant to Germany."

"Yes, but I'm just one man. We are swamped with responsibilities and desperate for help. Under the circumstances, I couldn't see Germany getting the bomb for another four or five year. Hopefully by then the war will be over. Of course if the war does last another five years then perhaps the bomb will be built by someone."

"So we've gone from impossible to four years. Is that what you have told your masters?"

"Niels, you have become suspicious. Hitler does not trust science; and scientists even less. It's war time. Germany has an energy crisis. We can do great things with nuclear fission besides building bombs."

"And have you made progress?"

"Enough to keep my masters happy, I hope. Germany will win this war; we are determined. If Hitler has to choose between dogma and the bomb, he will choose the bomb . . ."

Heisenberg paused again.

". . . Still, the war has done much personal damage. I miss my friends. Perhaps you could pass a message to them from me, unofficially of course."

"My connections are not what they once were, but if I get the chance . . ."

"You should take it without hesitation," Heisenberg spoke in earnest and then relaxed again and smiled. "Now, let's find a table and a glass of port. How about some music and song to cheer us up? We'll drink to absent friends. I wish I could see them all again and deliver my message in person, but perhaps you can, before this war makes prisoners of us all?"

The Gestapo who trailed them had no orders to eliminate Niels Bohr; they merely conducted a fishing expedition to try to catch Heisenberg in the act of treason. They knew that Heisenberg had indeed received permission to visit his old professor, and therefore they would simply report back what they had seen and heard.

The third man, an American named Morris Berg, Moe to his friends, also had no interest in Bohr. Moe had trailed Heisenberg since his arrival in Copenhagen; and Moe's orders extended beyond simply reporting on Heisenberg's movements. When not playing baseball for the Boston Red Sox, Moe worked as an assassin for the OSS, America's predecessor of the CIA. The OSS had assigned Moe a mission to find out just how close Heisenberg was to building the bomb and if necessary, prevent it by any available method.

Moe had spotted the Gestapo immediately, in spite of their stealth, for they performed no better than clumsy amateurs, but with a visible arrogance which oozed from them in all direction, and which made it impossible for them to move without detection. He concluded that Heisenberg must also have noticed them. That would put Heisenberg on guard, but would also misdirect his attention.

Moe thumbed the Browning .45 in his coat pocket. The presence of the Gestapo made his job neither more nor less difficult. Yes, they carried guns, but with their attention fixed on Heisenberg, they would never know what hit them.

In perfect Danish, free of any incriminating accent, Moe ordered a beer and sat at a table which allowed him to keep both the scientists and the Gestapo within his peripheral vision. He saw Heisenberg scribble on a piece of paper and hand it to Bohr. Was Heisenberg careless or brazen? Perhaps the Germans would save him the trouble and shoot Heisenberg first?

Moe looked around him, at the lights of Tivoli Gardens, at the park workers, singers and dancers, at the parents and their children, happy and smiling. Regardless of the German High Command's opinion of Heisenberg, the murder of two of their secret police would certainly bring reprisals against these innocent people. He decided against any immediate action. Heisenberg could live another day. Tomorrow, he would attend the lecture at the German Culture

Institute. Tonight, he would nurse the Carlsberg which smiled up at him.

"Werner," said Niels. "I fear for your safety also. Neither the allies nor the Nazis will allow you to complete your work if it is damaging to their cause."

"Me?" smiled Heisenberg. "No, Niels, you know that I lead a charmed life."

* * *

The two men reported back to their chief at Gestapo headquarters. They had heard no treasonous words fall from the lips of Heisenberg, but the matter of the paper which Heisenberg had given to Bohr required further investigation. They thought that Heisenberg had drawn something, a diagram perhaps, but unable to get close enough to see it clearly, they could not say with any surety. They recommended that the Gestapo interview Bohr.

Before the chief could respond to the recommendation, a call interrupted their conversation: all officers must assemble in the briefing room. After they had taken their seats, the German Commissioner to Denmark, Cecil von Renthe-Fink, entered the room. They stood to attention. The Commissioner waved them to sit. Renthe-Fink was a career diplomat who only joined the Nazi Party because he considered it expedient. Under his command, the Germans had followed a laissez-faire policy of non-interference in Danish affairs, but violent Danish resistance had increased and Hitler became impatient.

"I have a communiqué from Berlin," said Renthe-Fink. "Under the directive of Wilhelm Keitel, chief of the German Armed Forces High Command, I will read the following:"

"After lengthy consideration, it is the will of the Führer that the measures taken against those who are guilty of offenses against the Reich or against the occupation forces in occupied areas should be altered. The Führer is of the opinion that in such cases penal servitude or even a hard labor sentence for life will be regarded as a sign of weakness. An effective and lasting deterrent can be achieved only by the death penalty. Prisoners are, in future, to be transported to Germany secretly, and further treatment of the offenders will take place there.

By order of SS Reichsführer Himmler.

Heil Hitler."

The Commissioner departed. The chief stood and addressed them. "As you all know, under the Commissioner's hands-off approach, we have not had the opportunity to address the issue of Danish Jews in a manner consistent with policy in Germany. The new directive is clear. Danish Jews are directing the resistance against us and are a security threat. Under the orders of the new directive, Danish Jews are to be rounded up immediately and transported to Germany. Gentlemen, you have your orders; dismissed."

"What about Niels Bohr?" asked the two agents.

"Niels Bohr is also considered a security threat," mulled the chief. "He is Jewish on his mother's side. But let's proceed carefully; his disappearance will cause a diplomatic incident. I'll get further instructions from Berlin on how to handle him."

"In the meantime?"

"In the meantime we have our hands full with the others on our list. Bohr is not going anywhere; we know where to find him when we want him."

. . . *Flights of Angels*

"There are two gentlemen to see you, Sir. They are with Mrs. Bohr in the Pompeii Room."

"Gentlemen?" asked Niels.

"Yes, Sir, the Prime Minister and I understand, the Swedish Ambassador."

"Oh, oh, something's up. Were they smiling? Should I make a run for it?"

"I could not say, Sir."

Niels handed his coat to the butler and joined Margrethe and his visitors. They rose to greet him.

"Erik," said Niels to the Prime Minister. "I'm sorry, I didn't expect you; otherwise I would have been here to greet you."

"An opportunity to take tea with Margrethe, we could not resist," said Erik Scavenius. "May I introduce Gustaf von Dardel, Ambassador from the King of Sweden."

"My pleasure, Mr. Ambassador."

"But, in addition to that, we do have an urgent matter to discuss with you."

"Then I shall leave you to your business, Gentlemen," said Margrethe.

"Please stay, Mrs. Bohr," objected the Prime Minister. "Our news also concerns you."

"Bad news?" asked Niels. "Should I sit down?"

They sat.

"The Germans have shuffled the deck," said the Prime Minister. "Cecil von Renthe Fink is out. The new man, Werner Best, does not have the autonomy which Renthe Fink enjoyed. He is here to carry out Berlin's orders. Those orders included the arrest of all Jews."

"That is bad," agreed Niels. "But expected, given the German behavior. I hope you didn't agree to it?"

"My Cabinet has tendered its resignation to King Christian."

"Your news keeps getting worse."

"The Ambassador has some news to offset the worst of it."

"Sweden has agreed to grant immediate asylum to all Jews who present themselves at the Swedish border," said the Ambassador.

"A generous offer for which many will thank you," said Niels. "But at the risk of offending, I have to ask why you have come here to tell me this news? Surely your time would be better spent arranging for the evacuation of those poor unfortunates?"

"That is why we have come," said the Prime Minister. "Their evacuation concerns you."

"In what way?"

"Niels, I think it goes without saying that you love your country."

"Of course."

"And your country loves you."

"I'm glad to hear it."

"We have come here to ask you a favor on behalf of your country."

"What favor?"

"Leave."

"Leave?"

"Leave your country. Go to Sweden."

"Me? I sympathize with the plight of the Jews, but . . ."

"But you are a Jew yourself."

"No, my mother's family is Jewish, not me."

"The Germans do not differentiate; your life is in danger."

"I will not run. Let them lock me up."

"You must run."

"There are Danish patriots dying and suffering in Gestapo prisons. They did not run; neither will I."

"You must do what we ask."

"You don't understand . . ."

"No, Niels, it is you who fails to understand. Please let me explain."

Niels waited for an explanation.

"We have seen a copy of the German directive - thank God they are not all Nazis - they do not merely intend to detain you," said the Prime Minister. "It will be carried out within the week. We have consulted with the Jewish community leadership. It will not surprise you to hear that they are also patriots. Their answer is the same as yours: they will not run. But staying is not an option. If they stay, they fall into the hands of the Germans. We cannot protect them. And there cannot be an openly armed resistance at this time; the repercussions would be devastating."

"We must fight them at some point."

"And that point is coming, but for now, we must prepare - and you must run."

"I still say no."

"As I said, we have spoken to the Jewish leadership. We have some 8,000 Jews in Denmark. None will run unless their leaders order it."

"Naturally, they must order it."

"They cannot order what they will not do themselves. No one wants to be the first to go. No one wants to be called a coward. Niels, you must be the first."

"You cannot be serious. I am not a Jewish leader."

"The Germans consider you their leader. Do not forget that the Jews of Denmark are also Danish. You are a leader to all Danes; the most prominent and visible leader we have, besides the King. If you go, they will follow. You must be the first to go, to set the example."

"I need time to think. There has to be another way."

"We only have a few days at most. I need your answer immediately so that arrangements can be made."

"I need time to discuss this with Margrethe."

"8,000 lives hang in the balance."

Niels looked at Margrethe. Her smile told all. The discussion had ended.

"Make the arrangements," answered Niels.

* * *

They agreed on two signals. On hearing the first, planted in a morning broadcast on Swedish radio, Niels, Margrethe and their son, Aage, retrieved the small bags which they had previously packed and drove to the Physics Institute at the University. They took a route which Niels had driven many time and would not arouse suspicion. From the Institute, they walked their way south to a safe-house, near the Amager Beach. Forgoing the comfort of the house, they hid in a garden shed and waited for night to fall.

When night came, they left the shed and walked in the shadows to the beach, where they huddled together and crouched to make themselves as invisible as possible. Fortunately, no light threatened to betray their presence - except one which flashed briefly three times from out on the water. They broke cover and ran towards the water. A motorboat approached, breaking over the sound of lapping waves.

"How can the Germans fail to hear that?" they all worried simultaneously.

A man in the launch, not wishing to beach the boat, waved for them to wade out to him. They splashed forward. The sand shifted beneath them and threatened to spill them, but they kept their footing and reached the boat.

Once in the launch, their pilot turned and sped towards the darkness and a waiting fishing boat. Evading German Patrols, the fishing boat zigzagged through the mine fields and sailed across the Øresund to Sweden.

Upon Niels's arrival in Limhamn, the Swedes broadcast the second signal, 'Bohr is safe.' The evacuation of the Danish Jews began.

Sweden teemed with German agents, whose orders said find Bohr and shoot to kill. Every moment he stayed increased the risk that they would fulfill their orders, but it took several days and the certainty that the evacuation of the others had succeeded before Niels agreed to board the RAF plane sent to transport him to Scotland and then on to London.

The plane, an unmarked 2-man de Havilland Mosquito bomber, built for speed and high altitude, above the flak of the German guns, only had room for one passenger. Niels said goodbye to Margrethe and Aage. They would join him later.

When the plane touched down outside London, James Chadwick, a colleague from Niels's days in Manchester, stood there to greet him.

"Welcome back," said Chadwick. "Good flight I hope."

"We weren't shot down, so I suppose it could have been worse," answered Niels. "But I did have a little trouble with the oxygen mask. My head was too big for the helmet. The pilot told me I was unconscious for a few minutes, but no real harm done."

"Then that's all right. Still, it's good to see you. I've been asked to come fetch you and take you over to Whitehall. There's a chap we want you to meet, Sir John Anderson."

"Anderson?"

"Yes, Sir John is the Chancellor of the Exchequer; just got the job: Winston's having a bit of a reshuffle. But Sir John still keeps his old friends close."

"What's the meeting about?"

"Can't say; secret. But I do think you'll find it interesting."

At Whitehall, Niels and Chadwick passed through security checks and body searches before they at last entered the Chancellor's office.

"Before we begin, Dr. Bohr, I just need you to sign this," said Sir John. The Chancellor's secretary handed a single typed sheet to Niels.

"What is it?" asked Niels.

"What we discuss in this room is covered by the Official Secrets Act. We must ask for your surety than our conversation will go no further."

Niels turned over the paper in his hand. "It's a bit thin for an official document, isn't it? What exactly am I signing?"

"Yes, the complete Act is a bit longer. My secretary shall show you a full copy of the Act before you leave, but in the interest of time, we are at war after all, allow me to summarize the Act as follows: if you breath one word of our conversation to any unauthorized person, and that includes your mother, wife and children, we will toss you - and them - in the Tower and throw away the key. No trial, no appeal, no mercy."

"The word of a gentleman is not enough?"

"There are no gentlemen in government, Dr. Bohr."

Niels shrugged and scrawled his signature on the paper.

"Thank you. Sorry to brow-beat you, but rules are rules. Anyway, to business. Dr. Bohr, have you heard of a scientific project called Tube Alloys?"

"No, I can't say that I have."

"Good! If you had, some miserable sod would have felt the weight of the Official Secrets Act as it dropped on his head from a great height. Excuse my language."

Sir John and James Chadwick briefed Niels on Tube Alloys, the code name for the British effort to build an atomic bomb.

"So it's true, it can be built?" asked Niels. "I can't believe you have made so much progress."

"We've been working on the problem since Frisch arrived," said Chadwick.

"Robert is on the project?"

"Oh, yes, you'd be surprised at just how many of your colleagues are working on this. But as you know, the challenges are enormous; for every problem we solve, two more spring up. We need the best minds available if we are to succeed. We need your mind, Niels."

"I'm not convinced that I want to turn my mind to building a bomb."

"Before you make up your mind, there is someone else I'd like you to meet," said Sir John.

In a basement underneath the Office of Works at Whitehall, a mere 10 feet below street level and certainly no protection against a well aimed Luftwaffe bomb, Winston Churchill conducted the war.

And in a small office which led to Churchill's underground bedroom, Niels sat.

"Dr. Bohr," said Churchill. "We are honored to have you here. I am so glad to see you safely out of the clutches of the Nazis."

"Thank you, Prime Minister," said Niels.

"I trust that Sir John has filled you in on our endeavors?"

"With regards to Tube Alloys, yes."

"You can see the importance of beating Hitler to such a fearsome weapon."

"I can see the importance of preventing Hitler from achieving such a weapon."

Churchill seethed. "This is no time for schoolboy codes of chivalry. We call on you to help us - to help your own country, Denmark - to rid the world of this scourge. We need all hands."

"Sir John has told me that there are problems. These problems go to the heart of nuclear physics. They cannot be solved by one man alone, or even one country. It took the cooperation of many physicists from many nations just to reach this point. It will take continued cooperation. The Americans . . ."

"Ah, the Americans! Let me stop you there, Dr. Bohr," said Churchill. "Understand that Britain is not the only nation pursuing this weapon; America also realizes its worth. We are committed to cooperation with them where it benefits both our nations and our other allies. I take it that Sir John has not yet told you the service which we require of you?"

"The Americans have their own version of Tube Alloys," said Sir John. "Code name, Manhattan. We have agreed to explore the possibility of a joint project. We were hoping that you would act as our eyes and ears in America."

"You want me to spy on the Americans?"

"We want you to liaise with them," answered Sir John. "The Prime Minister and President Roosevelt have agreed in principle to the merger of Tube Alloys and Manhattan. We ask that you oversee the technical aspects of the merger."

"What about the Russians?" asked Niels.

"What's it got to do with the Russians?" roared Churchill.

"The Russians have some excellent physicists."

"You handle the physics and leave the Russians to me, Dr. Bohr."

"The safety of the world requires harmonious cooperation amongst nations. The Russians are our allies, are they not?"

"Comrade Stalin does not always see eye to eye with his allies. But let us set the Russians to one side for now. Are you with us Dr. Bohr?"

"You do not need the atomic bomb to win this war."

"We must use all means at our disposal; that is what Herr Hitler is doing."

"Germany cannot build the bomb."

"Are you sure of that?" demanded Churchill.

"How well do you know Heisenberg?" asked Sir John.

"No one knows Heisenberg. But it's practically certain that no substantial progress has been achieved by the axis powers."

"Lise Meitner believes that they are working on uranium," said Sir John.

"How do you know this?"

"Her nephew, Frisch. She still receives the occasional bit of gossip from Germany."

"She has kept in touch with Otto Hahn?"

"No, Hahn is not a Nazi, but he is still a loyal German."

"Max von Laue always had a way with words," explained Chadwick.

"The Germans are up to something. They have moved their scientists out of Berlin and to the South." said Sir John. "But let us suppose you are correct that they cannot achieve the bomb. Even limited progress may be useful to the Russians should they gain access to German knowledge after the war is over."

Churchill's secretary knocked and entered the office. "The Cabinet has assembled, Prime Minister. They are waiting for you."

"Damn it man, will you go to America?" snapped Churchill. "Yes or no?"

"Yes," said Niels.

* * *

On December 31st, a truck drove along an unmarked, unpaved road which alternated between hard and bumpy and soft and slippery. It followed a meandering course amongst the mesas and canyons carved out by the Rio Grande. The road climbed to 7,300 feet above sea level and the temperature fell below freezing, and as the truck had no heater, it made for an uncomfortable ride. In the back of the truck sat several men, stone-faced and quiet, watched over by 3 armed guards.

After an hour or so on the non-existent road, the truck arrived at a compound with a high barbwire fence, patrolled by sentries. The sentries and the driver exchanged words and papers, and the sentries peered in the back of the truck at the shivering men. After satisfying themselves that all was in order, the sentries opened the gate and the truck continued on its way until it reached the front of a group of buildings; a mismatched collection of old brick, wood and metal, where a group of men waited.

The truck stopped and the passengers climbed out and stretched. Niels surveyed the landscape before him and it did not warm his heart. Instead of the statues and marble columns of the university, he saw snow covered shacks, the snow turned black with soot. Instead of winter gardens to stroll, he saw paths of mud. Instead of a mansion in which to sleep, he saw the semicircular Quonset huts of galvanized steel.

"Margrethe is just going to love this place," he mused.

The new arrivals were greeted with the jeers of friendly, familiar recognition.

"About time the rest of you Brits got here," they shouted. "Did you bring the beer and steak and kidney pies?"

Niels recognized several faces, including that of Robert Frisch, who had arrived with the first wave of the British Contingent. A man stepped forward from the group and shook Niels's hand.

"Welcome to Los Alamos," said Robert Oppenheimer. "Happy New Year and who the devil are you?"

. . . Where Angels Fear to Tread

For 10 months, Otto also resided in exile. The picturesque village of Tailfingen made the perfect venue for walks in the Black Forest and skiing in the winter, but to Otto, the Kaiser Wilhelm Institute of Tailfingen didn't carry the same prestige as that of Berlin. He hated to live away from his home. He hated the lack of culture. He hated the cramped conditions and broken equipment. He hated that another war had destroyed Germany. Must he always be on the losing side? At least, he comforted himself, sleepy Tailfingen rested far away from the politics of the Nazis.

Except today. Today he received a surprise visit from Walther Gerlach. Otto knew the man well; a physicist by profession, but Gerlach heralded from the Munich contingency, not Berlin, and the rivalry between the two schools often led to friction. In a sudden but typically irrational burst of fickleness, prompted by the belief that Einstein had contaminated the Kaiser Wilhelm physicists beyond cleansing, Göring handpicked Gerlach to head all physics research, including the nuclear research which Otto conducted. The reason for the visit was that Göring had become angry at their lack of progress, which in turn meant that Gerlach was angry.

"Incompetence!" screeched Gerlach. "Treason! You're not too old to be drafted into the Territorial Army, you know." He waved a Swedish newspaper, the *Stockholms Tidningen*; the headline on the front page boasted of incredible news from London: the United States had a new weapon, a bomb with uranium at its heart, a million times more powerful than any bomb ever built.

"Propaganda," Otto shrugged.

"This is the very thing on which you are working. How did the Americans beat us to it?"

"Perhaps if you gave us the resources . . ."

"We gave everything asked of us. Heisenberg asked for a ton of uranium and 2 tons of heavy water, we supplied a ton of uranium and 2 tons of heavy water. Then Heisenberg said another half ton of uranium would do it. You got it. Now we have a new request for an additional 750 kilograms of heavy water. There is always a new request and a new excuse, but never any progress. Herr Göring is not pleased."

"He's not the only one."

"And where is Heisenberg, by the way?"

Otto shrugged and wished he knew. Gerlach had the wrong audience; to listen to petty tirades was not Otto's responsibility; bearing the brunt of Nazi anger and stupidity was Heisenberg's forte. But Heisenberg seemed to sense when trouble was near and had developed the ability to disappear into the shadows. When he had heard news of Gerlach's visit, Max von Laue had also made his excuses and departed; which left Otto to face the music alone.

"As a physicist, you should appreciate the difficulty . . ."

"Difficulty, difficulty, everything is difficult! The Führer does not understand difficult."

"What do you want me to say?"

"If we cannot build a uranium machine for energy or explosion, we at least need to satisfy Hitler that neither can the enemy. This newspaper report must be refuted."

"Isn't that the job of Ribbentrop?"

"Don't be glib. No more excuses. Göring wants results. We either build our own bomb or we explain why this story is a pack of lies, or we move the Kaiser Wilhelm Institute to the Russian Front. You have one week, Hahn."

The threat did not impress Otto. "Please, we both know the war is lost. When you return to Berlin, I'll wager that you find Hitler has fled back to Austria. One week, what difference will that make?"

Otto did not have one week. He did not have one second.

"Hands up, hands up!" the American GI screamed in German, as he burst into the room and pointed a machine gun directly at Otto.

"Hands up!" bellowed the second GI as he came in through the window.

The men looked as if nothing would make them happier than to brutally crush any resistance. Otto raised his hands in surrender. Gerlach did the same. More men streamed in: commandos from an operation dubbed Alsos, ahead of the advancing Allied Forces, behind German lines and on a mission to capture German scientists. A lieutenant entered the room: Moe Berg dressed in an army uniform.

With a perfect German accent, Moe spoke to them, "Professor Hahn, Professor Gerlach, you are under arrest. My men are a little edgy after all this excitement. I advise you do everything I say without hesitation."

Otto nodded; the horror of his capture tempered with the relief that he didn't have to kowtow to the Nazis any more.

"Where are all your reports and papers?" asked Moe.

"Right here," said Otto, tapping the side of his head with a finger.

"Okay, outside, move."

Outside the building, a line of American military vehicles, with tanks at the front and back, met Otto's gaze. He wondered at the ingenuity of the men who could move such a convoy of heavy metal and engines to his door with such stealth that he did not hear them arrive; perhaps if Gerlach had shouted a little less? He stopped, but was jostled from behind.

"I say, Otto, old man," said Max von Laue. "Would you mind moving along there? You're holding up the line."

"No talking," yelled Colonel Pash, the commanding officer. "Keep those men apart."

The Americans bundled Otto, Laue and Gerlach into separate armored scout cars, and assigned two guards to each man.

"We got everyone in the building, Colonel," said Berg. "Gerlach is an unexpected little bonus."

"But where is Heisenberg, Moe?" asked Colonel Pash. "Where is Heisenberg?"

* * *

Werner Heisenberg had requisitioned a bicycle, made his escape and come home to Urfeld. With the Allies close behind, he briefly considered continuing eastward, but a conversation in a bicycle repair shop changed his mind: rumors swirled that SS snipers hid in the woods to shoot any Germans who fled. So he had returned home.

In the distance, the thunder of artillery disturbed the peace, but Heisenberg ignored it. He sat in his study, in front of the window which overlooked Lake Walchen, ate some chocolate, sipped at a glass of red wine and contemplated the chess board on the table in front of him. The door to the study rocked gently.

"Come in," said Heisenberg. "I'm not armed," he lied, for a Schuster pistol lay on his lap.

A man emerged from the shadows, gun in hand.

"Have you come to execute me?" asked Heisenberg.

Sporadic gunfire erupted from somewhere near the house.

"Not unless I have to," said Moe Berg.

"American?" asked Heisenberg. Moe nodded. "Thank God for that. I have a pistol; I will place it on the table. Please don't shoot."

"You were expecting someone else?" asked Moe, his Browning .45 still aimed at Heisenberg.

"Russians; SS perhaps; I wasn't sure . . ."

Heisenberg pushed the pistol away from him. Moe lowered his gun, but kept his finger on the trigger. The gunfire continued outside.

". . . They don't give up easily, do they? Such fanatics."

Moe sat down opposite Heisenberg. "They want you almost as much as we do," he said.

"No, not really; it's just spite; if they can't have me then neither can anyone else," said Heisenberg. He indicated the board in front of him. "Do you play chess? It's a tricky one: mate in 6 moves. I can't see a way out."

"It looks as if your situation is hopeless," said Moe.

"Yes, I do believe that I am at an impasse. The wine has dulled my senses."

"Is there anyone else in the house?"

"Elizabeth and the children are in the cellar. I thought it safer for them there. I heard a disturbance and came up to check."

"I took care of the disturbance; your family is safe."

"Thank you."

"Lieutenant?" came a shout from outside.

"In here," responded Moe. "Heisenberg is with me."

Colonel Pash and a sergeant entered the study. "Hello, Professor, it's good to finally catch up with you."

A private entered and saluted. "Perimeter all secure, Sir," he said. "Two SS under arrest, wounded, but they'll live; a third one dead behind the house; the others got away."

"Sergeant," said Moe, as he put his gun away. "The Professor's family is in the basement; would you mind fetching them up. Try not to scare them."

"And bring another bottle of wine," added Heisenberg. "There are some glasses on the shelf behind you, gentlemen. Sadly, I can't offer you any hors d'oeuvres; we ran out of bread four days ago."

The sergeant went to fetch the family. A distant explosion rumbled.

"It's getting quieter now. I suppose it's almost over," said Heisenberg. "Will I be sent to America?"

"I don't know, Professor," said Colonel Pash. "I leave those decisions to others."

"Better to America than to Russia. I hope it's San Francisco; I like San Francisco. I wonder if they'll let Elizabeth come with me?"

A lieutenant entered and, reluctant to speak in front of Heisenberg, asked Colonel Pash to step out of the room. Heisenberg could only make out the Colonel's part of the conversation.

"How many? . . . Why do they have to surrender to us? . . . Tell them to surrender tomorrow at 10:00AM. In the meantime, get some reinforcements sent up, I can't accept the surrender of 3 platoons of German Infantry with only 10 men to guard them."

The colonel and the lieutenant returned.

"Okay, Professor," said Colonel Pash. "We are arranging an escort to take you to Heidelberg. But in the meantime, we shall have to stay here tonight, if you don't mind."

"Be my guest," replied Heisenberg. "How many can we expect for dinner? Oh, I forgot, we have no bread."

The sergeant, who now carried a suitcase, returned with Heisenberg's wife and children.

"Lieutenant," ordered Colonel Pash. "Take Mrs. Heisenberg to town and get some bread." He looked at the pistol on the table and picked it up. "Do you have a license for this?" he asked Heisenberg.

"I believe not," answered Heisenberg.

"Lieutenant, also arrange a weapons permit for the Professor." He handed the pistol back to Heisenberg. "I wouldn't want Mrs. Heisenberg to worry about you." Colonel Pash saw the suitcase. "What you got there, Sergeant?"

"Found it by the cellar door, sir."

"Planning a trip, Professor?" asked Colonel Pash.

"Just a few things for the journey: toothbrush, shaving soap, a change of clothes," replied Heisenberg. "I thought it best to prepare."

"There are some other things in the cellar, Sir, I think you should see," said the Sergeant. "Scientific things: equipment and notebooks."

"Berg, go check it out," said Colonel Pash. "Sergeant, go with him."

Moe went to the cellar. Besides using it to store wine, Heisenberg had converted it to a makeshift laboratory. Moe glanced around the cluttered room, but nothing seemed to require his immediate attention.

"Okay, Sergeant, our orders are to take everything with us. Only dismantle what won't come out in one piece."

"What about the blackboard, Sir?" asked the Sergeant.

"Blackboard?" Moe was not sure he understood the sergeant. Then he saw it, at the back of the cellar, the text on it barely legible in the dim light:

"Dummköpfe hetzen in wo Engel Angst haben zu treten."

"Hey, Sarge!" said Moe. "How's your German?"

"Not bad, Sir, but that looks kind of odd to me."

"It is odd. As if a foreign student of German wrote it. It's too literal a translation."

"That's what I thought, Sir. Shakespeare?"

"Alexander Pope. Who do you think is the intended recipient of such a message?"

"Must be us, he was expecting us. Maybe he's warning us that the house is booby trapped?"

"No, I don't think so, not with his kids in the house. And we're not so dumb that Heisenberg would try to tell us how to do our job. And he couldn't be sure that the SS wouldn't get to him first; I don't think a quotation from a dead English poet would have helped him there. Heisenberg sure does like to take chances."

"Still, pretty weird, Sir. I was expecting a blackboard full of equations."

"Heisenberg is a pretty weird guy. I'm glad I didn't shoot him when I had the chance."

Moe Berg knew what the message said, but why would Heisenberg say it in such a non-German manner? It was a warning, but to whom? Moe mouthed the words, as if to read them aloud would yield a clue to their meaning, '*Fools rush in where angels fear to tread.*'

... *August 6ᵗʰ, 1945*

Since the news of the alleged bomb had broken in the newspapers, the intrepid members of the Press had hounded Lise for her side of the story, which she steadfastly declined to provide. In Stockholm, where she worked at the Nobel Institute of Physics, the reporters' persistence had reached such a point of annoyance that Lise decided to escape the city for a brief respite in the tranquil security of the Bahr-Bergius' home in Kungälv.

The weather behaved perfectly. Gentle bird song filled the air and King Summer held court. Saturday passed in friendly, languid ease; and by Sunday afternoon, Lise had reached an exceptional state of relaxation. Eva had retired to the kitchen to prepare the evening meal. Niklas pottered about the house and performed the odd bit of maintenance here and there. Julia played on a swing in the garden.

Reclined in a garden chair, Lise read a book and wished that the day would never end. With the Nazis vanquished, the war in Europe had run its course and after more than a decade of nightmare and shadows, the sun had returned. Her optimism had returned. Her vacation had nourished her spirit and her flesh. She knew that in a few days she would have to return to the real world, but for now, time stood still.

Julia climbed from the swing and approached.

"What are you reading?" asked Julia.

"It's a book of English poetry. My nephew, Robert, gave it to me."

Julia looked over Lise's shoulder. "English? We are studying English at school. Can I see?" Lise handed the book to Julia and she read aloud, "*The Tyger* by William Blake . . . We don't have any tigers in Sweden."

"I should hope not."

"Except in the zoo."

"And that's where they should stay."

Lise sensed a sudden breeze on the air and looked up. The birds had stopped singing. Lise turned to Julia, but the girl had returned to the swing and with a hard push, set it rocking back and forth. The birds, suddenly startled, rose up into the sky en masse and flew away.

"They've all gone!" lamented Julia.

"What?"

"The birds; they've all gone. They are afraid of the tiger."

"Oh no, they've just gone in for tea. And we should go in too," said Lise. "It has gotten a little chilly out here."

Julia, with the poetry book in hand, sat on the swing and began to recite.

> *Tyger! Tyger! burning bright*
> *In the forests of the night,*

On the island of Tinian, in the Philippine Sea, the clock ticked over midnight to a new day, Monday 6th of August, 1945. At the North Field Airbase, the flight crews of the 393rd Bomb Squadron, from the 509th Composite Group, assembled for a mission briefing. Pilot and Commander, Colonel Paul Tibbets, was the only crew member who knew the details of the mission. Tibbets had visited Los Alamos.

"Just how powerful is this bomb?" Tibbets had asked.

"How many bombs have you dropped so far?" Colonel Pash had replied.

"My missions, I don't keep track."

"No, I mean in total, the whole US Air Force; how many bombs have the Air Force dropped in this war?"

"Can't say; more than a lot, I suppose."

"Well, this bomb is more powerful than all of them combined."

"So it's gonna make one hell of a bang, then?"

> *What immortal hand or eye*
> *Could frame thy fearful symmetry?*

At the Ujina fire station, Hiroshima, Japan, the clock ticked over midnight to a new day. Yosaku Mikami yawned. He had completed 16 hours of a 24 hour shift and tiredness had made him lethargic. He blamed the war - it made everyone tired. He wanted to go home, but he still had another 8 hours before the shift ended.

At least he had done his job and the time had come for someone else to take over, while he grabbed a few hours of sleep. In the time before the war, everyone in the firehouse had slept through the night. With the loudest alarm clock in the world to wake them, it wasn't overly negligent, but the chief had cracked down on the practice and demanded that somebody be awake and on watch at all times. With Yosaku's turn at watch over, he shook his buddy, Akira, awake.

"Come on, my turn in the bunk," he said.

"What time is it?" asked Akira.

"Just gone midnight. Come on, there's still some tea in the pot," he lied - the pot really held Yamazaki whisky. To their annoyance, the chief had cracked down on several of their time honored traditions, but he could not stamp out all their bad habits.

"Anything happening?"

"No, it's very quiet. No fires. No air raids. The city is asleep."

"Except for you and me."

"And let's hope it stays that way. Except for the you and me part; I hope it will soon just be you."

Yosaku and Akira exchanged places. As Yosaku lay in the bunk, and the only sound in the night was that of a thirsty fireman with a cup of whisky, his last thought before sleep took him was that Hiroshima was seldom so quiet.

In what distant deeps or skies
Burnt the fire of thine eyes?

2:15 AM. On Tinian, the teletype machine rattled out a message in code, which they quickly translated: President Truman says smoke 'em if you've got 'em.

The crews left the briefing room and walked across the runway to the waiting B-29 Superfortresses. Tibbets would fly plane number 82, named the Enola Gay after his mother. The ground crew had loaded the bomb earlier in the day, disarmed to avoid accidents. They would arm it during the 6-hour flight. Tibbets had personally selected his crew his from the finest which the Air Force had to offer.

"Pick anyone you want for this mission," they had told Tibbets. "And that goes for the ground crew, the control tower, the boys in the machine shop, the cooks and the barber."

Two other B-29s, the Great Artiste and the Necessary Evil, stood beside the Enola Gay, ready to accompany it on its journey; to film the event and to drop scientific recording equipment ahead of the bomb. Three more planes had left an hour earlier for advance weather reconnaissance.

On what wings dare he aspire?
What the hand dare seize the fire?

5:20 AM. The sun came up over the eastern horizon and Yosaku woke, rested and refreshed. The birds had begun to sing, but the men of the fire station still dozed. He heard Akira snore, another victim of Yamazaki whisky. Good job the chief never came round at this hour.

Yosaku climbed out of the bunk. His mouth felt parched. He wanted some tea, real tea this time, and he picked up the now empty pot, rinsed it out and filled it with water. The noise of running water stirred his friend.

"What time is it?" Akira mumbled as he rubbed his eyes.

"Sunrise. Here, have some tea."

Akira took the cup. "Thanks."

"I've never known anyone like you for sleeping," laughed Yosaku. "You'd sleep all day if we let you."

"What can I say? I need my twenty hours."

"Sleep when you're dead, that's my motto."

"Well you can keep your motto. When I get home I shall sleep some more. But not you, if I know your wife."

"No, not me; she has a whole bunch of chores lined up for me."

"I warned you not to get married."

271

And what shoulder, & what art
Could twist the sinews of thy heart?

5:26 AM. As the Enola Gay approached Japan with the rising sun, Tibbets handed control of the B-29 to his co-pilot, Captain Lewis, and crawled through the tunnel which connected the cockpit with the rest of the plane. The time had come to let the boys in on the secret.

"I guess some of you have already figured out what we're doing today?" said Tibbets.

"We're delivering bombs," they said.

"Yeah, but this one is a little bit special."

"Colonel," said the tailgunner, Sergeant Caron. "We wouldn't be playing with atoms today, would we?"

"Bob, you got it precisely right," said Tibbets. "You've been paying attention."

"Well that bomb is pretty peculiar; it ain't exactly standard Government Issue."

And when thy heart began to beat,
What dread hand? & what dread feet?

7:25 AM. The fire station radio, which Yosaku had turned on to rouse his comrades for breakfast, abruptly stopped its broadcast and the air raid siren blared.

"Too late," yelled Akira. "I'm already awake." He looked out of the window and up through the clouds, he saw a B-29, high in the sky. It had become a common sight over Japan. "Look at that! Another one flying over the city in broad daylight. How come we don't have some zeros up there to bring it down?"

Yosaku looked out of the window. "It's just an observation plane; it's not worth wasting the fuel; not for one or two. But they are up there for a reason. My guess is we'll be fighting off an invasion force any day now. Best conserve our resources for the battle ahead."

"Then we should shoot it down from here. What's the point of all those anti-aircraft guns if we never use them?"

"It's too high up; out of range of the guns."

"But it's an enemy plane."

"Don't worry; one plane can't do much damage. When the real fight comes, we'll be ready for it."

The air raid siren blasted the all-clear and the radio broadcast resumed.

"See, told you, nothing to worry about."

What the hammer? what the chain?
In what furnace was thy brain?

7:35 AM. With the Japanese fighter planes snug in their hangers, The Enola Gay crossed over the Iyo-nada Sea. The B-29 which Yosaku had seen, a weather plane, the Straight Flush, transmitted a coded message to the Enola Gay: cloud cover over the target less than 30%. Good enough for Tibbets, he informed the crew.

"It's Hiroshima."

What the anvil? what dread grasp
Dare its deadly terrors clasp?

7:45 AM. 30 minutes from the target. Tibbets ordered Captain Parsons and Lieutenant Jeppson to arm the bomb and remove its safety devices. He tried to remember all the mistakes he had made in his life, as a flyer, as a commander of men. He couldn't think of any. He sure as hell didn't want this to be the first.

When the stars threw down their spears,
And water'd heaven with their tears,

8:09 AM. His work shift over, Yosaku boarded the streetcar which would take him home to Sakaemachi. Because of the time, rush hour, he expected a crowd and he got what he expected; more than 100 people already occupied the car: Office workers, factory workers, dockyard men, sailors and mothers with babes in arms. Next to him, three schoolgirls conversed and giggled as they made plans to enjoy a rare holiday from student mobilization labor. Their laughter made him smile. In the midst of war, people could still laugh.

Did he smile his work to see?
Did he who made the lamb make thee?

8:12 AM. Tibbets broke radio silence. His orders said not to, but how the hell would the guys in the other two planes know the situation if he didn't speak to them. He started his bomb run and handed control over to his bombardier, Major Ferebee.

"One minute out," Tibbets intoned. "Thirty seconds out . . . Twenty seconds . . . Ten, nine, eight, seven, six, five, four, three, two, one."

The Enola Gay lurched, suddenly 10,000 pounds lighter. Tibbets took the B-29 down and away to the right, banking to an impossible 155-degree angle from the pending explosion. The B-29 groaned, shuddered and threatened to fall apart at the seams.

"We usually just fly straight ahead," Tibbets had said.

"You don't want to do that, or you'll be right over the top when it blows, and nobody would ever know you were there."

"How long we got before the blast?"

"You've got about 40 seconds to make the turn and outrun the shockwave."

Tibbets had rehearsed the maneuver over the salt flats of Utah. Although he had told his superior officers that he could handle the turn, the best he had managed in practice was 42 seconds.

Tyger! Tyger! burning bright
In the forests of the night,

8:15 AM. The streetcar approached the Miyuki-Bashi Station. A cry alerted the passengers to the presence of another plane in the sky. Yosaku looked up. He recognized the silhouette of the B-29; the same plane he had seen earlier or a different one, he couldn't say and he didn't care. He watched it turn and dive, as if something chased it. Perhaps the zeros had decided to challenge after all?

Then Yosaku saw something else in the sky. Not a B-29 or zero but a parachute. The Americans had dropped propaganda leaflets before, but they didn't need parachutes. What could it be? What had they dropped? Had the pilot bailed out? He squinted against the bright sunlight to try to identify it. Attached to the end of the parachute was the last thing he ever saw. And the sun was no longer the brightest object in the sky.

What immortal hand or eye,
Dare frame thy fearful symmetry?

In Kungälv, Sweden, the clock had ticked over midnight to a new day. Quiet had descended on the house. Everyone had retired to bed, except for Lise and Eva, who shared the last drops from a bottle of wine. Lise had wished that Sunday would never end, but she couldn't escape the fact that it was now Monday, August 6th.

Honor

"Whence come I and whither go I? That is the great unfathomable question, the same for every one of us. Science has no answer to it."

Max Planck

. . . *Robert, 1969*

At a table in one of the restaurants of the Connaught Hotel in Mayfair, Robert sat opposite Erik Rudberg, the Permanent Secretary to the Royal Swedish Academy of Sciences. Sir Paul Gall-Booth of the Foreign Office sat between them. They danced around the conversation in polite but measured tones, with Robert's entreaties constantly rebuffed by the non-committal language of the polished diplomat. Robert jabbed, Rudberg parried and Gall-Booth played the referee. Robert felt he had lost his power of persuasion: not once did they address him as Robert, only as Dr. Frisch.

"Dr. Frisch," said Rudberg. "I sympathize. If it was up to me, and if we had known then what we know today, she would have at least shared the prize in 1946."

"Then you agree with me."

"But none of the official evidence which the Academy received for review listed Dr. Meitner as a contributor. The prize was for chemistry and Dr. Meitner was a physicist. Your aunt herself never publicly refuted this assessment."

"I have two main arguments to that," said Robert.

"Only two?" said Gall-Booth. "I do believe that we are making progress."

"Only two for now," amended Robert. "First, although my aunt was, as you say, a physicist, the discovery of nuclear fission depended on the disciplines of both chemistry and physics, and a healthy dose of mathematics too."

"There is no prize for mathematics is there?" Gall-Booth digressed.

"No," answered Rudberg. "Alfred Nobel wanted to recognize advances which led to tangible benefits for humanity, not theoretical."

"My aunt was not a chemist," pressed Robert. "But fission was her discovery."

"Not according to the records."

"And here we have the second argument. The records were falsified. The Nazis removed Lise's name from her published works. They tried to rewrite the history books. But everyone knew that, didn't they? You say if only we had known, but the Academy did know; it was impossible not to know. Her discovery made the front page of all the newspapers, including the obscure Swedish ones read by the Academy."

"The Academy does not give awards based on gossip in the newspapers."

"She was nominated for the Nobel Prize on 15 separate occasions, before and after the war. Even Heisenberg nominated her, for Christ's sake . . ."

He paused; the gentle walls of the Connaught seldom heard such strong language.

". . . Everybody in the world knew, including the Academy."

"The Academy based its decision on the paper published by Otto Hahn after Dr. Meitner had left Germany. These are the facts. She was not there and her name was not on that paper."

"Her name was not on that paper because the Nazis forbid it, but that is irrelevant. Hahn's paper described the experiment, yet it was our paper, my aunt and me, published separately from Hahn's, but published at the same time, which explained the results of that experiment."

"The Academy determined that your paper was after the fact."

"Ha, you just proved my point. The Academy had the evidence in their hands that fission was my aunt's discovery, but they chose to downplay it, ignore it. Now why would they do that?"

"Are you suggesting that the Academy colluded with the Nazis? That is preposterous. Hitler's regime had already fallen before the decision was reached."

"I am suggesting that politics played a part. After the war there was a desire not to repeat the mistakes made in 1919, and a need to rehabilitate German science. Was Otto Hahn vital to that rehabilitation? Did the powers of the world sense an opportunity? Was this a snub for the sake of diplomacy over science? Did expediency win over truth?"

"I did not have the pleasure of working with Dr. Meitner at the Nobel Institute during her period there. And I did not become a member of the Academy until '54. So I'm happy to say that if politics played a role in the decision to omit Dr. Meitner from the award, I was not a party to it. But my predecessor, Arne Westgren, would certainly have worked with Dr. Meitner in Stockholm. I am sure that having known your aunt personally, he would not have condoned it either. No, I don't believe it."

"Niels Bohr believed it. From the moment the Prize was announced, until his death, he believed the Academy had done a great injustice to my aunt and he fought for the rest of his life to persuade the Academy to rectify its mistake."

"Ah, now if we are to consider Niels Bohr," interrupted Gall-Booth. "We must also take into account that after the war, Bohr himself was suspect and unwelcome in political circles. An unfortunate circumstance he brought on himself - he would insist on talking to Russian scientists. He did not make the best advocate for your aunt."

"Well, now I am her advocate," said Robert.

"Still to no avail, I'm afraid," said Rudberg. "Now that your aunt has passed, all the arguments you raise are redundant. As you know, we don't award the prize posthumously."

"Perhaps you should make an exception. Every day I hear a different excuse: she was only an assistant, she was not a chemist. Before the war, she was dismissed because she was a woman. After the war we needed to rehabilitate German science. How can we rehabilitate when we fail to start with the basic truth? The fascists sought to eradicate all mention of my aunt. They failed to take her life, but they did take her work. They removed her name from the papers she wrote. They credited her discoveries to others; and if the Nobel Academy has not colluded in this, they at least dishonor themselves by not joining in our fight to restore the truth."

"Dr. Frisch, my advice to you is to forget the Nobel. The Academy has never been known to change its mind. I know of your aunt's story. I am sorry for the hardships and prejudices she endured, but she is beyond all that now. Perhaps there was a time when the Prize, and its monetary attachment, would have comforted her, but that is also in the past. After the war, she did receive several other honors and much recognition. One more award, even a Nobel, cannot add to her reputation."

"Yes, I remember," said Gall-Booth "The Americans named her 'Woman of the Year.'"

. . . Farm Hall, 1945

As prisons went, the country estate near Cambridge, England known as Farm Hall would have disappointed those who expected burly warders and hardened criminals who contested for superiority in cell blocks of concrete and iron bars. Apart from the presence of prisoners, Farm Hall had nothing in common with such a place. Instead, Farm Hall had landscaped gardens, a tennis court and a grand piano. True, guards did patrol the perimeter of the estate, but they performed their duties as much to keep prying eyes out as to prevent any attempt to escape. The guards watched the prisoners to determine their usefulness, not because of any potential danger to society.

The ten prisoners, Otto, Heisenberg and Max von Laue amongst them, faired better than most who roamed free back in the wilds of Germany. They had clean sheets and 4-poster beds in which to sleep, in warm, wood-paneled rooms. They enjoyed bacon and eggs for breakfast and Chateaubriand steak for dinner; a vastly superior diet to that of their English hosts who still endured war-time rations. They had servants to clean their rooms and polish their shoes. They had teachers to help them learn the English language. They each had a personal batman to help them dress and to run errands to the post-office.

And they had a radio. And on the radio, the refined tones of the BBC newsreader wafted gently across the library where they had all assembled to listen. And they listened to the radio in stunned disbelief.

"The first atomic bomb has been dropped by a United States aircraft on the Japanese city of Hiroshima. President Harry S. Truman, announcing the news from the cruiser, USS Augusta, in the mid-Atlantic, said the device was more than 2,000 times more powerful than the largest bomb used to date.

The President said the atomic bomb heralded the *'harnessing of the basic power of the universe.'* It also marked a victory over the Germans in the race to be first to develop a weapon using atomic energy.

The President continued, *'If they do not now accept our terms they may expect a rain of ruin from the air the like of which has never been seen on Earth.'*"

Otto switched off the radio. No one spoke. Their astonishment hung on the air as a shroud. They bowed their heads and dared not look at each other, until finally the incessant tick-tick-tick of the library's grandfather clock proved too much to bear and Otto broke the silence.

"Impossible! It can't be an atomic bomb. They just called it that. It couldn't possibly be uranium."

"Why not?" asked Heisenberg. "After all, Hitler wanted us to build one for him."

"Take care what you say," admonished Walther Gerlach, who still believed that he commanded the group of German scientists. "For all we know the British may have installed microphones here."

"Microphones?" laughed Heisenberg. "Oh no, they're not as cute as all that. I don't think they know the real Gestapo methods; they're a bit old fashioned in that respect. But impossible, Otto? I think we know better. Given the same resources as the Allies, certainly we in this room could have succeeded."

"Well if the report is true, it shows at any rate that the Americans are capable of real cooperation on a tremendous scale," said Otto. "But I still say that it would have been impossible in Germany: envy and suspicion; each one downplaying the other's importance. We lacked the true cooperation necessary to accomplish such a feat."

"You can't say that as far as our Uranium Group is concerned," said Gerlach. "You can't say that."

"Not officially of course," said Max von Laue.

"Not unofficially either! Don't contradict me! There are far too many other people here who know," yelled Gerlach.

"Of course, Walther," soothed Otto. "But think of what it must have taken. We were unable to work on that scale. We never had the resources at hand."

"They may have had the resources, but we had the best scientists."

"Did we indeed?" asked Laue. "What makes you think that? Does the name, Einstein ring a bell? Fermi, Franck, Teller, Bohr?"

"I wonder how they did it?" Heisenberg mused. "How much uranium did they use? How did they trigger a reaction? The whole heavy-water business, which I did everything I could to further, cannot produce an explosive."

"Not until the reactor is running," added Gerlach.

"They seem to have the explosive before making the reactor and now they say, 'In the future we will build the reactor,'" said Otto. "Still, it must have taken more than just scientists, thousands of workers, perhaps, tens of thousands."

"We wouldn't have had the moral courage to recommend to the government in the spring of 1942 that they should employ 120,000 men just for building the thing," said Heisenberg.

"Perhaps if we hadn't wasted all our time and energy on the V1 and V2 rockets," said Otto. "How many thousands of men worked on that program?"

"I believe the reason we didn't do it was because all the physicists didn't want to do it, on principle," said Gerlach. "If we had wanted Germany to win the war we would have succeeded."

"Speak up, Walther," said Laue. "I don't think the microphones picked up on your air of moral superiority."

"I don't believe that, but I am thankful we didn't succeed," said Otto.

"Now, now, Walther has something there," said Heisenberg. "The point is that the whole structure of the relationship between the scientist and the state in Germany was such that although we were not 100% anxious to do it, on the other hand we were so little trusted by the state that even if we had wanted to do it, it would not have been easy to get it through."

"Ah, that makes more sense," said Laue. "Not superior principles, but superior distrust. We never lacked for that resource. If only Hitler had trusted us more, we could have put our principles aside."

"Even if we had gotten everything that we wanted, it is by no means certain whether we would have gotten as far as the Americans and English have now," said Otto. "There is no question that we were very nearly as far as they were, but it is a fact that we were all convinced that the thing could not have been completed during the war."

"Well, that's not quite right. I would say that I was absolutely convinced of the possibility of our making a uranium reactor, but I never thought we would make a bomb," said Heisenberg. "And at the bottom of my heart, I was really glad that it was to be a reactor and not a bomb. I must admit that."

"I don't think we ought to make excuses now because we did not succeed, but we must admit that we did not want to succeed," said Gerlash.

"No?" asked Otto.

"No!" insisted Gerlash. "I think it characteristic that the Germans made the discovery and didn't use it, whereas the Americans have used it. I must say I didn't think the Americans would dare to use it."

"Oh, stop making excuses and admit it," said Laue. "We failed because we are all second-raters. Poor old Gerlash, poor old Heisenberg. I heard that the Americans wanted to place us all in front of a firing squad while we were in Heidelberg. Why ever did the British talk them out of it?"

Gerlash bristled at Laue's jabs, but before a full blown argument could erupt, Otto returned to the radio and switched it back into life.

". . . And finally, in news closely related to the topic of the uranium bomb, the Royal Swedish Academy of Sciences has awarded the Nobel Prize for Chemistry to Otto Hahn,

the German chemist, for his discovery of
nuclear fission. It was this discovery which
directly led to the creation of the bomb."

"My God, congratulations, Otto," laughed Laue. "I take it back;
you, at least, are not second rate. And your discovery won the war for
the enemy. Germany is proud of you. We must celebrate. Let's have a
party."

"Knock it off, Max," interjected Heisenberg. "They dropped this
bomb on Japan, not Germany; they defeated Germany without any
help from Otto."

"Yes, you are correct, Werner," said a humbled Laue. "Sorry,
Otto, you are still second rate, but nonetheless, congratulations, your
Nobel is well deserved and long overdue."

"Congratulations, Otto," added Heisenberg. "I truly wish we had
heard the news under more pleasant circumstances. Max is right; we
must celebrate this honor as best we can. At least, I'm sure our hosts
will provide some Champagne for us."

Gerlash extended a hand, "My best congratulations, Dr. Hahn. It
is undoubtedly well deserved."

"The question is will Otto be allowed to travel to Oslo to receive
the prize?" asked Laue. "And will we all be allowed to go with him?
I'll drive."

Otto accepted his colleagues' congratulations with little
satisfaction; and not just because of the circumstances of his
imprisonment. He walked over to the drinks cabinet, poured a large
measure of cognac into a glass and gulped it down. This moment
should have stood as the happiest of his life, a magnificent tribute to
a glittering career. But the moment of which he had dreamt lay
destroyed by a nuclear bomb.

The other prisoners, with wide grins on their faces and well
intentioned delight in their hearts, moved to shake his hand, slap him
on the back and call him old friend, but he felt no joy nor warmth

nor camaraderie. He felt very much alone. The news left him sick to his stomach. That he should receive the Nobel for a discovery which had led to such ruin did not please him. Why did all his achievements have a stench of death about them? He wished that his glass contained cyanide instead of cognac. He longed for death to come and hide him. Thank God that the Nobel Committee had named him alone and excluded Lise from the Prize; at least they had spared her from this ignominy.

... *Woman of the Year*

L ise woke. The birds had returned and their song filtered in through the window with the sunlight. Her vacation had ended. She sighed. She must return to Stockholm, where the crude hammer of her alarm clock would replace the birdsong.

She heard voices from downstairs. Eva and Niklas had already started their day. She rose, dressed, smoothed the sheets on the bed and retrieved her suitcase from the top of the wardrobe. She placed the case on the bed, stared at it and willed herself to pack.

"Not before a cup of coffee," she conceded.

She opened the bedroom door to find Eva standing before it, coffee in hand.

"Here," said Eva as she handed over the cup "I thought you might need this."

"You read my mind," smiled Lise. "Thank you, but I could have come down; I don't expect breakfast in bed."

"I wanted to tell you - warn you - that we have visitors."

"You sound serious. Do you want me to keep out of the way until they have gone?"

"No, it's you they have come to see."

"Me? What it is it? What is wrong?"

"Come on down. They are in the kitchen."

Lise followed Eva to the kitchen, where she found Niklas and two other men, tweed jackets and narrow ties. They rose from their chairs as she entered, almost as if they stood to attention. The flash of a camera's bulb momentarily blinded her. Reporters! She sighed again: her vacation had certainly ended.

The cameraless man gently signaled to his comrade to forgo any more pictures for the present.

"Dr. Meitner," he said. "Hello, I am Hugo Strindberg of the *Tidningen* . . ."

"Yes, I know who you are, young man."

"Please, call me Hugo."

"I know who you are, young man, but what are you doing here. How on earth did you find me?"

"It wasn't easy."

"Couldn't you have waited until I returned to Stockholm? What is so important that you have to disturb my vacation?"

"My God, you don't know?"

"Young man, there is much that I don't know. What, specifically, do I not know that has brought you here to pester me and invade the home of my friends at this early hour?"

"Lise," said Niklas. "Perhaps you had better sit down."

Lise sat and prepared for the worse. The voice in her head said that someone had died; someone near to her; but someone so important that they had to hunt her down for her comments? No, that didn't make sense - in such a case, her opinions would add little value. What could it be?

"Dr. Meitner," said Strindberg. "We understand that you made the discovery which led to the uranium bomb."

"You have asked me these questions before; my answer is unchanged."

"You still maintain that you played no part in the creation of the bomb?"

"If such a bomb exists, I played no part in its creation."

"The bomb exists."

"Don't believe what you read in your own newspaper."

"The bomb exists. Yesterday, we received proof."

"What kind of proof?"

"There was a report on the radio," interrupted Eva. "We missed it."

"Report?"

"President Truman has announced that the atomic bomb was dropped on the Japanese city of Hiroshima," said Strindberg.

Lise looked to Eva and Nikas for confirmation. They nodded their heads in agreement. Nikas held up a newspaper with headlines which also confirmed it; and a sub-headline which read, 'Exiled Scientist Revealed as Heroine who Guarded Atom's Secrets from Nazis.'

"How many?" Lise whispered, the tears welling in her eyes.

"According to our records, Hiroshima was an industrial port city with a population of over 300,000."

"How many?" pressed Lise.

"Well that is hard to say. There is a great deal of confusion."

"But what reports are coming out of Hiroshima?"

"Dr. Meitner, we have no reports out of Hiroshima . . . Hiroshima no longer exists."

Lise wanted to scream, but only silence came out of her mouth; and the tears fell.

"You are called a heroine. We would like to . . ."

"I'm sorry," Lise stood up. "I have no comment."

"Just a few words will set the record straight."

"No, I'm sorry. I have to get back to Stockholm. I have a train to catch."

"We have a car; we can take you."

"No, I have to pack. I'll just go outside for a cigarette."

"Lise . . ." Eva began to warn, but too late, for Lise had already reached the front door.

Lise opened the door only to find the flashes of cameras and a dozen suddenly roused reporters who had gathered in the garden. As a pack, they closed in on her. She reversed her direction, closed the door and, impeded by Strindberg from a return to the kitchen, turned instead to the living room. Her head swam with unstructured thoughts and her ears rang. Strindberg and the cameraman entered the living room and asked questions which she could not hear. Eva and Niklas followed to protect her. The ringing in her ears continued. Niklas forced his way between Lise and the reporters and began to shepherd them from the room. The ringing continued until Eva picked up the telephone receiver.

"Hello, hello," Eva struggled above the questions of Strindberg and the responses of Niklas. "Hello . . . no . . . what? . . . speak up . . . who? . . . WHO? . . . No, she is here . . . Yes, I will fetch her, hold one moment please." Eva cupped the receiver's microphone. "Lise, someone else wants to speak to you."

"No, I have no comments. I don't want to talk to anyone."

"I think you should talk to this person."

"Why? Who is it?"

"It's the President of the United States."

* * *

In the clear sky, 12,000 feet above the Atlantic ocean, the Pan American flying boat, a Boeing B314 with a designation of NC18605, but affectionately known as the Dixie Clipper, headed towards New York City. It carried 28 passengers and 12 crew members.

Lise stared out of the window. She could see no land, but occasionally she made out the shape of a boat on the water. Near the end of the 20-hours flight, the passengers dozed and a quiet stillness floated through the plane; even the drone of the plane's engines added nothing more than a soothing background hum.

A flight attendant approached.

"We shall be landing in New York shortly, Dr. Meitner. Can I get you anything else?" asked the flight attendant.

"No, thank you," replied Lise.

"I trust you had a comfortable flight?"

"Yes, thank you, but it is also my first flight, so I have nothing with which to compare, except the train; and I rarely traveled in such luxury on the train."

"Well, we are honored that you chose to make your inaugural flight aboard the Dixie. You are lucky to have had the chance: sadly, the Dixie is to be retired. No more flying boats; they're not needed any more."

"That is too bad," said Lise. The plane hit a patch of turbulence and shuddered. Lise grabbed the armrest of her seat. "I think I still prefer the train, in spite of the difference in comfort."

"I understand, but really air travel is very safe."

"Yes."

"What brings you to New York?"

"My sisters, Frida and Lola, live there . . . And I am to visit with Mrs. Roosevelt."

"Wow, the Dixie and Eleanor Roosevelt all in the same trip. Maybe I should get your autograph?"

"Oh, no, I am not important or famous."

"You know, President Roosevelt sat in that very seat on his way to Casablanca to meet with Churchill and Stalin."

"No, I did not know that."

"Anyway, I'm sure your sisters will be happy to see you. Should you wish to freshen up a little before our arrival, the ladies dressing room is still available. We have to secure it for landing, but there is a little time yet."

"Thank you."

The flying boat looped to the north of Long Island, landed on the Sound and taxied to Bowery Bay and the pier in front of the Marine Air Terminal of the New York Municipal Airport.

Before the flight attendant opened the plane door, she approached Lise again. "I've been advised that you should remain on the plane until the other passengers have disembarked. So sit back and relax and I'll come back for you."

Lise peered out of the window, but the plane had its tail to the terminal and only water met her gaze. After a short wait, made longer by Lise's impatience to feel solid ground beneath her, the flight attendant returned.

"Okay, now we are ready for you. There are some reporters waiting and some well wishers, but we have arranged for an escort to help take you through the terminal."

Lise stood and walked towards the exit. The plane's engines had stopped, but the hum seemed to continue, if anything louder now. Then Lise stepped from the plane and a loud roar greeted her. A large mob, ten thousand, twenty thousand, Lise didn't know how many, cheered, waved and chanted her name. She froze and wanted to retreat to the safety of the plane.

"That's okay. Take your time," smiled the flight attendant. "Your sisters are inside. They are eager to see you. Now, take a deep breath and smile. Welcome to New York. Here is your escort."

"Robert? What on earth are you doing here?"

"Hello, Aunty. I thought you may need an interpreter."

Lise slowly walked the length of the pier with police officers at each side of her and Robert constantly whispered advice in her ear.

"Don't worry about the reporters; they'll ignore your answers and write what they want anyway, but as long as you smile and be nice to them, they'll write nice things about you. Oh, and if they ask for your opinion of Mickey Mouse, say you love him."

The mob massed on the promenade which stretched away from each side of the pier. The pier remained comparatively crowd free, but she still felt as if she walked the gauntlet. Inside the circular terminal building she passed quickly through customs and immigration. After years of dealing with autocrats, who scrutinized her papers in minute and lengthy detail, the informality and speed of the American immigration officers surprised her. They knew of her and had expected her. They welcomed her to America with a flamboyant stamp of her passport and wide grins on their faces.

Another police officer waited for her to identify her luggage and when she had done so, promptly disappeared with it. Lise expressed consternation.

"Don't worry, Dr. Meitner," they assured her. "We will transfer your bags to your hotel. They will be in your room when you arrive."

Then she moved to the terminal's public foyer. Lise hoped that she had left the crowd behind when she had left the pier, but the crowd inside the terminal seemed even larger than that which had greeted her on Bowery Bay. Robert linked her elbow and began to march her through the crowd, with the police escort close around. Cameras flashed and reporters yelled out questions.

"Is it true that you smuggled the plans for the bomb out of Germany hidden in your skirt?" asked a reporter.

"I never worked on the bomb." responded Lise.

"Can you comment on the rumor that you plan to go to Hollywood?" barked a second reporter.

"How does it feel to be the mother of the Atom Bomb?" asked reporter number three.

"Horrible!" shouted Lise.

Then she heard a familiar voice; it cut clear through the noise as a lighthouse beacon shone through the fog.

"Lise! Lise, over here," yelled Frida.

"Lise!" yelled Lola.

Lise wanted to break free of the police cordon and rush to embrace her sisters. They would not allow it. But their orders did include Frida and Lola and they joined the ever growing entourage of police, politicians and reporters. The sisters hugged briefly before the police parted them.

"Oh, Frida!" said Lise. "What a commotion. What is happening?"

"This way, Dr. Meitner," said a man in a suit and tie. "We have a car waiting."

"Then how did you smuggle the plans out?" demanded the first reporter.

"We'll have to hurry, Dr. Meitner, if we are to make the broadcast," said the man in the suit.

"Broadcast?" asked Lise.

"I'll explain on the way," said Robert.

"You are coming with me?" asked Lise.

"Of course," said Frida. "Don't worry; we'll be out of the worst of it in a minute."

"Is it true that you slept with a physics book under your pillow as a child?" shouted the second reporter, as the police pushed through the crowd inside the terminal and into a third crowd on the street outside the terminal.

* * *

On the street, the car waited with engine running; as did the police cars in front and back and the outrider escorts to each side. The police bundled Robert, Lise and her sisters into the car, and before they could settle back in their seats, the convoy set their sirens to wail and departed the airport for their destination: Rockefeller Plaza and NBC radio.

On route, Robert and the sisters took turns to explain to Lise of an obligation to participate in a radio broadcast with Eleanor Roosevelt. Mrs. Roosevelt had arranged the broadcast while Lise travelled from Europe. No one considered for a moment that Lise would decline the opportunity to appear on national radio with Eleanor Roosevelt. They all understood that she would be delighted. Mrs. Roosevelt had requested it and no one ever turned down Mrs. Roosevelt; she was most persuasive.

Robert lectured her on how best to handle her on-air performance. Lise, tired, unrehearsed and uncomfortable, wondered if she could make the best out of a bad situation, but the radio host offered only simple, friendly, gentle questions and Eleanor Roosevelt answered most of them, between frequent breaks for commercials.

So a grateful Lise minimized her air-time embarrassment, but it annoyed her that the host's questions sprang from so many delusions: that she had built a prototype for the bomb under the nose of the Nazi, Hahn; that she was Otto's secretary and had stolen the blueprints from his safe; that she had planted fake blueprints to thwart Heisenberg.

"Welcome back, Listeners," said the host. "Once again, we are honored to have in our studio, Eleanor Roosevelt and the distinguished scientist, Professor Lisa Meitner . . . Dr. Meitner, when you began your experiments into nuclear fission in the 1930's did you envision where those experiments may one day lead?"

"When the original research began . . ." said Lise.

"If you could just speak up a little, Dr. Meitner, if you please," requested the host. "Into the microphone."

"When the original research began before the war nothing was farther from our minds than the utilization of this energy for the manufacture of bombs. When the theoretical possibility of such utilization was discovered, I, like any other responsible person, hoped that its practical realization would not be possible. The scientist is ever awe-struck at the discovery of the laws of nature, and to use these laws for the construction of weapons which might lead to the annihilation of mankind is blasphemy to him. May the first two atom bombs to have been dropped also be the last."

"It is the responsibility of the women of the world to see that atomic energy is used for the benefit of man," added Eleanor Roosevelt.

"Would you agree with that, Dr. Meitner?" asked the host.

"Women have a great responsibility and they are obliged to try, so far as they can, to prevent another war. I hope that we will be able to also use this great energy that has been released for peaceful work," said Lise.

"And what is next for you, personally, Dr. Meitner?" asked the host.

Lise wanted to respond that her plans consisted only of a bath and a good night's sleep, but Mrs. Roosevelt fielded the question.

"We hope to show our honored guest something of our great country while she is here. Dr. Meitner has a full schedule planned, which includes a trip to Washington, where she will be honored by the President and the National Press Club as Woman of the Year."

"Thank you, Mrs. Roosevelt. Thank you Dr. Meitner; Mother of the Atom Bomb and Woman of the Year."

. . . A Thousand Suns

Eleanor Roosevelt took charge. She danced around New York society with Lise on display, back and forth, from breakfast speeches to power lunches to gala dinners, and round again.

"Lise," she would say, "You simply have to meet so and so."

But Lise would barely have time for a perfunctory 'hello' before she felt the tug on her arm as Mrs. Roosevelt eased her towards another introduction.

Mrs. Roosevelt's capacity for the work load seemed as boundless as her ability to work the room. Lise wondered about the purpose of it all. But Mrs. Roosevelt had an agenda beyond playing chaperone and Lise felt as empowered as a pawn on a chess board. Under the weather and weakened by the demands of the schedule, Lise wanted nothing more than to sit with her sisters and relax, but Mrs. Roosevelt had plans and no one ever turned down Mrs. Roosevelt.

Eventually, Lise had shaken the hands of all in New York and Mrs. Roosevelt announced that the time had come to move on to Washington, the White House and the Woman of the Year Award.

Harry Truman may have succeeded her husband as President of the United States, but for the night's gala dinner, and with the Truman's blessing, Eleanor Roosevelt, with her affiliation to the Press Club, still ruled as the First Lady of the White House.

And so began another round of introductions and hand-shakes. Lise remembered Robert's advice, smiled politely and let others lead the conversation.

"And of course, you already know this lady and these gentlemen," said Mrs. Roosevelt.

Before Lise stood Niels, Margrethe and Albert. Lise smiled. Even dressed in a tuxedo, Albert managed to look scruffy.

"I must go and say hello to a few people," said Eleanor Roosevelt. "But I leave you in capable hands." Mrs. Roosevelt, the other guests, the waiters with trays in their hands, even the walls of the White House, faded into a background mist and left Lise alone with her friends.

"Oh Margrethe, Niels, Albert!" she beamed and embraced them. "I am so happy to see you."

"You are looking well," said Niels.

"No I'm not. I have a cold and I'm exhausted. But you, Albert? Look at you! When have you ever looked such a gentleman?"

"Well . . . the President, you know . . . one has to make an effort," Albert muttered, in self-defense.

"Oh yes, of course, of course," laughed Lise at his discomfort.

A voice interrupted: "Ladies and Gentlemen, if you could please make your way to the ball room."

"And I had heard a rumor that a certain beautiful, young woman was going to be here," said Albert. "So I thought a clean collar and polished shoes couldn't hurt."

"And is she?" asked Lise.

Albert smiled. "Yes. And perhaps she will permit me the honor of accompanying her to dinner?" He extended his arm.

"I've had worse offers," said Lise.

"That is probably the only offer you will get from Mr. Einstein," said Niels. "I recommend that you take it."

"I once heard that the scientist only gets the girl in the comic books," said Albert.

Lise and Albert linked arms, and with Niels and Margrethe trailing behind them, they entered the ballroom.

"I see you have also chosen to wear black," Albert said to Lise. "An unusual color for you, but I think you pull it off nicely."

* * *

As the guest of honor, Lise sat at the President's table. Those seated around her included Albert, the Bohrs and Truman's daughter, Margaret.

"Ah so, you are the little lady who has gotten us into this mess," said the President.

"Let us hope, Mr. President, that our discoveries can be put to more constructive uses," answered Lise.

"Amen to that. But better that we have the bomb than the bad guys."

"Is it true that you are going to Hollywood to discuss a movie deal?" asked Margaret Truman. "Ingrid Bergman would be ideal to play you."

305

"No, that is not correct - There was some talk, but I saw the film of Madame Curie. I would be horrified if they did that to me."

"But Greer Garson was nominated for an Oscar for that role; and she got to kiss Walter Pidgeon."

"Exactly. But I have no time anyway: arrangements have been made for me to lecture at Harvard and Princeton Universities while I am here."

"Ivy league," said the President. "You're welcome to them. My education consisted of the trenches, the general store and the honest sweat of labor."

"My father is a man of the people," confided Margaret Truman.

"And damned proud of it," added the President. "That is not to disparage the accomplishments of the universities, please don't get me wrong. Your contributions to humanity are undeniable. After all, we've come here tonight, to celebrate the work of Dr. Meitner. But horses for courses, as they say."

"I find what you do so fascinating, "said Margaret Truman. "But I could never be a scientist; I'm afraid I don't understand any of it."

"Neither do I," agreed Albert.

"And your work in particular, atoms and bombs. How can something so tiny cause such a great big explosion?"

"Then permit me, perhaps, to explain," said Albert. "The President is correct - we are here to celebrate a practical application of science, are we not?"

Lise shuddered. She knew of Albert's penchant for argument and she did not wish to see a belligerent Albert unleashed on an unsuspecting audience. But the President spoke, "Please enlighten us, Mr. Einstein."

And Albert began.

"As the President once said on a previous occasion; the damage caused by a nuclear detonation is equivalent to perhaps twenty thousand tons of TNT, yes? But how is that achieved? How does the bomb do so much damage?

"A conventional bomb is crude and brutish, more bluster than power, but our bomb is subtle. Our bomb knows physics. A single neutron fired into the heart of the nucleus, bypassing the atom's defenses, is all it takes. A single neutron is not very big, not much of a threat. And the nucleus, even a nucleus split in two, hardly a concern. But the beauty of the process is that by splitting this atom, we have set some fragments, particles, in motion.

"Imagine a bullet hitting a window; the glass is shattered and shards of broken glass fly through the air, yes. Now, imagine those shards fly at the speed of light, because that is what our particles are doing. Instead of one stationary, harmless nucleus, we have these fragments moving at the speed of light. They crash into other atoms and split them also. The number of particles in motion continues to increase; two becomes four, four becomes eight, and so on, until the heart of our bomb, a lump of uranium, is transformed into an army of particles in motion.

"This whole process takes a millionth of a second. To an observer, the bomb would seem suspended in mid air, but to use a scientific term, the cat is now out of the bag.

"So what? One neutron or a billion, what harm can they do, even if they travel at the speed of light? If during their flight, they hit nothing, then they are harmless, but they are not that careful; they are blind; they run about and bang into each other and the steel casing of the bomb's interior. All that commotion causes friction.

"What does friction lead to? Rub your hands together, they get warm, yes. If you could rub your hands at the speed of light, how hot do you think they would become? The friction causes the metal to heat; it rises beyond the boiling point of water, beyond the boiling point of steel. The bomb begins to melt. The temperature continues to rise; five thousand degrees - the temperature of the sun - a million degrees - ten million - the temperature of the universe at its creation.

"And now, one ten thousandth of a second after that first, tiny, insignificant neutron hit the nucleus, that energy is unleashed on an unprepared world. Our observer would witness the birth of a star, no bigger than the bomb which originally housed it, but it burns a thousand times brighter than the sun. The star hangs in the sky for a few seconds, serene, beautiful and beguiling. But a star in the middle of our sky? That cannot be right, it should not be there - go away, shoo.

"And as the star realizes that it is not welcome in our sky, its serenity turns to wrath. Its wrath takes different forms and moves out in all directions. First, as a shockwave of ultra violet, which moves so fast that it boils the air through which it travels. Any creature caught in this first wave will fare no better than the bomb casing. Within milliseconds, all within a perimeter of a mile, ten thousand of our fellow human beings perhaps, simply cease to exist.

"Now the wrath takes a second form, a wave of high pressure which pushes all before it, even the air. The star transformed to a hurricane. Those unfortunates yet alive would still not know what has occurred. Perhaps they saw the bright light appear in the sky, but the speed of destruction advances much faster than the capacity of sound to keep up with it. Mere seconds after the light appeared, their world suddenly explodes around them; windows shatter, doors implode, and cars are picked up and thrown through the air; buildings, bridges, trees crash down on their heads. And so, perhaps another fifty thousand are killed and twice that number injured.

"And thus the energy of the bomb is discharged. But didn't I say that the hurricane had pushed all before it, even the air? Yes, what does that leave? A vacuum! The winds reverse their direction to fill the vacuum and even more are killed.

"And we are done. Except of course, where did all those billions of particles go? Some find homes in the bones of their still living victims, who will die in the weeks and months ahead of gamma ray poisoning.

"And now, our observer can look back across a scorched, twisted landscape, covered with wreckage and a small fire here or there. And in the center of this landscape, a great cloud rises to the heavens; and in the center of the cloud is a written a message; and the message says, 'God was here.'"

Truman nodded to the Master of Ceremonies, who rose to address the assembly. "Ladies and Gentlemen, the President of the United States."

"You're a hard act to follow, Mr. Einstein," said the President, as he rose to his feet to deliver a few prepared remarks and present the Awards.

* * *

Dinner over and awards handed out, Lise, Albert, Niels and Margrethe shuffled back to the foyer. Lise held a small silver bowl, her award for Woman of the Year.

"Another feather in your cap," said Margrethe. "And deservedly so."

"Thank you," said Lise.

"And with Otto Hahn to get his Nobel, it has been quite the year for the Hahn-Meitner Research Department."

Niels bristled. "I think it's a disgrace that your name is not along side his; and I told the Committee so in no uncertain terms."

"I agree," said Albert. "They told me the Prize for Chemistry should not concern us physicists."

"But Otto is a great chemist," defended Lise. "His Nobel is long overdue."

"And you are a great physicist and your Nobel is long overdue," countered Albert.

"And the discovery of fission belongs to the discoverer; only the Nobel Committee could think otherwise," said Niels. "As soon as I heard of the oversight, I nominated you for the Prize for Physics."

"Thank you, Niels. I appreciate that very much, but they have awarded the prize for the discovery. I don't think they can award a second prize."

"It won't be a second prize. It will be the Physics Prize for the discovery of fission. If Otto can get it for chemistry, you should get the Prize for Physics; it is simple. I believe we can make an undeniable case that fission is more important to physics than it is to chemistry."

"I tried to make that case to the President," said Albert.

"Albert! That was very naughty of you," said Lise. "Teasing Miss Truman like that."

"What? I was merely keeping the conversation flowing. These affairs can be so dry. Still, Woman of the Year; you did all right for yourself?"

"Yes. I am honored. What a nice prize."

"The silver bowl? Very pretty. Did you steal anything else? I managed a few spoons and a coffee pot, but that was all: too many eyes."

Eleanor Roosevelt floated in with a photographer in tow.

"Ah Lise, there you are," said Mrs. Roosevelt. "We are going to have a little photo for the press, if you don't mind, with tonight's other honorees."

Mrs. Roosevelt herded Lise away from Albert and the Bohrs to another part of the foyer, where several other women had gathered for the photograph. Lise moved to the back of the group.

"No, Dr. Meitner, you come over here, front and center, between Georgia O'Keefe and Ingrid Bergman," said the photographer. "Ok, let's see those awards. Everybody smile."

. . . Nobel Prize

"Professor Hahn. The discovery of the fission of heavy nuclei has led to consequences of such a nature that all of us, indeed the whole of humanity, look forward with great expectations, but at the same time with great dread, to further developments. I am convinced, Professor, that just as your great discovery has been a result of your far-reaching researches on atomic nuclei, irrespective of any eventual practical applications, the further ardent development of research in this field as a consequence of your work will be of particularly great pleasure to you. With regard to its practical application I am also sure that you share all our hopes that this application will serve in the end as a blessing to mankind. Professor Otto Hahn. Whilst offering you the sincere congratulations of the Academy, I ask you to receive from the hands of His Majesty the King the Nobel Prize for Chemistry."

Arne Tiselius, Nobel Awards Ceremony,
December 10, 1946

Otto, dressed in tuxedo and white tie, waltzed into his suite at the Grand Hotel, Stockholm. Technically, he remained under arrest, but his military guard had behaved with discretion, so as not to spoil his big night; and now they lingered outside in the corridor.

"What a night, Lise, what a night!" he cried. "Come in, let's have a nightcap."

"It was a good night for you," agreed Lise, as she followed him into the suite.

"For us; don't forget the part you played. But, yes, it was a good night; a great night!" He took the gold medal from its black, velvet lined box and held it up so that the light made it sparkle. "And I think perhaps it marks the end of an ignoble period and a bright new beginning. I pray that we can now begin to rebuild the reputation of German science."

He sang a snippet of an old Brahms duet as he put down the Prize and uncorked a bottle of Champagne and wondered if he could ask his guards to hunt down some ice, or whether that would prove too much of a mischievous liberty.

But Lise did not join in the song and she did not smile; which caused Otto to frown.

"What is wrong?"

"How could you do it?"

"Do what?"

"You did not achieve this Prize on your own."

"Of course not; I thanked you and Fritz for your contributions. It was a team effort. I pointed that out. I was careful to say, 'we' instead of 'I.'"

"I did not expect you to set the record straight, but you stood up there at that podium, in front of that audience, and referred to me as your assistant. I was Head of the Physics Department for twenty one years. I was never your assistant. I thought we were partners?"

"Lise, calm down; you are upset that you were not also nominated. I know the awarding of the Prize to me alone has carried some controversy, but as the Academy has been at pains to point out, the Award was for chemistry and I am the chemist in our partnership. But I'm sure that you shall also win the Physics Prize; your time will come. In the meantime, you have also been recognized: Member of the Swedish Royal Academy, the science and arts prize from your home town of Vienna and Woman of the Year; these are great honors. I wish I could have been there in Washington to see you honored, but they would not permit it. You must not be upset with me."

"I'm upset that you alone are recognized for work we all did."

"You were gone. What was I supposed to do? Close the laboratory and retire? Had you stayed perhaps the Academy would have seen it differently. I stayed and carried on with our work. I did the experiments."

"My experiments! I suggested them. I interpreted the results for you."

"Had you stayed . . ."

"Had I stayed, I would be dead!"

"Look, I didn't nominate myself for the award. You know how fickle the Academy is. The Prize was theirs to give, not mine. Should I have turned it down?"

"But you kept quiet about our involvement. What about poor Fritz?

"Strassmann shall share the prize money with me. You both shall share."

"I don't want your money. I want my name back on the papers I authored. I lost my home. I lost my friends. I was forced to leave my work behind. I've spent the last year listening to people who believe that I was no more than your typist. Why did you remain silent? Why do you remain silent still? Why do you allow the lies to be perpetuated? I lost everything except my memories. And now you, of all people, seek to rob me of those."

"No, don't exaggerate. You know how complicated the world has become. The rehabilitation of German science must be handled with delicacy. The future of science is in the balance. In a way, we are both victims of circumstance, but now the war is over. This is a new age. Come back to Berlin and help us rebuild. Did you hear that we are to rename the Kaiser Wilhelm Society to the Max Planck Society? You will be restored as the Head of the Physics Department. Come back to Berlin."

"After everything that has happened, how can my answer be anything but, 'no?' How can I work along side Germans without being reminded of what Germany did to me and my family and the others? And how will I make them feel if I work along side them: shame, resentment, anger? What kind of working relationship will that foster?"

"Those feelings will pass with time."

"For you, perhaps, but I don't have the ability to put the horrors out of my mind. And you know my return is impossible for another reason."

"What other reason?"

"You! I see the man you have become. What have you turned into? You have broken your oath to truth and justice . . ."

"No, no, wait a minute. The years have tested us, but I was never a Nazi, you know that. I always . . ."

"You dined with party members. You did not even try passive resistance."

"We had to move with care. Max Planck tried to oppose them and where did it get him?"

"You dare speak of Max? Erwin Planck was tortured and murdered for standing up to them. What did you do? Fritz Strassmann stood up to them; Fritz hid Jews in his apartment. What did you do? You never once spoke out. Now, you worry about the stain on the reputation of German science. I cannot rest. I cannot sleep; I think about Belsen and Buchenwald and I begin to cry and lay awake all night. As long as your sleep was undisturbed, you didn't care."

Lise broke and cried. As much as she wanted to, she could not hate Otto. He moved to comfort her. He held her until the sobs subsided, then he lifted her chin and brushed the tears from her cheek.

"What has made you so bitter that you blame me for the crimes of the Nazis?" he said gently. "I don't know what to tell you. You are upset, I understand that. It was quite a night; perhaps we have drunk too much and everything is blown out of proportion. Please don't be angry with me. We shall call it a night. Get some rest. You will feel better in the morning. I shall see you at breakfast. When you've had a chance to reflect, you'll see that you have wronged me. We are old friends. How many years have we known each other?"

"Our friendship lasted forty years."

"And we shall be friends for many more." Otto released Lise from his embrace, but continued to hold her hands. "I am also tired. Let us both get some rest and start fresh in the morning."

Lise could not hate. In time, she may forgive. She could not speak, but duty spoke to her. She slowly backed away. Otto felt her fingers slide away from his hand, but something remained. He looked at his hand to see that he now held a small envelope.

"What's this?" he asked.

"The ring: your mother's ring, which you gave me for emergencies. The emergency is over and so I return it."

"Lise?"

"Goodbye, Otto."

. . . Cambridge, 1968

R obert usually took her to the grocery store once a week, in spite of her protestations that she could manage on her own. In defiance, and to prove a point, she would occasionally walk to the city center and map out a route around the shops and stalls of King's Parade and Market Square.

Sometimes she would purchase a small item or two; most of the time, she just enjoyed the stroll and fresh air. The busy streets, lined with pubs, tea rooms and other student hangouts, reminded her of Vienna and made her forget her age. But, not that she would ever admit it to Robert, some days her legs seemed as if they did not wish to cooperate.

Today was such a day.

"Yes, Deary?" asked the congenial waitress.

Lise ordered coffee.

At the other end of the café, some students argued, politely but loud enough for Lise to hear.

"I tell you," said one, "The Brezhnev Doctrine will be the beginning of the end."

"Politics?" mused Lise. "Some things never change."

She finished her coffee and moved to exit the café, but her legs refused to obey.

"Are you okay, Deary?" asked the waitress. "You look a little pale. Can I get you some water?"

"Oh, no, thank you," said Lise. "I'm just not as light on my feet as I used to be. Once I'm up I shall be good to go."

"Here, let me help you."

With the firm support of the waitress's arm under her elbow, Lise managed to stand.

"Thank you," said Lise.

"You go careful now."

"I will."

Lise reached the café door and halted. She sensed something wrong. She did not feel good to go. She felt as if her legs moved out of synch with the rest of her body. Her head hurt. The watching waitress moved towards her and a student sprang into action, but she saw them out of focus, as if she viewed them through the lens of a camera. To steady herself, she reached for the door handle, but it evaded her and she crashed hard to the floor.

317

* * *

The phone in Robert's office rang. The papers on his desk demanded priority and his instincts told him to ignore the phone, but he seldom followed his instincts.

"Hello?" he answered.

"Hello," said Ulla at the other end of the line.

"You never call me at the office. Did I forget something?"

"No, it's your aunt, Lise. She's had an accident."

"Accident? Is it serious?"

"She has a broken leg, but the doctor would like to talk with you."

"Did he give you a number for me to call?"

"I think it best if you went 'round and spoke to him in person. I'll meet you there."

* * *

Robert and Ulla stood in the hospital corridor, as the doctor explained Lise's condition.

"She has had a stroke and as a consequence, she fell and fractured her hip," said the Doctor. "By all appearances, it is not the first time this has happened."

"No," agreed Robert. "When she broke her hip about nine years ago, we persuaded her to move to England, so we could look after her, but it's hard to watch her 24 hours a day; she is very stubborn and independent; always has been."

"I wasn't referring to the fracture; I meant this is not the first stroke she has suffered."

"No, she had a heart attack four years ago. I told her to slow down, but if it was up to her, she'd be out climbing a mountain somewhere. She has never been content to sit back and relax."

"She is resting comfortably now; and not in much pain. She is weak, however. I doubt that there is any more mountain climbing in her future."

"Can we see her?"

"Yes, of course. She may not be completely focused, and there is a little paralysis."

"You go," said Ulla. "I'll join you in a minute."

Robert entered the ward. Lise appeared to be asleep, but her eyes opened as he reached her bedside.

"Oh, Robert, hello. What are you doing here? You should be at work."

"All these years you have called me Robert. My name is Otto. Every one else calls me Otto." He reached for a tissue to wipe away the saliva from her chin.

"You shall always be Robert to me."

"How are you feeling?"

"I've felt better. The nurses here are not gentle at all."

"Can I get you anything?"

"A cigarette; they're not allowed on the ward. I would go outside, but they won't let me out of bed."

"You should quit smoking; those things will kill you. Are you causing trouble?"

"I never caused trouble. I wish that I had."

"Oh, I think you made your share."

"Well perhaps, but not as much as others . . . Now they are all gone: Boltzmann, Niels, Laue, Albert, Eva . . . Max . . . All gone. People pray for a long life. The trouble with that is one loses so many of one's friends along the way."

"We are still here, Aunty."

"No, I have been split so many times I no longer exist. And you? You are just a nephew; you do not count."

"No, no, I do not count."

"Still, I have hope that one day you'll turn your life around and make me proud. There is some promise left in you yet."

"Thank you Aunty; coming from you that means such a great deal. And if you say it, it must be true; I've never heard you tell a lie."

"Don't take it personally. I believe there is some promise left in everyone."

"How can you be so optimistic after what you have been through, after what the world has done to you?"

"Some say it is a savage world and to survive it we must be more savage. I never believed that. I do not want to live in a world of savages."

"Then you should not have chosen physics for a career."

"I did not choose it; it chose me. It spread its arms around me and enclosed me. But how small the circle has become. I don't want to lose any more friends before I myself am on that list . . . There is still Otto; I should write to him."

Robert did not have the heart to tell her that Otto had already taken his place on that list a mere few days prior.

"That time is a long way off yet."

"No, my time has come. I can tell. It's as if you have struggled with an experiment and the results suddenly become clear. Now I understand."

"I wish I did."

"Boltzmann told me to seek the truth. I thought he was talking about science, but now I know better. There is a universal truth; it is hidden from us, but it is there. I am lucky to have had a glimpse of it. My heart is full and happy."

"So there is no regret, no disappointment? You are not sad that Otto got the Nobel Prize and you did not?"

"No, I was never unhappy about that. I did not want the prize for that. For my other work, it would have been nice, but not for that."

"I still think you should have shared it."

"If I could have shared, it would have been with you. We made that discovery together, you and I, little nephew."

"On a snowy winter's day," laughed Robert.

"On Christmas Day," said Lise. "What were we thinking? What a gift to the world." She tried to reach out her hand, but could not lift it and Robert took it up. He felt no strength in her grip, no warmth in her fingers. "What a gift to the world."

* * *

In Lise's cottage, surrounded by cardboard boxes, Robert held a photograph of his aunt.

Monica entered the room.

"Father, the taxi is here; we have to go back now."

Robert replaced the photograph on the mantel, but as he did so, he noticed that Lise, above her frown, also wore a straw boater. He had missed it the first time, for people usually see only what they expect to see. Ah yes, the hint of playfulness was still there - always there for people to see - for the ones who really knew her. He smiled.

He would continue tomorrow, refreshed and cheerful.

. . . Fade out

T he lecture hall in the Türkenstraße building of the Institute of Physics at Imperial University of Vienna smelt of decay, as it had always done, even when it was new. Robert stood at the podium and scanned his audience: a mixture of colleagues, staff and students, male and female, but no reporters. He imagined he could see her sitting there, a young woman who tried to be as innocuous as possible, wanting acceptance and hoping to blend in, as she scribbled furiously in a notebook.

Robert addressed the audience, "I want to tell you the story of Lise Meitner."

"When Lise Meitner . . . when my aunt first sat in this very hall, more than 60 years ago, and listened to a lecture by Ludwig Boltzmann, even the very existence of the atom was still under debate. Today, thanks in part to the great contributions of my aunt, not only do we know more about the atom, but we have harnessed its energy, for good and for bad.

"Her story is that of a woman who overcame every obstacle in her path. The academic community tried to deny her because she was a woman. The Nazis tried to deny her because she was a Jew. The Nobel Committee tried to deny her because . . . well, who knows their reasons? Perhaps because of political expediency; perhaps some combination of all the above. Her name was removed from her work. Her equipment was listed as belonging to others. Her status and contributions downplayed.

"But she was resolute of purpose and tireless in the pursuit of her dream; and history will not deny her. Albert Einstein, Max Planck, Niels Bohr; she was their contemporary and their friend. Her seat with them at the table deserves to be recognized and preserved.

"Here is the irony. Had the Nobel Academy done the noble thing and awarded her the prize for her discovery of fission, I would not be here today talking to you. She would take her place, rightfully so, on the list of the great scientists and that would have been the end of the story. But they failed to do that and as a consequence, she will now always be known, famous or infamous, as the woman who was denied the Nobel. So once again, she stands apart - as she did all her life. They tried to make us forget her, but in doing so they have assured that we shall always remember.

"Many who knew her tried to set the record straight. I once asked myself what was the point. Now I realize that I had asked the wrong question; in my search for answers to the wrong question, I almost missed the bigger picture.

"I now understand that our humanity lies in the little things, not the great. The small, often overlooked, seemingly insignificant things are the catalysts of the earth shattering changes. Small - whether it be a single electron or a single woman who faces down a dangerous and hostile world. Small, yes, insignificant, no; and certainly not powerless. I now understand that it takes something small to break through powerful defenses. What we cannot smash, perhaps we can squeeze.

"Max Planck and Niels Bohr fought to have my aunt's accomplishments recognized. I have taken up that sword from their hands. At first, I did so because I was angry at the injustice done to her, but anger is hard to sustain and easy to give up once the fire subsides. Only after the anger has gone, do you know if a cause is really worth the fight.

"When I stopped to wipe the anger from my eyes, I saw more than just a snub by a few old men on a dusty committee. I saw a life unfold. I saw a woman who overcame the sexism and bigotry to live the life she wanted to live. That is the real success of Lise Meitner, and the story I wanted to tell. Yet, then I saw that there was even more to her story; for when I looked at her life in the context of the age in which she lived, I saw a woman resolute in a world of chaos, the collapse of empire, war and destruction on an unimaginable scale, a downward spiral of the worst excesses of mankind. But through it all, as the great and powerful waged wars to annihilate the world, it was the small but determined people, such as my aunt, who preserved our humanity. This is the story I wanted to tell.

"She always told me to follow the truth, wherever it may lead. As a single, small neutron which starts a chain reaction, Lise Meitner started me on a search for truth which must inevitably overwhelm and obliterate all the lies, hatred and bigotry. So now this story is no longer about Lise Meitner; it is about us; you and me. It is about standing up to injustice when we encounter it and calling a lie a lie. It is up to us to follow her example.

"Some will take her accomplishments and say, 'See what a woman can achieve,' but she was not a feminist; she was an individual. She would have told you, 'It is not what a man or a woman can do . . . Not what a German or a Jew can do . . . Not what an industrialist or a socialist can do . . . It is what I can do.' And anyone who thinks that she did it for fame and glory, or for money, or for vanity . . . or for the Nobel Prize . . . they did not know my aunt, and they do not understand, as I did not understand for the longest time, that bigger picture.

"They did not want her life to be remembered, but I am here to celebrate it. They did not want her voice to be heard, but I am here to honor her and tell her story. They wanted her story to end with a whisper, but I will shout it from the roof tops.

"Lise Meitner, my aunt, born November 7th, 1878, died October 27th, 1968, but her discoveries . . . and her humanity live on."

Although based on real events, fission remains a work of fiction, and many liberties were taken. Truth, as with beauty, remains in the eye of the beholder. I encourage everyone to pursue the truth, wherever that may lead.

Regards,

Tom Weston

36826281R00197

Made in the USA
Middletown, DE
12 November 2016